RUM
& Coke

A Saddles & Racks Novel, #4

USA Today bestselling author

Kimberly Knight

COPYRIGHT

No portion of this book may be reproduced, scanned, or distributed in any print or electronic form without permission.

This book is a work of fiction and any resemblance to any persons, living or dead, any places, events or occurrences, is purely coincidental. The characters and story lines are created from the author's imagination or are used fictitiously. The subject matter is not appropriate for minors. Please note this novel contains profanity, explicit sexual situations, and alcohol consumption.

Copyright © 2018 Kimberly Knight

Published by Knight Publishing & Design, LLC

Cover art © Okay Creations

Cover Photographer © by Sara Eirew Photographer

Formatting © by Mermaid Publishing House

All rights reserved.

DEDICATION

To Verlene Landon:
Thank you for your continued support of this series and your friendship.

AUTHOR NOTE

Please note that you can read this book as a standalone. However, it is recommended that you read it after the first three books to avoid any spoilers.

ONE
Vinny

Present Day

"WE'LL ALWAYS HAVE THE DODGERS."

I took a sip of the rum and Coke I was nursing at the hotel's bar. I should have been drinking something stronger than rum, or I should have been drinking the 151 proof version that would fuck me up. However, Bacardi had discontinued it, and I was left drowning my sorrows with my usual eighty proof drink of choice even though nothing was going to prepare me for today. Not even alcohol.

Especially since it was *her* wedding day.

When I got the invitation on my doorstep last night, my world came to a screeching halt. Three and half months ago, she'd left me. One minute we'd just started dating, and the next minute she was moving in with the asshole. I tried to go talk to her, but I was never allowed. He lived in a gated community, and she told me on the phone that she was with him of her own free will.

Nothing added up, but in the end, I couldn't get her back.

"We'll always have the Dodgers." Those were the last five words Tessa ever spoke to me. The truth was, we didn't have the Dodgers. She hated the Dodgers, and I knew it was code— an S.O.S.—but I couldn't get to her. Couldn't confirm if it was a cry for help because I was never able to see her again.

I tried.

Now, she was marrying the guy, and I felt as though I was living in some sort of twilight zone. The funny thing was that I had been planning to take a break from escorting for Tessa. I wanted to see where things were headed with her because she was the first and only woman I'd ever loved. If she were to come back to me, I'd give it all up right now and whisk her away.

If I could.

But I couldn't.

I drained the rest of my drink and then went in search of the room that would feel more like a coffin to me because watching Tessa walk down the aisle was going to be the death of me. My heart was already breaking, and I hadn't even seen her yet. Just the mere thought of her taking someone else's last name was enough to put a crack in my heart, shatter it into a million fucking pieces and prevent me from ever being whole again.

Why did I even come? Why did I get out of bed this morning? Why did I drive the forty minutes to Henderson and get out of my car? And why was I about to walk into my worst nightmare?

All the questions had the same answer: Because I loved her.

I loved Tessa enough to put her happiness before mine and let her go because now I understood that she *did* leave me on her own. Maybe I'd never move on. Maybe I'd find someone new and eventually quit escorting and start a family. Maybe. But truthfully, after today, I'd never open my heart to anyone else.

When I found where the wedding was being held, I realized it wasn't in a room. It was a courtyard, and even though I wasn't going to feel as though I was suffocating, the hundreds of flowers scattered around, and the altar in the center, taunted me. I made sure to get a seat in the back by the door to the hotel in case I couldn't handle it and needed to leave.

I pulled a flask of rum from my black suit jacket and took a swig as people started to take their seats. I needed more alcohol to numb the pain. At any moment, the wedding would start. Tessa was going to walk in on her father's arm, and he'd give her away.

And no one would know that he wasn't the only one giving her away.

Tessa

Six Months Prior ...

THE BEAT OF THE MUSIC THUMPED IN MY EARS. I WAS ON AUTOPILOT AS I stared at the people in front of me who were cast in a red hue from the lighting. There was one group of guys who were regulars; every day after they got off work at a construction site, Brent and his co-workers would come in for a few beers. Brent was more my regular than the other guys because he was the one who always wanted a lap dance from me before he headed home. It had been like that for as long as I'd been working at Red Diamond, and I'd heard from the other girls that the group had frequented RD for a few years. I wasn't complaining, because Brent was a good tipper. Plus, he was easy on the eyes with his buzzed head of dark hair, his green eyes, and his rock hard body.

As I danced, all I could think about was that my kid was sick again, and that meant he was missing school and important therapy time. It was hard being a single mother, and I'd never planned on struggling in life. Never planned on getting pregnant before marriage.

But it happened.

Five years ago, I found myself knocked up after a one-night stand. I was *that* person. The one who was barely twenty-one and got drunk, slept with a Marine during Fleet Week in San Francisco, and was left to raise a baby on her own. I was able to track Scott down after I found out I was pregnant but, to make matters worse, he'd died in combat before I could tell him I was carrying his child. Since he didn't know, that meant the military didn't know and, therefore, all medical bills were on me and only me. All expenses were my burden alone, and now that I was a dancer, the club didn't offer benefits because we were contract hires.

I lived in San Francisco at the time, struggling to survive without a child even though I worked at the front desk of one of the high-end hotels. It only got worse when I had Colton. Three months after he was born, we moved in with my parents. We were there for three years before I couldn't take living under their control any longer. So, my son and I moved to Las Vegas because I'd heard the cost of living was cheaper.

Not long after we relocated, Colton was diagnosed with autism. Medical bills and his specialized preschool were covered by the state, but not his therapy. I had every intention of working the front desk at one of the hotels on the Strip when I'd moved, but so did a lot of people. As a result, when I met my neighbor who worked at Red Diamond, I decided to become a stripper. I needed the money and had no other options. Stripping was the only way for me to make ends meet.

At first, I thought I was dealt a shitty hand, but I wouldn't change it for anything. Colton was my life, my world, the reason I got out of bed each morning.

Even in the dimly lit club saturated with red lights, red walls, and red plush seating, I'd always catch my boss, Sebastian, watching me during several of my sets from his office overlooking the stage. It made me nervous, but I figured he did it to make sure the girls were doing their jobs and getting people to stay as long as possible—and ordering several drinks.

None of the girls I worked with actually loved stripping, including me. We did it for the money, plain and simple. And honestly, if the pay and hours weren't so good, I would have left a long time ago. Every week I dealt with drunks trying to cop a feel during a private dance, drinks accidentally being spilled on me, or guys who felt they didn't need to pay a dime and only wanted a free show.

As I continued to sway my hips, doing the same routine I always did, I smiled at the men and women watching me, anticipating the moment I would untie my top and show them what they came for. I was on autopilot. You could say I was acting in a way.

Brent stuck a bill into my G-string. "Lap dance?" It was the same request every Thursday and Friday. Brent would wait until it was my last set and then want his lap dance for the road. I didn't know his story, but at least he was cute and not like a lot of the men who smelled of booze and cigarettes with beer bellies.

I grinned. "Meet you in five."

After I finished the lap dance for Brent, I was in the dressing room, changing into my clothes to go home, when Honey, one of our managers, came into the room.

"Ladies, listen up." Honey closed the door behind her, and all seven of us turned and looked at her. She kind of reminded me of Dolly Parton in a way. She didn't have the southern drawl, but her rack and blonde hair were both huge. "Anyone up for making a little extra tonight? I got a call from a friend, and there's a bachelor party that needs a girl."

There were groans all around. After hours of being on display, all we wanted to do was go home and sleep. Most of the girls were married and wanted to get home to their husbands and family, and I wanted to get home to Colton. No one wanted to work more than what we needed to (even if the money was good), but given all the therapy bills on top of the standard living bills, I needed the extra cash. I decided to take the extra money because I'd make more in an hour stripping than I'd owe the sitter to stay extra.

"I'll take it."

Honey smiled and walked toward me. She handed me a small piece of white paper. "Here's the address."

I sighed as I took the paper. Bachelor parties were the worst. All the guys assumed we wanted to sleep with them as though it was written in the rules or something.

Her grin widened, and I started to think she didn't have our best interest in mind after all. "It's not your typical bachelor party, Scarlett," she stated, using my stage name and the one I used around the club. "It's for a male escort."

I balked then blinked. Then blinked again. "A male escort?"

"One of the guys from Saddles & Racks is gettin' married."

"One of the guys from Saddles & Racks is getting married?" I repeated, not believing I'd heard her correctly. I'd heard of S&R around the club because women talked. Some wanted to join the company, and I'd thought about it too, but everyone knew what really went on behind closed doors and that wasn't for me.

"A male escort is settling down?" Sommer asked from across the room.

"I don't know all the details except they need a girl to dance for about thirty minutes. It's a surprise party."

"Why would a guy want to see tits at his bachelor party when he sees them as his job?" Crystal asked. Crystal, aka Melony, was my neighbor, the one who got me the job. She was also my best friend. And she had a point.

"I didn't ask questions," Honey stated. "It's a job, and it pays five hundred." She turned back to me. "Do you want it or not?"

"Yes. Of course." At least this way I didn't think the guys would be horny and looking to score since they did *that* every day—despite what they said in public.

"Perfect. Be at the address by eight." Honey patted me on the shoulder and then left to check the floor.

The moment I stepped up to my apartment door, I heard the episode of *PAW Patrol*. It was the same episode that had been on repeat for the last month. That was my life. Every day. All day. The only break from *PAW Patrol* was when there was a San Francisco Giants baseball game on. Colton was obsessed with the team and the game itself. He would watch the same game over and over until he knew what the next play would be inside and out. That was one obsession I enjoyed. Growing up in San Francisco, I was a diehard fan, going back to their Candlestick days. Now that I lived in Vegas, I only watched them on TV. That was how Colton became obsessed.

But the current season hadn't started yet, so it was *PAW Patrol* and nothing else.

After unlocking the door, I opened it to see my son sitting on the floor in front of the TV, a baseball in his hands as he stared at the cartoon. My gaze moved to the couch where my sitter and neighbor, Sophia, sat reading. I entered, and we smiled at each other.

"Good day?" I asked, closing the door behind me.

Sophia was a sweet old lady who I'd first turned to when I moved into the apartment complex. I'd run out of milk the first week I lived here. It was before I found the job at Red Diamond and I had no money to my name because it went to our first month's rent. She took me under her wing, cooking dinner for Colton and me each night. She was the one who suggested I talk to our other neighbor, Melony, because she worked as a stripper and made a lot of money. When I worked at RD, Sophia took care of Colton. She didn't mind that I had to work Friday and Saturday nights until early the following mornings. She was amazing. I loved her and would be lost without her.

"It was." She smiled.

"Does he still have a fever?" I asked as I put my keys and purse on the table near the door.

"No. Broke a few hours ago, and I think he's feeling better."

"That's good to hear." I bent down beside him, but he didn't turn, so I moved in front of him and compressed his ears with both hands until he looked up at me with his steel-blue eyes. "Hey, Slugger. Want pizza for dinner?" It was generally pretty difficult to get Colton's attention, and eye contact was out of the question, but when I used the gentle compressions, it always brought his attention to me.

He hummed in agreement and rocked back a little as he flapped his hands in excitement.

I smiled. "I'll make sure it's cheese, your favorite."

My gaze met Sophia's again as I stood. "I hate to ask, but I was offered an extra gig for tonight."

"Oh, sweetie. I don't mind."

I smiled up at her. "Thank you so much. You're a lifesaver."

I arrived at the address right on time.

I'd assumed it was going to be a house, but when I pulled into the parking lot of a building with party style buses out front, I realized I was wrong. The handful of times I'd done bachelor parties, they were held at either a house or a hotel room. This was obviously different. I wasn't sure if I should go inside or what, so I stayed in my car until I saw a group of guys walk out of the double doors of the building. They were laughing and high-fiving like a bunch of frat guys. *Shit.* One or more of them was definitely going to try to hook up with me. Of course, I wouldn't do it. I was tired and just wanted to get my time done, get my five hundred dollars, and go home.

After taking a deep breath, I grabbed my purse and stepped out of my car. When I beeped the car alarm, it caused the group of four guys to turn and look in my direction. Out of nowhere, butterflies entered my belly, and my nerves skyrocketed. This wasn't the first time I had approached a group of guys in next to no clothing—a black halter top dress over a sparkly red bikini, black fishnet stockings, and black stilettos—but it felt as though it was. Maybe it was because they were male escorts and saw naked women all the time. Would they judge me? Compare me to all the women they dated? I felt as though they would.

I didn't think I was bad looking. Hell, Red Diamond didn't hire ugly women, but what if these guys preferred blondes? What if the guy getting married wanted a chick with green eyes? What if he wanted a girl with bigger boobs than mine? I tried to shake off my insecurities as I moved closer, telling myself that these guys liked any and all women—they were escorts. It didn't matter because I was only entertainment and not going to a dating interview. They had hired a stripper, and I was a stripper.

"Is this her?" one of the guys asked as I stepped within a few feet of the group.

I wasn't sure which one it was, but a guy stepped forward and asked, "Are you from Red Diamond?"

"Yes, I'm Tessa." I stuck out my hand with a warm smile. I didn't know why I said my real name because usually when it came to an RD gig, I used Scarlett. It just slipped out.

The guy smiled back and took my hand in his. "I'm Paul. This is Bradley, Vinny, and Nick."

"Which one of you is the lucky guy?" I asked as I shook Paul's hand.

Each one protested, snapping that none of them was that much of a pansy to settle down. I chuckled, shaking my head and moved to take Vinny's hand in greeting. Our hands lingered as his gaze peered down into mine. My belly fluttered again, and my pulse quickened. At that moment, I wished it wasn't dusk so I could tell what color his eyes were, but it was eight at night, and all I could make out from the light coming from the one-story building was Vinny's strong jaw and killer smile. A smile I wanted to stare at for hours.

"We're going to pick up the schmuck," Nick stated as my eyes moved to him.

"Tessa. Is that short for something?" My attention turned back to Vinny as he spoke, still holding my hand.

I blushed. "Teresa, but everyone calls me Tess or Tessa."

"All right, dude. Let's go." Paul slapped Vinny on the back.

"Yeah, man. Leave the poor girl alone. It's bad enough she has to put up with Nick and his asshole ways," Bradley joked. At least I thought he was joking. I hoped Nick wasn't an asshole. I hoped none of them were since I was going to be stuck on a small bus with them.

Vinny let go of our lingering hands and gestured for me to walk up into the black bus after the three other guys had entered. As I made my way down the center of the bus, I could feel Vinny's eyes on me. I didn't mind. He was gorgeous, but a thought struck me that he must get a lot of clients because he was so damn good looking—even in the dark. I tried to shake off my insecurities as I walked past the pole in the walkway and sat on the bench-style seat.

"Want a drink, sugar?" Paul asked as he grabbed a bottle of tequila from the bar in the back. The other three guys were each making their own drinks too.

I shook my head. "I better not. I'm assuming I need to dance on that pole while the bus is moving?" I waved my hand in the direction of said pole.

Paul cracked a smile. A smile that wasn't as spellbinding as Vinny's. "Exactly."

"What *is* the plan exactly?"

Paul finished pouring his drink and then took a seat across from me. "You're going to hide in the bathroom while we pick up my man

Gabe. Then, when we've been driving for a good ten minutes or so, come out and do your thing on the pole."

"You want me to hide in the bathroom?" I asked.

"It's a surprise," he stated as though I'd asked a dumb question.

My gaze roamed over the guys as they walked down the aisle with their drinks. Bradley and Nick sat next to Paul, and I held my breath as Vinny took a seat next to me. I felt stupid for feeling any sort of attraction toward Vinny. He was a male escort after all, and I was ... me.

"Do you all work for S&R?" I asked. They nodded. "Why did you hire a stripper then?" I questioned, looking directly at Paul, who seemed to be the one in charge of the party.

"Because it's a bachelor party," Nick stated as though the answer should have been obvious and I'd asked another dumb question.

"Don't be an asshole," Vinny snapped.

I turned my head to look at Vinny, and we smiled at each other then I turned my head back toward the three other guys and asked, "Okay ... but you see tits all day, right?"

"Sugar," Paul leaned forward and placed his hand on my knee. "We honestly hired you because that is what men do for bachelor parties. But that's not all we're doing. We just want Gabe to think you're the only entertainment."

"You have more strippers coming?"

He shook his head. "No. We're driving up to go camping."

I balked at his answer. "Camping?"

"Don't worry, it's not far," Vinny affirmed. "Once we get there, the driver will bring you back to your car. Shouldn't take longer than a few hours—tops."

Few hours? Honey had said they needed a stripper for thirty minutes, not two hours. But it was five hundred bucks, and now that I thought about it, that was a lot of money for thirty minutes. Honey must have not understood correctly, but it was too late now.

I nodded silently as the guys started to talk again amongst themselves. I wasn't paying any attention to the words. All I could think about was that seeing Vinny in the brightness of the bus's lights was one million times better than in the darkness of night earlier. He had a buzzed head of what seemed like light brown hair and brown eyes that twinkled when he laughed.

I hadn't felt this way toward a man in a long time. I never dated because my time was spent taking care of Colton, but as we drove, I had that weird butterfly thing happening in my stomach. I didn't want to think about what that meant. Plus, I also needed to call Sophia and tell her I'd be later than I'd thought.

"Now," Paul spoke with a grin, "this is what we need you to do."

THREE

Vinny

TESSA.

Fuck, she was beautiful.

In my line of work, I'd met hundreds of women. None of them had ever caused that stupid lingering thing to happen like you see in chick flicks. But Tessa …

I never wanted to let go of her hand.

There was something different about her, and I couldn't explain it. When I'd first stared down into her big, beautiful, blue eyes and she stared back as though she was reaching into my soul, I knew insta-love could be real. I wasn't in love with her—far from it—but there was definitely insta-lust going on.

I wanted to ask her anything and everything as we drove toward Gabe's house, but I decided against it. The guys would harass me. Not a single one of them knew what it was like to be in a relationship. Hell, I didn't either. Saddles & Racks allowed me to have the best life I could have. It allowed me to have the money I needed for travel and concerts, and all the things I wanted to do.

But being a male escort wasn't my only job. It was my nighttime job—my side hustle. My daytime job was being a special education teacher. Working in special education was very demanding and required me to juggle many responsibilities. I began each day with the standard requirement of responding to parent emails when I arrived at school and preparing each child's specific schedule, but then it went deeper than just teaching. I was a case carrier for each student. Each child had their own individual education program, and my job was to delegate the different learning groups with my assistants, have intensive one-on-one academic and behavioral support for each student, as well as collect data to add to the individual education programs that the assistants prepared throughout the day when they'd interact with the students.

The eight to nine hours I spent at the school were demanding, so being a male escort was a stress reliever. I could go to a bar and pick up a woman for the night, but this way I'd get paid to do it.

Plus, it was fun.

We only had sex if the vibe was right—and the vibe was *usually* right. That was why we were hired the majority of the time. The trick was to take the client's money when the date started, so whatever happened after was between two consenting adults. It was illegal to take the money *after* sex or when sex was mentioned because that was considered prostitution. Of course, I could see where a parent of one of my kids would have an issue with it. That was why I had an alias for S&R: Duane Wood.

The bus pulled up to Gabe's house, and Paul left to go inside to grab him. Tessa went into the bathroom as planned, and while we waited, the driver dimmed the lights, painting us in multiple colors as the LED lights shined on the baseboards and ceiling. Nick moved to the bar and poured what I assumed was a whiskey and Coke for Gabe.

"What did you do?" I heard Gabe ask from outside.

"Did you expect me not to drink tonight so I could drive your ass around?" Paul replied.

"I guess not," Gabe answered.

"Gabe, this is Alfred," Paul said, and I was confused. *Who's Alfred?*

"What?" Gabe chuckled slightly.

"I'm kidding," Paul exclaimed. "His name's Roberto, but Alfred is better for our little adventure."

Oh, he was talking about the driver and was referencing Batman?

"Adventure?" Gabe asked.

"Get on the bus, Gabe," Paul groaned.

Brad stood and moved to the doors. "Party's up here, man," he cut in.

He returned to his seat while Gabe finally stepped onto the bus. As soon as the guys and I saw him, we hooted and hollered and stood to greet him with bro hugs. Without any words, Paul guided Gabe to a seat across from me, and Nick handed him the drink he was making. The doors closed and music started to play as though we were a club on wheels.

"Where are we going?" Gabe questioned as the bus started to move.

"Around," Paul answered, making everyone except Gabe laugh. We knew the plan. Tessa was going to come out in a few minutes and talk Gabe into getting down to his boxers all while he was handcuffed to the railing behind him. It was part of a master plan. Brad's master plan, actually.

"Are you going to be in a shit mood the entire night?" Nick asked.

Gabe glared at him. "I just want to know where we're going."

"It's a surprise. Now drink your drink, loosen the fuck up and have a good time. This is your night." Paul gestured with his head toward the drink in Gabe's hand.

He cracked his neck to relieve tension, nodded, and took a long gulp of his drink. Paul moved beside me, and I knew the show was about to start.

I smiled. Not only because I was getting to see Tessa again, but because Gabe was in for a real treat. Hell, so was I. Sure, I'd seen more titties than I could count, but never had I been this excited before. I was dying to know what was under her bikini top. Dying to know what was under the bottoms too, but I knew that wouldn't happen tonight. Tessa worked for a tittie bar, not a full nude club, so she'd only take her top off.

Tessa sauntered down the hall, the dress she arrived in gone. She wore a sparkling red bikini with fishnet stockings and stilettos, her hands on her hips as her ass swayed past me, and her long brown hair in a ponytail. Good Lord, she was stunning, and my mouth started to water as I stared at her. I took a sip of my rum and Coke. It was my go-to. I was the rum guy, Gabe was a whiskey man, Paul loved tequila, Nick was a vodka guy, and Bradley liked his gin.

"What did you do?" Gabe hissed.

"Me?" Paul asked, bringing a hand to his chest as if he was innocent.

I grinned. When we came up with this plan, Bradley had asked if we were good at lying. Paul was playing his part well.

"Autumn knows about this?" Gabe waved a free hand up and down the length of Tessa's body as she stood in front of him.

My gaze moved to her ass, and I had to take another sip of my drink to wash down how much I was salivating. I wanted to drop to my knees and bite her plump ass.

"Well ..." Paul started to say, and we all laughed. Paul had mentioned that Autumn knew about the camping, but not about the stripper.

"Just relax," Tessa cooed and knelt before him. The sight of her on her knees made my dick twitch in my pants, and I wished she'd turn around and pretend I was Gabe. I wanted her to work my belt buckle free, pull down the zipper of my jeans, and then take my dick in her mouth.

"Look, lady—"

Tessa stood and straddled his hips. I watched her whisper something into his ear as my gaze locked with Gabe's. I couldn't hear what was said, but Gabe grinned. My eyes narrowed out of anger. I wanted her to straddle me, ride me, make me feel good. Whisper into *my* ear.

She leaned back, and Gabe asked, "What's your name, sweetheart?"

"Tessa."

"Well, Tessa ..." He looked over her shoulder at Paul, narrowing his eyes as if to say he was finally going to take the stick out of his ass and said, "Do your thing." He flipped Paul off and then moved his attention back to Tessa.

So did I. Her back was still toward me as she stayed straddled on his lap. Then button by button, the plan started. She undid his button-up dark blue shirt, and once she had it off his body, Gabe reached up as though he was going to untie her bikini top. I silently wished she'd turn around so I could see her tits.

Tessa slapped his hand, and I smiled. "No touching."

"Are you serious?" Gabe protested.

She stood and threw Gabe's shirt at Nick. "I am."

"Sweetheart," Gabe chuckled, "you promised me your tits."

"I vote for tits," I chimed in before I realized what I was saying.

Gabe's gaze met mine again, and he nodded approval. "See, we want to see your boobs."

"All in good time, boys."

"Let the woman work," Brad stated.

"Now ..." Tessa knelt again, and my dick twitched as I watched her grab Gabe's belt buckle. "You won't be needing this."

"Whoa!" He started to crawl away, but before he could move, Tessa was back on his lap.

"Someone needs to be handcuffed so he can't move."

Gabe shook his head. "You're not handcuffing me."

I grinned. This was part of the plan. We needed Gabe handcuffed so he couldn't chase after us once he realized what was happening.

"Yes, I am," Tessa stated matter-of-factly. *Good girl.*

"You're stripping me of my clothes before we go to a club? That defeats the purpose," Gabe groaned.

"You don't know how to dress yourself?" she teased, and I couldn't fight my chuckle any longer. In fact, we were all laughing. He had no clue.

"I ... You don't need to handcuff me."

No one said anything while Gabe looked at each and every one of us. Finally, he removed that stick that was up his ass and let Tessa handcuff him. She cuffed one wrist and then the other above his head. Bradley had worked it so that the cuffs were on a long chain and the chain was the part wrapped around the bar. The guys moved to get a refill on their drinks, but I couldn't move. Didn't want to move.

Tessa removed his belt and then stood just as *Pony* by Ginuwine blared through the speaker. "That's my cue," she stated, and her hips started to sway and roll as her hands glided across her upper body. I took another sip of my drink, finishing it off, and then sucked an ice cube into my mouth, needing to do something to distract me from how much I wanted to be Gabe.

She moved to the pole and walked around it, looking at each and every one of us. Seducing us. She was for sure getting to me, and when her gaze lingered on mine for longer than the few seconds she gave the other guys, she reached over, grabbed my head and brought it between her breasts. My tongue slipped out, and I tasted her skin. It was sweet, salty, and dangerous. I knew that if we were alone, she'd learn all my tricks I use on clients. I wanted to show her how I could make her moan, scream, and lose herself as I worked her body.

Tessa released me after a few seconds and moved back to the pole, turning until she was facing Gabe again. With her back against the pole, her hands glided up her breasts to her neck and then behind her nape where she finally untied her top. I watched the strings come loose, and I had to adjust the way I was sitting because I was itching to switch to the other side. To have the front view of her removing her top.

Her hands cupped her breasts, keeping the top from falling down, and I watched as she bent toward Gabe and let it fall with her chest in his face—the chest I wanted to lick again without the fabric around each globe. The chest I wanted to put my face into and never leave.

What was wrong with me? I'd just met this girl, and I was bursting at the seams.

Tessa's hands moved behind her back, and she loosened the rest of her top and finally removed it completely. I jumped slightly as she flung it at me, and then I smiled. Was she feeling something for me, too? I was the only one she'd touched beside Gabe, and she *had* to touch him.

Still not turning, she knelt in front of Gabe again and began to work on the button and zipper of his jeans.

"You're not going to do pole tricks?" he questioned.

"In a moving bus?" She chuckled.

He laughed. "Oh, right."

My gaze stayed on Tessa's bare back as I played with the strings of her bikini top in my hands while she worked Gabe's shoes and pants off.

"Finally!" Paul boomed as soon as they were off.

"What do you mean *finally*?" Gabe asked.

"Well, we're about to be at our destination in three minutes. Tessa, put his shoes back on."

"My shoes? You mean my clothes. Nick, give me my shirt, asshole."

"Sorry, man. No can do," he replied.

The bus pulled to a stop, and everyone stood except Gabe. Brad moved toward him and released the bar above his head where he was handcuffed, causing his handcuffed arms to fall into his lap. Paul sprinted out the door as soon as it opened, and Gabe started to chase after him, but Nick stood in his way, blocking him and allowing Paul time to get his paintball gun that was in the front seat.

I smiled at Tessa and handed her back her top. I had no idea what to say, but I knew I had to say something. "Thank you for coming."

Thank you for coming? What the fuck? Did we just have a dinner party or something?

She grabbed the fabric from my hand, our fingers touching for the briefest of seconds, and chuckled before replying, "Yeah. Uh, thanks for having me."

Before I could say anything further, Nick handed me my paintball gun, and the guys and I deboarded the bus.

"Are you going to shoot me?" Gabe asked Paul.

"This is how it's going to go," Paul replied. "You're going to run, and we're going to chase you—"

"You want me to run in the woods naked?" He laughed sarcastically.

Nick shot a paintball near Gabe's foot as though we were some mob and he needed to intimidate Gabe. "Let him finish."

"Are you fuckers for real?" Gabe groaned.

"Yep," Bradley stated.

"Like I was saying," Paul said, "you run, we hunt. Think of it like hide and seek."

"Motherfucker, I'm gonna kick your ass." Gabe moved as though he was going to strangle him with the long handcuffs, but stopped when all of us pointed our guns at him. They, of course, weren't real, but being hit by a paintball hurt like a bitch.

"Boss, you need to hurry up before a car comes," Roberto interjected.

"*Alfred!*" Paul shouted. "Jesus, I know. We're parked on the side of the road. I get it. Now if everyone will shut the fuck up, we'll be on our way in two minutes!" He paused for a second. "Okay, you'll be running, yada-yada, and if we catch you, we shoot you with these." He gestured to the guns. "There's a campsite just behind me that you need to find."

"How am I supposed to find it?"

"Don't give me that shit, Captain Hastings."

"You're serious?"

Paul bobbed his head.

"And I don't get a gun?"

"Nope, but you get a flashlight."

We laughed.

"You know paybacks are a bitch, right?" Gabe questioned.

Paul chuckled under his breath. "Shit, I'm never getting married."

"Maybe not, but I know where you sleep."

"Touché. We'll give you a thirty second head start."

I only had thirty seconds to make my move with Tessa, so while they released Gabe and he ran off, I went back into the bus. I was nervous and scared, but I was going to try.

"Hey," I called out.

Tess looked up from her phone. She had put all her clothes on and, I had to admit, I was bummed. "Hey," she replied.

"I don't have long, but I was wondering if I could get your number?" I stepped in front of her, and she stood. We were inches from each other, and I wanted to lean down and taste her lips.

She smiled up at me, and I instantly relaxed. "Well, I don't usually give my number to clients."

"Oh," I breathed, defeated. We stared at each other for a few beats. I wanted to beg. That wasn't me though. Sure Tessa was gorgeous, and I wanted to get to know her better, but once she got wind of what—wait, she did know what I did on the side. She knew we were S&R guys. At least, I assumed she knew. I was about to wish her a good life because she was obviously in the same mindset as all other women I dated, but then she spoke.

"I'm not looking for a boyfriend."

"And I'm not looking for a girlfriend."

"But I could use a friend."

"So could I."

"I have baggage."

I chuckled without sound. "Don't we all?"

She stared at me for a beat, and I knew my thirty seconds were almost up. "Okay, give me your phone."

FOUR

Tessa

WHEN I TOLD VINNY I COULD USE A FRIEND, WHAT I REALLY MEANT WAS I needed a male figure in Colton's life. I wasn't planning on introducing them anytime soon because I wasn't in the habit of bringing any strangers around my son until I felt as though they were good people, but in the short amount of time I was near Vinny, I liked him and wanted to get to know him. I didn't know why. I had barely spoken to him. Maybe it was the look in his eyes that told me he was a good man, or maybe it was the way he didn't grope me. All the Saddles & Racks guys seemed genuine and special in their own way. Especially Vinny. I didn't know what his way was yet, but I wanted to find out. I hadn't been interested in a guy for a very long time. My main focus was taking care of Colton and surviving. Parenting was hard—especially alone—and then to throw in his special needs … I sometimes questioned if I was strong enough. I'd cry myself to sleep, wondering where I went wrong, forced to show my tits for money to survive. Still, I made more money than my parents, and I only worked four days a week. There was no way I could stop stripping and get a *real* job because of the money and the hours.

After I got home from the bachelor party, I lay in bed and replayed the night over and over in my head. It was by far the best bachelor party I'd ever danced at. It was fun teasing Gabe and not being touched. Usually, the guys would try to fondle me even if I told them no, but the more they'd feel me up, the more they'd throw dollars at me. Last night wasn't that type of party, and I honestly felt as though I could hang with them for a beer or something outside of work.

Maybe I *should* work for Saddles & Racks. They couldn't force me to sleep with clients; I was sure they had rules about that, right? Maybe if Vinny called, I'd ask him about it. That was, of course, *if* he called.

The next morning, I woke to the sounds of *PAW Patrol*.

Colton amazed me every day. In six months, he would turn five, and I swore he had the smarts of a ten-year-old. He was able to control the TV easily, and he knew what he wanted and was able to find it on Netflix without any problems. He was also starting to read despite being unable to communicate like *typical* children his age. Therapy was helping him, and he was currently in an early intervention program, but after the summer months, he'd move on to a special needs kindergarten class. I knew that since he was progressing and meeting or sometimes even exceeding his goals, I was doing something right. Even if I had no idea what I was doing.

After getting out of bed, I used the bathroom before going into the living room to check on Colton. He was in front of the TV, a baseball in his hand, and the cartoon dogs on the screen. I kissed him on the head before I went into the kitchen to make a cup of coffee and breakfast. He didn't look up as I walked past because all of his focus was on the TV in front of him.

My cell phone started to ring, causing my stomach to dip in the hope it would be Vinny.

Instead, it was my mother.

"How was last night?" Sommer asked as we sat in the dressing room getting ready to go on stage.

"It was fun. Easy."

"Were they hot?" she asked as she curled her long, blonde hair.

I stopped applying mascara and looked at her through the reflection of the mirror. "What?"

She rolled her blue eyes. "They have to be hot to be escorts."

"Do they?" It made sense, but I still questioned it.

"I don't think anyone would hire an ugly escort."

I snorted. "No, I don't think they would."

"So, they were hot?"

I smiled, remembering all the guys, especially Vinny. "Yeah, they were."

"What did they look like? Give me the details."

"Why don't you just look at their website?" Ginger asked from my other side.

"I have," Sommer admitted. "But I want to know if they're better in person."

"I've never looked at their website," I confessed.

Ginger poked at the screen on her phone and then handed it to me. "Here, look at their bios and tell us who's cuter in person."

I grabbed the phone from her as she went back to spritzing hairspray in her short, red hair. Everyone except Gabe was listed, and I realized Vinny used the name Duane in his bio. "They all are, but Gabe isn't on there anymore," I stated. They really were. The photos didn't do them justice.

"Is that the one getting married?" Sommer asked, taking the phone from me.

"Yeah."

"What does he look like?" she questioned.

"Tall, bald, and handsome."

"Whoever he's marrying is a lucky lady. Can you imagine the moves he knows?" Ginger fanned herself as though she was hot just thinking about it.

My brain instantly went back to Vinny and the fact that he must know some moves too. Moves I hadn't thought about since I was twenty-one. Maybe I was only having those thoughts about Vinny because I was sex deprived and he had sex for a living?

"I bet they all have moves," Sommer stated.

"Who was your favorite?" Ginger asked.

Before I could respond, the door opened and Honey walked in. "Sommer, Sebastian wants to see you in his office."

In the time I'd worked at Red Diamond, I'd never been called up to his office. Maybe Sommer wasn't cutting it? All of the dancers were independent contractors, which meant we had to pay him to dance, but that didn't mean he'd hire anyone off the street. I'd seen him turn plenty of women away. Most of them were pretty, but you had to be strong to work in this field, and have a thick skin, because not every man or woman would like who you were on the outside. I was lucky I suppose. I was medium height, had decent boobs, long, dark brown hair, and blue eyes.

My gaze met Sommer's, and she gave me a small smile. "Hope I'm not fired," she jested. At least I assumed she was joking. I'd never known her to be anything except one of the top dancers. She was the one who taught me how to use the pole, and she was amazing at it.

She left, and I finished getting ready for my first set of the night. When it was time, I stood backstage, dressed in my signature sparkling red bikini and sky-high black heels, and waited for the DJ to introduce me.

"Ladies and gentleman, please welcome to the stage, Scarlett." I'd chosen the name because I only wore red when I danced. It was my color.

There were no cheers after he announced my name. The only thing I heard when I took the first step up onto the stage was the beat of the drums of "West Coast" by Lana Del Rey. I strutted out from behind the black curtain and into the lion's den. It was early enough in the day that the place wasn't packed, but there were enough people that I knew I'd make enough for gas money with my two dances for the one set.

I made my way down the stage, the lights dimmed, and swayed my hips to the beat as I walked. When I got to the end, my gaze moved up to Sebastian's office, and I almost stumbled backward, not believing what I was seeing. Sommer was on her knees in front of him as he sat in a red high-back chair that was angled to the side. Her mouth was working his cock.

His gaze locked with mine, and then he winked.

After my ten or so minutes were up, I collected the money that had been thrown onto the stage and turned to leave, glancing one more time over my shoulder to see that Sommer was gone. In the year I'd worked at Red Diamond, I hadn't known any of the girls to hook up with Sebastian. Hook up with the bouncers? Yes. The DJ? Yes. Customers? Yes. But never the boss.

Until now.

When I finally made it to the dressing room, where I'd change and freshen up for my next set, I expected Sommer to be in there, but she wasn't. Ginger was out on the stage, and Nicole was the only other person in the dressing room who I had some sort of friendship with, but we weren't close. Melony was my best friend, the only one I trusted, and she wasn't coming in for another hour, so I couldn't tell her what I saw just yet. I wanted to ask Nicole if she knew about Sommer, but I thought better of it. The girls talked shit about each other, but that wasn't me. Of course, I'd listen to all the drama, but I would never get involved. I needed the money too much to risk an altercation that would get me fired.

So, I kept my mouth shut again.

When Sommer came back into the dressing room, she looked as though she was the cat that ate the canary. I didn't question her. If she wanted to tell me, she would.

By the time I got home, I was bursting at the seams, wanting to tell someone what I'd seen during my first set. I wasn't able to talk to Melony when she arrived at work, and while I wasn't one to spread gossip, I was one to tell my best friend everything. Before I left, I told Mel to come to my apartment when she got home because I needed to tell her something. She was intrigued and said she would.

To my surprise, when I walked in through the front door, Colton wasn't watching the same cartoon he had for the past month. It was still *PAW Patrol*, of course, but not the same episode. "A new one?" I asked Sophia.

"His idea," she responded as I closed and locked the door behind me.

Change was good. Change was growth.

After Sophia left, I spent time with Colton, playing cars with him —well, it was more that we were both doing the same activity and playing side by side, not together. While I drove the cars around on the table or the floor, he lined them up in a row. We ate dinner, and I put him to bed, watching the clock for when I knew Melony would get off.

Finally, there was a quiet knock on my door. I stood, and after checking the peephole, I opened it.

"What do you need to tell me? Everything okay?"

"Yes, come in."

She did, and we both sat on the couch, facing each other. "Don't repeat this."

She snorted and rolled her green eyes. "You know me better than that."

"But this is huge."

"Well, stop prolonging this and spit it out."

"You know how Sebastian can see the stage from his office?"

She nodded.

"And you know how we can see into his office when we dance?"

She nodded again.

"Have you ever seen him …" I trailed off, trying to think of the right words.

"Seen him what?"

I just went with it. "Have you ever seen him with one of the girls up there ... pleasuring him?"

Her eyes grew wide. "Pleasuring him?"

"Giving him a blow job," I whispered.

"Shut up! Who?"

"Sommer."

"No way," she hissed. "Tell me everything."

"There isn't much to tell except that was what I saw. Oh, and he winked at me while she was doing it. She didn't mention it at all." I wrinkled my nose at the memory.

"Well, why would she?"

I shrugged. "I don't know? I mean, Sebastian isn't bad looking, and he is the boss."

"Would *you* brag about it?"

I chuckled slightly. "No, I don't think so."

We were silent for a few moments. "I can't believe he winked at you. I wonder how long it's been going on," Melony pondered.

I leaned against the back of the couch with my shoulder. "I have no idea, but I don't think it was the first time."

She furrowed her brows. "What makes you say that?"

"Because she wasn't in his office that long. It's like she walked up the stairs and he said, 'get on your knees.'"

"Maybe he did?"

Shit, maybe he did.

"So ..." Melony grinned. "Do you want to tell me about Duane?"

I drew my head back slightly because I hadn't told her that Vinny had texted me earlier and I was slightly confused. "Duane?" I asked, wondering why she had used his Saddles & Racks name.

Her smile widened. "He came looking for you."

My smile instantly matched hers. "He did?"

"He did."

"What did you tell him?"

"To come back tomorrow night."

FIVE

Vinny

As soon as we were back in town, I showered and then drove straight to Red Diamond. I couldn't get Tessa out of my mind. Even when we were chasing Gabe through the woods. Even when the guys and I were sitting around a fire, drinking beer, and shooting the shit. Even when the Montgomery brothers drove us back to the city.

After getting out of my Lexus LX, I walked into the brick building. I hadn't been inside Red Diamond before—hadn't needed to. It was early evening by the time I arrived, and the moment I stepped inside, my eyes had to adjust to the dim lighting. Strip clubs were notorious for being dark, the light mainly focused on the bar and stage. But if you thought about it, it made sense it would be brighter in those spots so we could see the goods better.

I scanned the area for any trace of Tessa. My plan was just to talk to her again. If she were on stage, I'd give her a few bucks, making sure she knew I was there. If she were giving a guy a lap dance, I'd wait in line, and then pay for five in a row. But as I scanned every inch of the visible area, I didn't see her. There were a few girls around, but none of them was the girl with the long brown hair and steel blue eyes I couldn't get out of my head.

So, I waited.

I went to the stage, took a seat, and waited for the next dancer to come out. It wasn't her. This girl was a little shorter than what I remembered Tessa being, even with her heels on. She wasn't in a red bikini, and her hair wasn't brown either. As I watched this girl work the pole, I threw her a few dollars to get her attention. She smiled and then came toward me. I held up a twenty and motioned for her to come closer. She bent at the knee, opening her legs as though I could actually see her pussy, and started to stand again.

"Wait," I called out.

She got on her knees and began to rub her hands up her chest.

"Do you want this twenty?" I asked, raising my voice slightly so she could hear me over the loud music.

She rolled her green eyes as though she didn't have time to work for it.

"I'll give you this plus another twenty if you help me out."

"With what?" she questioned, still moving as if she was putting on a private show for me.

"Is Tessa here?"

She wrinkled her brow. "Tessa?"

"Yeah, I need to speak with her."

The girl shook her head. "She already went home for the night."

"Oh." I leaned back in my chair as hope died in my stomach.

"She works the mornings on Thursdays."

I nodded and handed her the twenty. She eyed it and then I smiled, reaching into my wallet and pulling out another one for her as promised.

"Why are you looking for Tessa?" she asked, stuffing the bills into her bottoms.

I smirked. "Because she's my favorite." That was true. I didn't know any of the dancers except Tessa.

"But you know her real name."

I cocked my head to the side. "What do you mean?"

"Her stage name is Scarlett."

"Oh." I chuckled. "I met her last night at my buddy's bachelor party."

She stopped dancing and leaned closer to me. "You're an S&R guy?"

My grin widened. "Yeah."

"What's your name?"

Because this chick knew me as an S&R guy, I went with my own fake name. "Duane."

The girl started to dance a little. "She didn't mention you."

Well, fuck. Though Tessa met me as Vinny and not Duane. "Guess I didn't make an impression on her."

"I wouldn't take it personally."

"Why's that?"

Before she could answer my question, her song ended, and the DJ was announcing the next dancer. "Come back tomorrow night. She'll be here."

There was no way I was going to be able to wait even if it was less than twenty-four hours. I nodded to the woman—I never got her name because it didn't matter—and fished my phone from my pocket. I sent a text to Tessa as I stood to leave:

Hey, it's Vinny. Wanna go to dinner tonight?

Before I could start my engine, my phone dinged with a text.

Tessa: **Hey! Sorry, I can't tonight.**

I groaned because I *would* have to wait almost twenty-four hours.

Me: **Lunch tomorrow then?**

I watched the dots on the screen dance and then stop. Dance and then stop. Finally, I got a reply.

Tessa: **Are you buying?**

I chuckled and responded back: **Yeah.**

Tessa: **I can't be more than an hour. I need to run errands before my shift.**

Me: **An hour works for me.**

Tessa: **I'll meet you at noon in the parking lot of Red Diamond.**

Me: **See you then.**

Paul: *Getting a new roommate next week. I think we should haze him or something.*

Me: *Haze him?*

Paul: *I'm assuming he's transferring from another S&R. We should give him the Vegas welcome.*

I laughed as I read his text.

Me: *What's the Vegas welcome? You and Gabe didn't get hazed.*

Paul: *New ritual then.*

Me: *Then you think of something to do.*

Paul: *Already planning it.*

The next day, I went into work, made sure my class was set for the day, and then told Principal Fitzgerald that I was still feeling ill from my sick day prior. I'd never skipped work for a woman before, but Tessa agreed to a lunch date with me and I wasn't going to cancel it. It was a date, right? When she gave me her number the other night, she said she only wanted to be friends, but yet, she agreed to go to lunch with me. Maybe we were only going as friends? Time would tell.

I arrived at Red Diamond ten minutes before noon. I hadn't been that nervous since the night of my first date as an escort.

Ken had asked me to cover for him. Somehow he'd overbooked his time, and instead of canceling with one woman, he offered up a friend to be her escort. That was where I came in. He knew I needed the money. My entire life was dedicated to turning pro and going to the Olympics for men's beach volleyball. I'd obtained a full ride to The University of Southern California, but it was short-lived because I'd gotten hurt two years ago during my sophomore year. They took my scholarship away, but I didn't want to be a quitter, so I stayed enrolled, decided to become a teacher, and received a few grants. But I was broke, eating ramen noodles, five dollar pizzas, and PB & J's to survive.

"It's two fifty an hour," he said.

I could eat a steak dinner with the extra money, so I agreed to do it. "What do I do?" I asked.

He grinned. "Meet her at the bar, talk to her, go up to a room she books, and you know. It's easy."

"Wait," I stammered. "I have to have sex with her?"

"What is it that you think I do?"

"Go on dates," I answered honestly.

"I do, but I also get to do a little extra."

"Every time?"

He shook his head. "No, but if you're horny, do it. There are no strings."

"No strings." I tested the words on my tongue. I wasn't looking for a relationship, but sex without the added stress of wondering if a chick would want more would be nice. I wanted to be a bachelor my entire life. I craved the chance to travel the world whenever I desired. Granted, I knew I couldn't do it on a teacher's salary, but I was going to find a way to have the life I sought. Maybe this was it?

He told me where and when to meet the client and how to prepare for my night. I shaved, trimmed, and lathered my entire body with lotion. For some reason, even though I was nervous, I wanted to impress whoever I was meeting because who knew what this opportunity would bring.

I couldn't believe I was going to do this.

That night, I'd done just that. Shelby became a regular, and I escorted her on numerous occasions with an LA-based company before I moved to Vegas five years ago for a teaching job and joined S&R. And while I knew going to lunch with Tessa was nothing like escorting Shelby or any of my clients, I was still nervous. I hadn't *dated* since high school, which was ten years ago. And that wasn't dating—it was fucking.

The moment I saw Tessa walk out of the side door, a smile spread across my lips. Dressed in jeans, boots, and a sweater, she was still gorgeous. I didn't need to see her in a bikini, topless or even naked to appreciate her beauty. I got out of my SUV and started for her so she'd see me. Once she did, her smile matched mine.

I wrapped my arms around her as soon as we were within inches of each other. "Hey," I greeted.

"Hi," she replied.

We broke apart. "Hungry?"

"Starving." She followed me to my SUV.

"Do you like Bonefish Grill?"

"Never been there."

I opened the passenger side door for her, and she slid inside. I went to my side and did the same. "Do you like fish?" I cranked the engine after buckling my seatbelt.

"Yeah."

"Good. Bonefish Grill is one of my favorite places."

"Sounds good, and just a reminder that I only have an hour."

"Have another hot date?" I teased as I drove out of the parking lot and toward the restaurant.

Tessa chuckled. "No. I have errands, remember?"

"Oh, right."

"Are you working tonight?" she asked.

"Yeah, a little later." I did have a date. Because of Gabe's bachelor party and trying to organize everyone's schedules, I had taken Thursday off from school, and now half a day on Friday. We had the shindig on a Wednesday night because most guys had their dates on the weekends and didn't want to pass up the opportunity of making money.

"Is it true? Do you sleep with your clients?"

I turned and smirked at her. "You'll have to hire me to find out."

She laughed, and then a few minutes later, I pulled into the parking lot of the shopping center where the restaurant was. After we were seated in a booth, Tessa said, "I heard you came looking for me yesterday."

I grinned. "I did. I wanted to make sure you made it home safely after you left us in the woods."

"You could have called."

"But I wanted to see you," I admitted.

She sighed. "Vin—"

"Friends can want to see friends," I stated, already knowing she was going to mention the whole not looking for a relationship thing.

She stared at me for a beat. "Just so we're clear, I'm not looking for a boyfriend."

I held up my hands. "And like I mentioned, I'm not looking for a girlfriend. But I want to be your friend, Tess."

"Why? You don't even know me."

"Why does anyone want to be friends with someone? Because they think a person is nice, funny, whatever. And I think you're nice and a cool chick."

She took a deep breath. "As long as we're on the same page and you're not expecting anything."

"Nope. Who knows, this may be our one and only lunch."

I wasn't sure why I'd said that. Maybe it was because Tessa was so adamant about us only being friends and I hadn't had a girlfriend—ever. I wasn't used to being turned down because women usually wanted more from me, thinking just because I made them feel good for an hour, that I'd form some sort of attachment to them. It wasn't the case at all, and either they accepted that fact, or I'd never book with them again.

"Doesn't need to be that way," she replied. "Do you like baseball?"

I balked at her change of subject just as the waitress walked up to take our order. After we ordered, I replied, "Yeah, I like baseball. Why?"

Tessa grinned. "Who's your team?"

"Why? You like baseball?"

She took a sip of water. "Just tell me. This will determine if we can be friends."

I chuckled and draped an arm on the back of the booth. "Dodgers."

"Oh, God!" she shrieked. "I need to call a cab and get out of here."

"What?" I laughed nervously and leaned forward, ready to grab her hand so she couldn't leave.

"I'm a Giants fan."

Being a huge Dodgers fan, I knew that the Giants and Dodgers were big rivals. So much so, fans had come to blows over games in the past.

I grinned. "No need to leave. You just made this friendship more interesting."

SIX

Tessa

STRIPPING HAD TAUGHT ME A LOT ABOUT RELATIONSHIPS, SEX, POWER, and intimacy—or the lack of, in my case. Men told *Scarlett* their private fantasies and desires hoping for more than just a dance or boobs in their face. While I was staring across the table at Vinny, I wanted to tell him *my* fantasies and desires and that I didn't want to be only friends. That I wanted to see what would happen if I told him I'd lied and wanted to be more. But then, I wasn't sure if I could be in a relationship with someone who had sex for a living. We used our bodies in two different ways to make money, and that thought made me not tell him the truth.

It was better that we were only friends because I had Colton to think about. He was starting kindergarten in a few months, and I needed to focus on his progress to get him ready. Next week I was meeting with his teacher to discuss a plan for the new year even though this year wasn't completed yet. If Vinny and I did become friends, and hang out for more than just the one lunch, then maybe I would tell him I wanted a male figure in Colton's life, but I had to do it when the time was right.

That wasn't right now.

The following Wednesday, I was at Red Diamond, ready to do my third set when Sebastian stopped and stood next to me, his hands in his pocket as we both looked toward the curtain. I slowly turned my gaze as I looked up at him and wondered to myself why he was backstage. I only saw him up in his office or on the floor greeting customers or whatever.

"Tessa," he greeted.

"Mr. Delarosa."

He grinned down at me, and I noticed his slicked-back, dirty blond hair was perfectly in place like it always was. "How long have you been dancing for me? Ten months?"

"A little over a year," I corrected.

"How are you liking it?"

It wasn't my dream job, but I wasn't going to tell him that. "I love the money and the flexible hours."

"Good. I like seeing you out there."

I gave him a small smile, not sure if I should respond or not. All I could think about was what I saw in his office a few days before. Luckily, the DJ announced me before I felt any more awkward.

"It's time to bring out the lady in red. Ladies and gentleman, please give it up for Scarlett!"

Before I took a step up, Sebastian said, "If you ever need anything, Tessa, let me know."

I nodded with another small smile and walked out to "Double Tap" by Jordin Sparks blaring from the speakers.

After my shift, I picked Colton up at school. We went home, where he instantly turned on the TV and put on his cartoon. As I stared at the cartoon dogs, I kept replaying my interaction with my boss over and over in my head. The conversation was weird and awkward. I had been at Red Diamond for over a year and he'd barely spoken to me in that time. I needed Melony. I needed to pick her brain.

Me: *Can you come over before you head to RD?*

She texted me back right away: *On my way over.*

A few minutes later, there was a knock on my door. Peeling my eyes away from the TV, I went to greet my best friend.

"Hey."

"What's up?" she asked, walking inside.

"Let's go to the kitchen table."

"This must be serious," she stated and walked toward the kitchen.

I closed the door and locked it. After sliding into one of the dining chairs, I said, "It's not serious, but something's up with Sebastian."

"What do you mean?" She arched her brows.

"He talked to me today."

Melony chuckled. "And?"

"Is that normal? He's barely said two words to me the entire time I've worked there."

She thought for a moment. "I mean, I see him talking to the girls."

"You do?"

She stood and went to my fridge, grabbing a bottle of water. "Well, yeah. He's our boss."

"What does he say to you?"

I watched her move back to her seat and thought for a moment before answering. "Actually, I can't recall anything."

"See," I stated. "This is weird."

If I hadn't seen Sommer on her knees in his office, I wouldn't think twice about it. Now, I was questioning everything. It wasn't normal. The girls and I went in, danced, and left. We paid our dues to Honey and not him directly. It was as though he was Big Brother and only watched us from afar.

"What did he say, exactly?" she asked.

I took a deep breath. "Just asked how long I'd been at Red Diamond, if I was liking it, and told me that if I ever needed anything, I could come to him. Oh and, he likes seeing me dance or something."

We stared at each other for several moments.

"Do you think that's how he got Sommer on her knees?" I asked.

Melony shook her head slightly and blinked a few times as though she was still thinking. "Maybe. I mean, it's not like she's straight like us."

"I can't," I breathed, knowing that *straight* meant we didn't do extras. Melony and I never crossed over a line with anyone at the club. Of course, there were those who only saw dollar signs and wanted to do the extra stuff. I couldn't. And with our boss? No way.

"You shouldn't have to."

"But what if? I can't get fired. I need the money."

She took a sip of her water. "If he does, tell Honey or something."

I went to the fridge for my own water. "You think she'd do something?"

"I don't know, but he can't expect that from us."

I moved back to my chair and sat down. "It's a strip club. People think we're whores already. What makes you think he's any different?"

"Because he knows we're not."

I wasn't sure if that was true. We had rules at the club, and if a customer tried to touch us or anything, we got Honey or a bouncer. Anything under clothes wasn't permitted, and I knew Melony and I stuck to that. Not all of the other girls did because they'd get more money for other things. That wasn't me.

"You'll let me know if he tries anything with you?" I asked.

"Of course. He may be decent for a guy in his forties, but he's not my type."

He wasn't mine either.

Vinny: *Remember Paul?*

I smiled as I read the text from Vinny. I'd been thinking about him a lot, but I'd never tell him that. My heart did a little flutter, and I typed back: *Yeah?*

He texted back right away: *He's in love.*

My mouth hung open.

Me: *Seriously?*

Vinny: *Well, maybe not in love, but he has a girl roommate he can't stop talking about.*

Me: *Is that a new thing?*

Vinny: *Yeah, she works for S&R too.*

I paused before replying. Did that mean that Paul and his roommate had sex all the time or not at all because they were too tired after working all day by having sex with clients?

Me: *Maybe you'll need to hire me again for his bachelor party?*

Vinny: *I wouldn't mind seeing your tits again ;)*

Me: *You know where to find me ;)*

Vinny found me the next night during my second set. I was dancing to "Me & U" by Cassie when our eyes locked. Each set, I danced to the same songs and did the same routine more or less depending on how many people were wanting to stick dollars in my G-string. We each did at least five sets. Each set was once an hour or so depending on how many girls were working. The rest of the time we worked the floor and did private dances—or in some cases, girls did extras.

Usually, I tuned out the words of the song because it was on endless repeat for me, but as Vinny and I smiled at each other, the lyrics became clear as day. It was as though I *had* been waiting for him. The look in his eyes and the smile on his face told me he wanted me just like the song was saying.

I worked the stage, taking off my top and teasing everyone sitting nearby. My gaze met Vinny's again just as the words talked about me making a move, that it would be a secret we could keep between the two of us. We stared at each other, never breaking eye contact, and I wondered if he heard the same words—if he thought the same thing— if he wanted the same thing. If I didn't have Colton, I was sure I wouldn't hesitate to tell Vinny how I really felt because I did want him. It had been over a month now since we'd met, and every time I saw his name on my phone or his chocolate eyes, my belly dipped. He had that effect on me.

Before the song ended, Vinny beckoned with a crook of his finger for me to come closer. I didn't hesitate as I crawled toward him, topless. He held out a twenty between his fingers, and when I got to him, I leaned back on my heels, thrusting my hips forward so he could slip the bill into my bottoms. But he didn't. I narrowed my eyes at him in a playful manner, silently asking him what he was doing. He motioned for me to come closer again and this time I placed my hands on the stage and got within inches of his face.

"How much to get you to go to dinner with me?"

I chuckled. "You don't need to pay me to have dinner with you."

"Then come to dinner with me."

"I can't. I have more sets to do."

"I'll pay whatever you'd usually make—"

"Vinny …" I sighed. I could leave. If I did, I would have to pay the house more for missing my sets, but it was possible. But I needed every dime I made.

"Tess—"

"Scarlett," I corrected.

He grinned. "Fine, Scarlett. How much for a private dance?"

My second song of the set was ending, so instead of prolonging our flirting, I whispered, "For you, I'll do it for fifty."

"Then I want two."

I nodded and stood. After grabbing my top, I left the stage and went into the dressing room to change into a fresh red bikini and spritzed myself with my body spray that smelled like cotton candy.

When I came out from the back, Vinny was waiting near the door. As soon as he saw me, his face lit up. I had to admit I would never tire of that look on his face. I motioned for him to follow me, and I took him into one of the private rooms. Across from the entry, a red leather loveseat spanned the small space. Red wallpaper with black metallic roses lined the walls, and a crystal chandelier hung in the center of the room.

"Do you want a drink?" I asked.

"Can't. I'm on my lunch break."

I closed the door behind me. "Escorts get lunch?"

Vinny chuckled. "A man's gotta eat Tess—Scarlett."

I grinned back. "You can call me Tessa in here, and you're not eating."

He got more comfortable, spreading his legs as he leaned back on the couch. "You're the one preventing that."

"How?" I asked.

He furrowed his brows and cocked his head to the side as though I was an idiot for asking such a question, then he slowly grinned again. "Do your thing, Tess." He motioned with his head toward his lap instead of answering my question. Then it dawned on me, and I swallowed.

I wasn't nervous until now. I'd done plenty of lap dances in the past year, but none of them were for a friend. Taking a deep breath, I pushed my nerves aside and did what I always did by running my hands up my sides as I sashayed toward him. His brown eyes lowered from my face to my hips, and he licked his lips.

"No touching," I reminded him and myself.

He held up his hands. "I'll try."

I chuckled and turned my ass toward him. I slowly rotated my hips in a circle and ran my hands under my hair, bringing the long brown curls off my shoulders and neck. "What made you come in tonight?"

"I wanted to see you."

I stilled my movements.

"Friends visit friends at work."

I turned and faced him. I was about to argue with him, but then I realized maybe he was right and I was reading more into it than I should. While some of Vinny's actions and words implied he wanted there to be more between us, he hadn't come out and said it, nor had he actually made a move. So, I went with it as I continued my dance on his lap.

"I like when you visit me at work."

"You can visit me at work too," Vinny stated.

I laughed, throwing my head back as I moved onto his lap facing him. "I can't afford you."

"I'd give you a discount."

"Oh yeah? You have a friend's discount?"

"Only for you."

"I'm flattered."

"Maybe we can do an exchange," he suggested.

"How so?"

He shrugged and placed his hands on my hips only to remove them quickly when we both looked down after I'd stopped moving. "Sorry."

Even for that brief second, his touch felt good on my skin, and I reminded myself once again that we were only friends and couldn't be anything more. At least not now. "It's okay. Just don't let it happen again or I'll have to tell Titus."

Vinny grinned. "I'll try not to."

I started moving again. "So, Paul's in love?"

"Apparently. He's taking his roommate on a date."

"Who pays for that?" I asked.

He scrunched his eyebrows in confusion. "I imagine he does."

"I mean since they're both escorts."

"Oh." He laughed. "I'd think he would because there are two things a woman shouldn't touch on a date."

"What are those?"

"The door and the check."

"And what *should* she touch?" Because most of the time a man got an erection while I rubbed myself on his lap, I hadn't realized that Vinny was hard until those words left my mouth. I usually tried not to think about it, but now I was all too aware how turned on he was.

"Don't tease me like that because my imagination is already fucking you right now."

I swallowed, not able to respond because I wanted his fantasy to be my reality.

SEVEN
Vinny

I WAS PLAYING WITH FIRE.

I couldn't stay away from Tessa. I tried. I really did, but before I realized it, I was pulling into the parking lot of Red Diamond and then sitting in front of the stage waiting for her to come out. I didn't have to wait long.

When I saw her, I wished I hadn't. Not because I didn't want to see her, but because all the other men in the room were looking at her too. I wanted to pick her up off the stage, walk out the front door and never let another man look at her again. But that couldn't happen because she wasn't mine. So, I did the only other thing I could think of to get her away from other eyes. I asked her to dinner, but she turned me down. I went one step further, not ready to give up on getting her alone, and asked her to give me a lap dance. And she did. Twice.

Now, I was hard as a fucking rock and on my way home, by myself, thinking about how I'd have solved my problem if it had been a job for S&R. Hell, even if Tessa hadn't said she only wanted to be friends, I would have been able to fuck her in that tiny room, but she *had* said that—multiple times. I also got the impression she wasn't one of the strippers who did *extras* because the moment I touched her, she'd stilled as though she wasn't used to men touching her at work.

As I drove home, I made myself a promise that I wouldn't ever set foot inside Red Diamond again because going home to rub one out, thinking about Tessa, was torture.

I wanted the real deal.

The following Wednesday afternoon, I was at school—my day job —preparing next year's case load for all the incoming children transitioning into kindergarten. It was only the beginning of April, but a lot went into preparing each child's education plan. I was so engrossed in the scheduling that I barely heard the faint knock on the classroom door.

"Come in," I called out. The door opened, and I stood, smoothing down my tie. When I looked up, I shook my head slightly. *Was I daydreaming?*

"Mr. Reed, this is Teresa Stewart," the principal, Alan Fitzgerald, stated. "She's here for her three o'clock classroom transition meeting for her son, Colton."

I blinked and stared at Tessa for a few beats, then cleared my throat and stuck out my hand. "Right. It's nice to meet you."

Tessa took my hand. "You too."

There was an awkward silence until Alan said, "All right, if you need anything from me, Ms. Stewart, please come to my office, but your son will be in good hands with Mr. Reed."

"Thank you," Tessa replied, and we watched Alan leave and shut the door behind him. Her blue eyes locked with mine again. "Why didn't you tell me you were a teacher?"

"Why didn't you tell me you had a son?" I countered.

"Because I wasn't ready. I thought you only worked—"

"The school doesn't know," I informed her.

She walked a few feet and sat on a mat where the kids played. "I get it now."

"Get what?" I asked, confused.

"Why you use a fake name for S&R."

I nodded. "Yes, but my picture is on the S&R website, so technically they could still find out."

"Then why bother using a fake name?"

I shrugged as I sat next to her. "It's just another step to hide it. And no one has found out—until today."

"To be fair," she chuckled, "I only found out because I'm a stripper."

I felt hope in my chest at the sound of her laughter. At that moment she held my career in the palm of her hand, and I was preparing myself to do whatever I needed to prevent her from going to Principal Fitzgerald. "Please don't tell anyone."

She stared at me for a moment. "I would never do that to you, but what do we do?"

"What do you mean?"

"You're going to be my son's teacher."

"Working at S&R doesn't affect my work here," I assured her.

"I mean us."

I cocked my head to the side slightly. "Us?"

Tessa laughed again. "I mean, I gave you a lap dance." Her eyes widened as the words left her mouth. "Oh, God. I gave my son's teacher a lap dance."

I reached over and touched her hand and grinned. "And his teacher paid for a lap dance and frequents a certain strip club."

"Is that supposed to make me feel better?"

"Yes?" I *was* trying to make her feel better. No one needed to find out anything. Tessa didn't say anything further, so I continued, still touching her hand. "Look, Tess. I'm technically not your son's teacher yet. So what if we have a friendship? So what if you gave me a lap dance? No one needs to know, and no one can know about S&R. I will lose this job, and I don't want that. I love all my kids."

"Why did you become a teacher?"

I chuckled slightly. "Let's get off the floor, and I'll tell you whatever you want to know."

"Okay," she agreed.

I helped her stand and then moved behind my desk. I motioned for her to take a seat in one of the chairs. Leaning back in my chair, I said, "All right, here's the short version of why and how I became a special ed teacher. I went to USC on a full ride for volleyball. Specifically, I wanted to do beach volleyball, but I tore my ACL my sophomore year. I recovered after surgery and had a year of rehab, but in the end, the doctors didn't clear me to play again, so I continued with my education to become a teacher."

"Aw, that sucks. Why did you pick special ed? It has to be challenging, right?"

"It is. I couldn't play volleyball anymore, but I wanted to coach. The Special Olympics in L.A. needed volunteers, and the rest is history. I got my bachelor's degree, and I got credentials in special education."

"That's amazing. Do you still volunteer?"

I smiled. "I do."

"What made you want to be an escort?"

I leaned forward and rested my elbows on the desktop. "Why are you a stripper?"

She snorted. "Because I need money to survive and raise my son."

I nodded. "Right, because of the money. You could easily do something else, right?"

"Well …"

"Tess, I make *a lot* of money being a part-time escort. I like to travel, not live paycheck to paycheck, and I like to have fun. After I lost my scholarship in college, I was eating ramen to survive. I know how hard it is, and I get it. My buddy was working as an escort and needed me to help him one night—"

"Help him have sex?" She scrunched her face in confusion.

"No." I laughed. "Well, yes, but not with him. He'd overbooked and needed me to take out one of the ladies. After that date, I realized it was easy money, I got laid, and I never ate instant noodles again."

Her face softened, and I knew she finally understood why I did both jobs. "So, what do we do?"

"What do *you* want to do?"

"I don't know." Tessa shrugged and looked away from me.

"Can I tell you what I want to do?"

Her gaze met mine again. "Okay."

"I suggest we go over what I have planned out for your son, and I won't go back to Red Diamond anymore so there's no line crossed."

"And we're no longer friends?"

I frowned. "We can still be friends."

"How?"

"Friends go to lunch, dinner, movies, whatever. I'm sure we can figure something out."

"Can you get in trouble once the school year starts?"

"Well, they can't tell me who I can and can't be friends with, but it's probably best we don't say anything."

"Okay."

"Okay?"

"Yeah. I agree to everything you said."

"Great." I reached for the folder to go over everything with her, but then stopped. "You know, I was going to text you tonight because the Dodgers and the Giants play in L.A. next weekend. We should go."

"I can't leave Colton."

"Bring him."

"To L.A.?"

"Sure, why not?"

"But the drive, the noise."

"I know what to do." I smiled. "Remember, I specialize in this."

"Right, but I don't think he'll be able to ride there and back in one day, plus a baseball game."

"We'll make it a weekend trip and get a hotel—"

"I can't get a hotel room with you."

I grinned. "Two rooms, of course."

"Let me think about it. Our last road trip was when he was three and we moved to Vegas. It didn't go so well."

"We'll make stops along the way. We'll bring snacks, his favorite toys, noise-canceling headphones, an iPad, and whatever else I can think of. We'll be fine."

"Okay."

I was starting to really love that word as it left her lips. "Okay?"

Tessa smiled, and after a few seconds she agreed. "Yeah, let's do it. It will be good for him, and he loves the Giants."

I smirked. "Not after he sees how much better the Dodgers are."

She tsked. "That will never happen because it's not true."

"Only time will tell, Tess. Only time will tell."

Holy shit. What the hell was I doing?

Before Tessa left my classroom, I told her I'd buy the baseball tickets and book our hotel rooms near the stadium. Sure, friends did that, and it shouldn't be a big deal, but being friends with her was fucking with my head. I wanted to be more than friends. I wanted to only have one hotel room—alone. I wanted to know what she looked like fully naked, not just her tits.

I wanted her.

But now that I was going to be her son's teacher, there was more of a chance it would never happen. Maybe it was the universe telling me we were only meant to be friends. I didn't like that idea, but I was going to have to deal with it. I didn't want to cross the line and lose my job. I was already walking on eggshells because it would only take one co-worker or a parent of a student to book a date with me through S&R and my career in education would implode.

I had a feeling shit was going to go down, and it wasn't going to be good for me.

Since Tessa needed to work Friday night and tonight, I decided we would go to the Sunday game. That way, we could drive after Tessa got off work Saturday night, and Colton could sleep on the drive, which would make for a better car ride in general. Tessa gave me her address and asked me to be at her apartment an hour after her shift ended.

After parking, I made my way to her apartment number and knocked on the door. When it opened, I expected to see her smiling face. Instead, it wasn't her. It was the stripper I'd paid forty bucks to tell me Tessa wasn't working.

"Ah," I stuttered, glancing at the apartment number on the door again.

She smiled. "It's good to see you again, *Duane*."

"Um…"

The door opened wider, and Tessa was there. "Hey." She smiled.

"Hey."

"This is Melony, my best friend and co-worker."

"Oh!" Everything was making sense. I stuck out my hand and Melony took it.

"Should I call you Duane or—"

"Vinny is fine." I winked.

She smiled and blushed at our little secret joke. "It's good to officially meet you."

"Same, and thanks for the info the other week."

"Not a problem."

My gaze moved back to Tessa. "Colt is sleeping," she said, "but if you want to carry our bags, I can get him."

"No, let me." I didn't know how heavy he was, but for some mysterious feeling, I felt as though I should do it.

"Are you sure?" Tessa asked.

"Of course."

"I'll grab the car seat," Melony stated.

I followed Tessa to a bedroom with a nightlight that projected the illusion of water onto the ceiling. "Wow, this is cool," I whispered, looking up at the rippling image.

"It calms him."

"I bet." I was already in awe of her parenting skills. Sensory processing disorders for children with autism were a huge issue, and it was vital to find or develop what worked for each child, and many needed something to focus on while going to sleep. It was beneficial for his sensory therapy.

"Go ahead and grab him. I'll unplug the light so we can bring it with us."

There was an odd feeling in my chest as I picked up the sleeping boy. It was as though all the pieces of my life I didn't know were missing were finally being put together.

But I didn't know why.

EIGHT

Tessa

I WAS NERVOUS.

The man beside me made me that way, but at the same time, seeing him carry my sleeping son melted my heart. The only other man to hold Colton was my father, and it had been four months since we'd seen my parents at Christmas. I knew Colt would eventually need a father figure in his life—someone to teach him sports, how to shave, whatever. And while I thought Vinny could maybe be that person in a friendly capacity, I didn't realize how much my heart wanted it to be more.

When I went to the school to have the meeting with Colton's teacher, I never in my wildest dreams thought the teacher would be Vinny. He was shocked to see me, too, and to learn that I had a son. Colton was supposed to come as well, but he was having a meltdown and I couldn't get him into the car. At the end of the day, I suppose it didn't matter. Now Vinny would interact with Colt longer than thirty to forty-five minutes, and hopefully, that would make the transition better.

"Are you excited?" Vinny asked as we drove down the dark freeway in the desert toward Los Angeles.

"So excited. I haven't been to a game in years."

"I go a few times a year."

"Really?"

He nodded. "Yeah. Love my Dodgers."

I snorted. "I love my Giants, but having Colton has made it difficult to go."

"I can imagine." There was a brief pause, and then he asked, "If you don't mind me asking, is his father around?"

I took a deep breath. "No. He was in the Marines and died before I could tell him that I was pregnant."

"I'm sorry."

I smiled tightly to myself. "It's okay. I mean, it's not okay that Colton's father died, but I didn't know him. It was actually a one-night stand during Fleet Week, and before I could get in contact with him, he died in combat."

"How'd you find out if he was fighting in the war?"

"The night I met him, he and his Marine buddies were living it up because, after Fleet Week, they were being deployed. When I realized I was pregnant, I searched for him on Facebook, but I didn't know his last name. Hell, I didn't even know his real name because they were all using nicknames. It took me months to locate him. Then, before Colt was born, the USO posted a picture of his father on their Facebook page. A friend of his commented on the picture that it was the last one of him and his fellow Marine, Corporal Scott Colton. I messaged his friend and told him who I was and that I'd met *Jameson* during Fleet Week in San Francisco and I was trying to get in contact with him. Weeks later he messaged me back that Scott, who went by the nickname Jameson because he loved the whiskey, had died in combat not long after being deployed."

"Wow," Vinny breathed.

"Yeah, it's been tough raising Colt alone. I saved the image from the USO page, and when he's old enough, I'll tell him the story and show him the only picture of his father that I have."

"Did the military help with medical bills or provide health coverage for Colton?"

I shook my head. "There's no proof he's the father even though I know he is because I wasn't dating or sleeping with anyone else during that time."

"What about Scott's family?"

"Scott's friend said he contacted the family on Facebook, but they never got back to him or something. I don't know. Never heard from anyone again after he told me Scott died."

"That's horrible."

I shrugged. "Yeah."

"Even though I haven't officially met Colton, I can tell you've done an amazing job raising him."

"Thank you." There was a stretch of silence until I spoke again. "Thank you for setting this up. I hope Colt will be fine with all the people at the stadium."

"The noise-canceling headphones will help."

"Hope so because I'd love to take him to a game at AT&T Park. That ball field is amazing."

"I've never been to it."

"Maybe we can go later in the season when the Dodgers play in San Francisco?" I suggested. "The food is incredible."

"And you can show me all your favorite places from when you were a kid."

I chuckled. "Yeah, I'll be your private tour guide."

"If you're good, I'll give you a *big* tip."

My eyes widened. "Guess we'll find out, won't we?"

"Yeah, Tess. We sure will."

I stayed in the car with a sleeping Colton while Vinny checked us into the hotel. It was almost seven in the morning by the time we arrived, and I was worried that the hotel wouldn't let us check in, but a few minutes later, he came back to the car, smiling.

"So." He rubbed the back of his neck. "They only have one room left."

"Are you serious?"

"No." He laughed and moved to the back of the car.

I chuckled, opening my door and following him. "That was mean."

He opened the back hatch of his SUV. "Would it be so bad to share a room with me?"

No, it wouldn't. "I'm not sure what Colt would think if he woke up and there was a strange man in the room."

"True, but after the school year, we're going to be best buds."

"I hope so." I grinned and reached for our bags. "He loves baseball —you can teach him how to throw."

"I love baseball too, but I'm better at spiking a volleyball." He motioned with his head toward the bags as though to ask me if I could get them by myself. I nodded, and he opened the back door of the car. "How tall was his father?"

I shrugged. "Not as tall as you, but not short."

Vinny reached in and grabbed my son as I closed the back door. "Good. I hope he'll be tall. I'll teach him everything I know."

"Then you'll need to get him a volleyball." We started toward the lobby.

"I'll do that on Tuesday and bring it by your place."

I was trying not to read into his words, but I couldn't help it. I liked that he was making future plans with us. I knew if our relationship went further than friendship, I wouldn't be okay with him sleeping with other women. Having men stare at my breasts while I danced on stage was *much* different from Vinny bringing a woman to orgasm with his body.

When the elevator arrived, we stepped inside, and he hit the button for our floor. As the lift ascended, he handed me a key packet. "Rooms are next to each other. I'll get him in bed and then let you get some sleep. It's going to be an exciting night."

"Yeah, because the Dodgers are going to lose."

"Should we make this interesting?"

"How so?" I was smiling. I couldn't stop myself. I liked that we had this little rivalry of sorts.

The elevator dinged after coming to a stop. The doors opened, and we walked out into the hallway. "Well, it's a three game series, and since the Dodgers won game one, and the Giants won last night's game, whoever wins tonight's game is the winner. Loser cooks dinner for the other person?"

I nodded, still smiling. "I hope you know how to cook steak and lobster."

I took a quick shower as soon as I got into the hotel room. Colton was still asleep, which was good, but as I crawled into bed, he woke and started to panic about being in an unfamiliar place. I compressed his ears, and he looked up at me. "It's okay. We're in a hotel. Remember I told you we were going to a baseball game?"

He blinked rapidly to let me know he understood.

"Mommy needs to get some sleep. Can you go back to sleep? I'll turn on your waves."

He hesitated for a moment and then slid back down, resting his head on the pillow.

"Good boy. When we wake up again, you can play on the iPad. Okay?" He blinked quickly again, and I moved to plug in his nightlight.

I crawled into bed beside him before drifting off to sleep.

I could have sworn I'd just fallen asleep when I felt a little hand shaking me. I opened my eyes in the dark room with blue waves on the ceiling to see Colton staring at me. "What's wrong, Slugger?"

He pointed at the TV, so I sat up and looked for the remote. Going to bed at eight in the morning wasn't the best idea, but at least we arrived in L.A. with no problems. Now, I just needed Colt to watch TV or play on his iPad for a few hours more.

After spotting the remote next to the TV, I crawled out of bed and turned it on. "I don't think we can get *PAW Patrol* on this TV. Do you want to watch it on your iPad?" He reached out as though I was holding the device, so I switched off the television, got him a banana, apple juice, his baseball, and the iPad from our bag, and then put him back in bed beside me with pillows propping him up. "Mommy needs a little more sleep, okay?"

He didn't respond as he pulled up Netflix and went straight to his cartoon.

I woke again, but this time it was because there was a knock on the door. Looking at the clock, I noticed that it was a little after eleven. I crawled out of bed, glancing briefly at Colton who was engrossed in his iPad and rolling the baseball in his hands. Looking through the peephole, I saw it was Vinny holding a tray of what looked like coffee. Before opening the door, I ran my fingers through my long dark brown hair and prayed that one of the coffees was for me so I could mask my morning breath.

"How are you awake?" I asked as soon as I opened the door.

"Figured we could go to lunch and then hang out here for a few hours before we head to the field. That way, Colton can have a nap."

"I'm going to need one too," I admitted, and opened the door wider so he could step in.

"I brought you coffee. Not sure how you like it or even if you do."

"Love coffee, and cream and sugar are fine."

Vinny set the tray on the dresser next to the TV. "I brought this guy chocolate milk." He turned and faced Colton who was still immersed in his iPad. "Hope that's okay."

I smiled. "That's perfect." He handed me the cup with a coffee lid on it, but the moment I touched it, I realized it was cold and must be the chocolate milk. I took it with me to the side of the bed and got on my knees. "Hey, Slugger. This is Mommy's friend Vinny. He brought you chocolate milk."

He didn't look away from his iPad, and Vinny moved to kneel beside me. He cupped Colt's ears as I normally did. "Hey, Colton. I'm Vinny. I'm going to be your teacher in a few months. Can I get a handshake?"

Colton's blue gaze moved to Vinny, and I expected him to ignore Vinny and go back to his cartoons, but instead, he blinked rapidly to communicate his okay. Vinny grinned and stuck out his hand, and I watched as my little man greeted Vinny.

"That was amazing," I gushed. He really did know how to work with children. We stood, and Colt's attention went back to his cartoon. "Thank you for the coffee. I can get us ready and come to your room in thirty or forty minutes if that works?"

"I'll be waiting."

Lunch wasn't going as planned.

I was hopeful Colt would be okay in a restaurant, but he wasn't. He had a hard time sitting still for more than thirty minutes at a time unless he had something to focus on, and his iPad had died. So instead, we got our food to go and went back to my room to eat and charge the iPad so he could have it at the baseball game. After getting Colton situated with his cheese quesadilla in the center of the bed, I took a seat at the desk, and Vinny sat in the chair near the window.

"Thank you again for all of this," I said to Vinny after taking a sip of my drink.

"Of course. I'm having a good time."

"Even with the lack of sleep?"

He grinned. "Even with the lack of sleep."

"Me, too," I admitted. "I honestly can't wait to see Colt's face when he sees the players take the field for the first time."

Vinny took a bite of his taco. "Some people assume baseball is boring, but when your team's doing well or two rival teams are playing each other, it's electric."

"I used to go with my dad, and not because the Giants were good. We were decent, but as you know, hadn't won a World Series in years."

"Helped that you had Barry Bonds hitting all those home runs."

"True." I took a bite of my own taco. "I'm hoping Colton can grasp the excitement when everyone cheers after a home run."

"You mean after the Dodgers hit a home run."

I chuckled. "I'm going to be cheering whenever the Giants hit a home run."

"You'll be the only one."

"Please," I tsked. "I won't be the only Giants fan there this afternoon."

Vinny smiled and stuck a chip into his mouth. "I'm going to be so embarrassed sitting next to you."

"Not when the Giants win. You'll be crying."

He threw his head back, laughing. "Even if they do lose—which they won't—the season is only beginning."

"True, but I still want steak and lobster when the Giants win." I smirked, feeling good about my Giants and already thinking about the steak and lobster feast.

NINE
Vinny

WHEN I BOUGHT THE TICKETS FOR THE BASEBALL GAME, I GOT US THREE seats in the outfield in the front row. Not because they were cheaper than a lot of tickets but because, in my opinion, they were the best seats. The bleachers in the outfield were where home runs were hit—home runs that needed to be caught by fans. Hopefully, I could get Colton a game ball and switch it out with the one he was currently playing with.

Tessa was booed for wearing her orange and black Giants jersey, but when the crowd saw Colt in his, the jeers turned to a collective aww. I had to admit Tessa had made a cute kid even if she was teaching him to like the enemy. I was in my Dodgers blue and gray jersey and, in our group, was the odd man out, but I didn't care. I wasn't sure if my Dodgers were going to pull off a win because as soon as we went ahead, the Giants answered back with a run. Our only saving grace, if the situation continued, was that we were last at bat because we were the home team. If we scored the final run, they wouldn't have a chance to tie the game.

The game was in the fifth inning and tied. Tessa and I were sitting with Colton in between us on the bleacher. Colton had his baseball in his hands and his noise-canceling headphones on. Each time a new person would get up to bat, he would repeat the stats that were on the scoreboard over and over as though he was committing them to memory, and he probably was. He didn't speak conversationally but only in random and sometimes repetitive ways—a symptom called echolalia.

"I can't believe he's talking so much," Tessa stated.

"That's good," I replied because it was. His treatment must be working.

"Cotton candy! Get your cotton candy here!" a vendor shouted as he walked down the aisle of the bleachers.

I raised my hand, indicating I wanted one. After I paid for it, I handed it to Tessa.

"You don't want him to sleep tonight, do you?" She chuckled.

"He's not in my room," I teased.

"If he's up, I'll make sure you are too for feeding him all this sugar." Colton had already had a hot dog and a soda, and he was getting now cotton candy. I didn't think it was so bad. I wanted nachos myself.

"It's what you do when you're at a game," I stated.

"I guess." She laughed and opened the clear bag. Tessa tore off a chunk of the pink spun sugar and handed it to me. I took a small piece, got in front of Colton the best I could, what with being on the bleachers, and stuck it onto his lips. "Mmmm, cotton candy." I stuck the rest into my mouth and watched as Colton's little tongue slipped out, tasting the sugar candy. His eyes widened with surprise. "It's good, right, Colton?" He blinked in response, and I smiled as I returned to my seat.

"You really are good with him," Tessa stated.

"I've learned a lot of behavior strategies. We'll get him there."

She smiled a warm smile. The sweet smell of cotton candy blew in the wind, reminding me of what she smelled like when she gave me the two lap dances. I cleared my throat and adjusted myself before turning my attention back to the game.

"Want some more?" she asked, extending another chunk.

I took the piece from her and stuck it into my mouth. It melted to nothing almost instantly, and all I was left with was a sweet aftertaste. Leaning back, I crooked my finger, asking for her to move closer to me behind Colton. She did, and I whispered into her ear, "Do you taste like cotton candy too?"

Her blue eyes widened. "What?" she whispered, only a few inches from my face.

I leaned in again. "You smell like cotton candy, Tess. I want to know if you taste like it too."

She pulled back slightly again, both of us still balancing our weight behind Colton. Our gazes locked and slowly, not able to hold back my inner feelings for her any longer, I brought my mouth closer to hers, wanting to get my first taste of her lips. Wanting to find out if she was as sweet as spun sugar. Just as our mouths were within millimeters of each other, there was a crack of the bat, and everyone around us stood as though the ball was hit at us. The moment was lost as we stood quickly and turned our attention to the field just as a ball flew above us. Someone on the Giants had hit a home run and put them in the lead.

"I like my steak cooked to medium." Tessa smirked up at me.

I grinned. "We still have four and half more innings. The evening's still young."

So, the Dodgers lost.

I'd normally be bummed, but I'd never been so happy to lose a bet in my entire life. Okay, maybe I *was* pissed the Dodgers lost, but the season was still early, and the Dodgers and Giants played each other a bunch of times. I planned to make a bet with each game.

By the time we got back to the hotel, we were all exhausted. Colton did amazing, and I was proud of him for being able to be around a shitload of people without any problem. Granted, he didn't talk to anyone, focused mainly on his iPad except when a new batter would get up. That was okay. I knew it was progress from what Tessa had told me.

"Get some sleep. Check out's at noon, and we can leave then if you'd like," I whispered after putting a sleeping Colton into bed. The sugar had done nothing to him because once we were in the car, he was out.

Tessa yawned. "That works."

There was a brief moment of silence. I wanted to try kissing her again. I hadn't been able to think of much else since the moment we almost did. But instead, I walked to the door and opened it. "See you in the morning. Good night."

"Good night," Tessa replied right behind me.

I turned around and she was looking up at me with her blue eyes. An image of her looking up at me as she sucked my dick flashed through my head. I couldn't wait any longer, I needed to know what her lips felt like, what they tasted like.

Fuck it. I was going to do it.

Even though she'd told me she only wanted to be friends, I was going to kiss her and show her I wanted more. I liked being with her. I loved getting to know Colton, and I didn't want to spend a day without seeing them.

We stared at each other as Tessa held the door open. I licked my lips, she swallowed hard, and I leaned down just as my phone in my pocket started to ring.

"Fuck," I muttered and pulled it out of my pocket. Once again, the moment was lost. "It's Paul," I said out loud.

She smiled warmly up at me. "I'll see you in the morning."

I nodded and swiped my screen to answer it as I walked toward my door. "Yo."

"I'm getting married!" Paul shouted into my ear.

I stopped walking. "What?"

"I'm getting married," he repeated.

"To who?"

"Andi. I mean, Joss."

I blinked and tried to clear my head. He wasn't making sense. The last I'd heard from Paul a few weeks ago, he was taking his roommate Andi on a date. Then he told me he thought he was falling in love with her. Now he was saying a different woman's name. "Who's Joss?"

"Andi."

I slipped my key into the lock of my room. "You're not making any sense."

He sighed. "Shit went down last week. I'm not at liberty to tell you except Joss is FBI."

I stopped walking again just inside my room. "FBI?"

"Again, I can't tell you details, but yes, she's FBI and was using an alias."

The door closed behind me, and I moved to sit on the edge of the bed. "She's FBI and was working for S&R?"

"Undercover."

"What?" I breathed, drawing out the word.

"Again, I can't tell—"

"Whatever. I get it, but I want to know everything when you can tell me."

"Of course. It's crazy, man, but yeah, the case is still going on, and actually, her best friend from D.C. is here to help."

"She's still undercover?"

"Yeah, and shit, I probably shouldn't have told you her real name until I cleared it with her. I'm just so excited."

"I won't tell anyone. Congrats, dude."

"Thanks, man."

"Did you set a date yet?"

"Not yet. It all depends on the case."

"Right. Well, let me know when you do."

"You going to bring Tessa?"

"What?" I snorted.

"Don't play coy. I know you have a thing for her. You're in L.A. now with her—"

"As friends," I stated—or lied. I wasn't sure. Tessa and I were getting closer, but at the same time, we were still just friends.

"Did you fuck her yet?"

I rolled my eyes. "No. It's not like that."

"But you want to."

"Of course I want to. Who wouldn't?"

"Well, seal the deal, man. Bring her to my wedding."

"You don't even know when you're getting married."

"If it's up to me, it will be soon."

"Let me know."

"I will."

First Gabe got engaged, and now Paul was too? And I was starting to have feelings for a woman, too? What the fuck was in the water at Saddles & Racks?

The next Friday, Shelby booked an evening with me. She was my first regular client and lived in L.A., but she came to Vegas at least once a month. When she did, we both knew what the date was all about. We'd meet at a bar, have a few drinks, and then go back to her hotel room where I'd give her several orgasms before calling it a night. It was easy, familiar, and I knew exactly what she wanted and liked. It helped that we'd had a *relationship* for almost ten years.

Most of my other dates were a shot in the dark when it came to pleasing them in the bedroom. Some wanted to be in control; they knew what they wanted. Some wanted me to figure it out on my own and made me try everything until I got them humming. Others wanted shit that their exes or whoever would never do.

One chick told me her ex never went down on her because he didn't like it. I told her that all straight men loved eating pussy, and it wasn't because we were eating pussy. It was because it made us feel good to make the woman feel good. We were in control and making them squirm from the pleasure we were giving to them.

They say women are complicated, but when she was grinding against your mouth and holding your head against her pussy, you'd just figured out what made her tick, and it was only a matter of time before she came with the swipe of your tongue. Even though I'd never been in a relationship before, I knew that if I were to ever get in a fight with a chick, I'd just have to make her come with my mouth and the fight would be over. So, ladies, if a man says that he doesn't like going down on you, that means he doesn't like pussy.

End of fucking story.

I walked inside the Velveteen Rabbit in the art district. It had an eclectic vintage feel to it and was where I met Shelby every time. I spotted her in the back against the wall, sitting on one of the velvet couches. When she saw me approach, her eyes widened, and a smile graced her face.

"Hey," I greeted as she stood, and I pressed my lips to hers.

Shelby was in her forties with strawberry blonde hair and blue eyes, with a little meat on her bones. Over the years she'd had many relationships, but none were the forever kind. It was better for me that way because it meant she'd keep coming back—and had. "Hey, Duane, I ordered you a Bacardi and Coke."

"Thanks, honey." I took the drink from her and then sat next to her on the couch, resting my arm on the back and turned slightly toward her. "How's work?" Shelby worked as an entertainment attorney and did a wide variety of things such as labor law, intellectual property law, and reviewing contracts. Being in L.A., she worked with a few actors, filmmakers, and musicians.

She sighed. "Busy."

I grinned. "Busy's good, right?"

"Means I have a job."

"Exactly."

"What about you? How are things?"

I smiled, thinking of Tessa. "Things are good."

"Who is she?"

I balked. "What?"

She snorted and rolled her eyes. "Come on. I've known you for at least a decade, and I've never seen you smile like that."

"You've seen me smile."

"Not like that." She motioned with her finger at my face.

"Like what?" I took a sip of my drink.

"Your eyes twinkled."

I threw my head back, laughing. "They did not."

"They did." She took a sip of her drink. "So, there isn't a woman?"

I grinned again. "Well—"

"See. Told you. Who is she? A client?"

I shook my head. "No. Just a friend. Met her a little more than a month ago at my buddy's bachelor party."

"You didn't seem this glowy the last time I saw you."

I shrugged. "We've gotten closer."

"Tell me about her."

"You want to know about another woman?"

She took a sip of her vodka and cranberry. "I want to know about the woman who has gotten into your heart. I've never known you to have a girlfriend before."

"Well, she's not my girlfriend," I corrected.

"But you want her to be?"

I shrugged and took a sip of my drink. I wasn't sure if I wanted a girlfriend, but I knew I wanted more with Tessa. "I'm not sure," I replied.

"What's holding you back?"

"My buddy who's getting married quit S&R—"

"And this girl will make you quit?"

I lifted a shoulder again. "I'm not sure."

Shelby took a sip of her drink, and after a few moments she said, "I hate to say this, but if I was interested in a guy and found out he was an escort, I don't think I'd be okay with it."

I bobbed my head. "I know that. I've seen it through the years with friends of mine."

"Maybe she'll be different?"

"Maybe," I replied, but I knew better.

Even if I was a straitlaced escort and only gave them dates, I wasn't sure if Tessa would be okay with me *dating* other women and I wasn't sure if I was ready to give up the game for someone I'd only known a month.

Even if she was all I could think about.

TEN

Tessa

THE WEEKEND WITH VINNY WAS AMAZING. THE GIANTS WON TWO OUT of the three games, I won the bet between Vinny and me, and I was on cloud nine. Something was changing between us. I'd always been attracted to him, but now, with Vinny was making me fall for him.

But I was still keeping it to myself.

I wasn't okay with him working for S&R and starting any kind of romantic relationship with me. He hadn't mentioned anything about his clients, but I had to assume he was still escorting. I was scared to bring it up to him because I wasn't sure if he wanted more with me, and if he was still working for S&R, I couldn't bring myself to be okay with him sleeping with other women. I knew he was attracted to me because of how turned on he was when I gave him a lap dance, and because he'd tried to kiss me twice. But that didn't mean he wanted a girlfriend, and I wasn't looking for a friend with benefits. I was just going to see what happened.

And that was what I told Melony when she came over on Tuesday while Colton was at school.

"Hey," she greeted when I opened the door. "Brought you your favorite salad from Peppermill."

I sucked in a breath, and my eyes bulged with excitement. "I love you."

She laughed and walked inside my apartment. "I know."

"Thanks for bringing me lunch. I'm starving," I stated as I closed the door then followed her into my small dining room next to the kitchen.

"I was craving a giant salad, so I figured I'd bring you one too."

I slid into a chair across from her. "Is that the only reason?"

She furrowed her brow. "Yeah, why?"

I tsked and rolled my eyes.

"What?" she asked with a smirk. "I've brought you lunch before. I'm being nice."

I chuckled. "I know you have, and you are, but I also know you, and I know your real motives."

"And what are those?" She handed me the box with my favorite salad— spring greens with chicken, blue cheese, slices of pears, walnuts, and a pear vinaigrette.

"You want to know about yesterday and Sunday."

She grinned. "Well, I was here when you were freaking out before he showed up Saturday night."

"I was not." I totally was. I'd never gone on a weekend trip with a guy before. It didn't matter that we had two separate rooms because I wasn't sure what to expect. But being with Vinny was like being with someone I'd known my entire life. He made me feel comfortable. He made me happy. He made me excited, and he made me feel like a woman and not another pair of tits to stare at.

"Please. You couldn't sit still while you waited for him to pick you up. You like him, and I know you like him as more than a friend."

I took a deep breath and sighed. "I do."

"I knew it. I knew it. I knew it." Melony stabbed a piece of chicken from her salad.

"But I can't do anything about it."

"Why not? Because of Colt?"

I took another deep breath. "No. He's great with Colton. I mean, of course he is since he's a special ed kindergarten teacher." After I found out about Vinny being a teacher, I'd told Melony. Hell, I'd told her everything because she was the only true friend I had in Vegas and I could trust her with anything.

"Then why not? He's hot."

"I know he's hot."

God, he sure the hell was. His buzzed, short brown hair looked soft, and every single time I saw him, I wanted to run my hand across his head. I swore his chocolate brown eyes twinkled when he looked at me. I wanted to feel his fucking perfect lips pressed to mine. Even his thick neck and Adam's apple turned me on. I had no idea why. Maybe it was because I wanted to wrap my arms around his neck while he fucked me against a wall—any wall. I knew he'd have no problem because his arms looked strong. I also knew— even though I'd only seen it in pictures on the S&R website—that he had at least a six-pack, maybe even an eight-pack, and said abs were dusted with dark hair that went all the way into his pants. And the V. Good Lord, the V. I wanted to run my tongue down his entire body as I explored every inch of him and found where that V pointed to.

Melony snapped her fingers in front of me. "Did you hear me?"

I blinked as I focused on her. "Um, no?" I was too busy daydreaming about the man who seemed to be perfect in every way.

"I said that since you know he's hot, and he's obviously interested in you, why aren't you riding him?"

I forked a piece of lettuce and a piece of pear. "Because other women do."

"Oh." Her shoulders fell. "Right."

"Yep. Just thinking about it makes me sad because I would want to be the only woman even if he doesn't have feelings for any of them."

"I totally get it," she agreed around a mouthful of food. "But let's say he quits and is just a teacher. Do you think he'd be okay with you showing your tits and giving other guys lap dances every night?"

I shrugged. "I don't know. Usher seems to be okay with it."

Melony stared at me for a beat, and then we burst into laughter at my reference to Usher's song, "I Don't Mind." "Maybe you should talk to him?" she suggested.

I took another bite of salad. "I can't." I wasn't sure if I'd be okay if he didn't sleep with his clients and only took them on the dates.

"Why not?"

"What if he only wants to be friends with benefits?"

"I think he wants more than that. He's spending time with you and Colton. Friends with benefits is just what Bailey and I are."

Melony wasn't looking for a relationship. She and the guy she was sleeping with had an understanding that it was only for sex. Melony was okay with that because she was going to school to become a nurse and didn't want to get involved with a guy until she was set in her career. I had nothing to fall back on, and if I found a guy who wasn't okay with my stripping, then I didn't know what I'd do. And if that guy was Vinny, it would break my heart if he was okay with me stripping because I needed the money.

"I'll just see what happens," I replied.

"Okay. Now, tell me everything that happened from the time you left until he dropped you off last night."

I laughed and took another bite of salad before I told her what she wanted to know.

After I picked Colt up from school on Friday and made sure he and Sophia were good for the night, I went to Red Diamond. Having my talk with Melony made me realize I needed to do something other than strip because I wasn't going to be able to do it forever. Hell, I didn't *want* to do it forever.

When I walked in through the side door, a feeling of sorrow washed over me. This was all I had to survive. Most of the girls were stripping to pay for college, medical school, whatever. I was doing it to pay therapy bills and to put food on the table for Colton and me. I wasn't hurting by any means; stripping was good money. But I wanted more even though I wasn't sure what *more* was anymore.

Sommer walked into the dressing room not long after me. I was sitting at a vanity doing my makeup, and I smiled tightly at her. "What's wrong with you?" she asked.

"Nothing," I replied, and she sat next to me at an open vanity.

"You seem gloomy or something. Sure hope that doesn't affect your tips."

I rolled my eyes. "It won't."

"Whatever. More money for me."

"Do you not listen? I said it won't affect my tips."

"Bitchy much?" she barked.

I turned toward her and glared. "I always give my best performances because not all of us get extra *perks* from the boss."

Sommer threw her mascara down and turned toward me. "What the fuck does that mean?"

I snorted and rolled my eyes again. "Nothing."

"That's what I thought."

I stood, scooting the stool back as I did. Sommer was a friend, but because I was in a bad mood, not wanting to bite my tongue anymore. "Tell me, did he pay you for your extra time?"

She stood and got within inches of my face. I faintly heard the other girls trying to calm us, but we didn't pay them any mind. "I don't know what you're trying to say, but whatever it is, it's none of your business," she hissed.

"You're right. I don't give a fuck whose dick you suck."

Her eyes widened, but before she could respond—*or slap me*—Melony stepped between us and pushed me back. "What the hell are you doing?" she asked. "This isn't like you."

"It's shark week or something," Sommer jabbed.

"Is it?" Melony whispered.

I rolled my eyes. "No. That was last week."

"Then why are you all—"

"Bitchy?" Sommer cut in, still seething as she glared at me.

I groaned and stepped around Melony. I left the dressing room and headed straight into the restroom that was only for dancers. Melony followed me. "Okay, what's going on? Vinny said he only wants to be friends with benefits or something? Broke your heart?"

"What? No," I groaned. "I haven't said anything to Vinny, just like I told you I wasn't going to."

"Well, it seems like you need to get laid," she teased. "Release some of that sexual tension."

While that may be true, it wasn't the reason I was in a bad mood. "I need to be a better mother."

"What?" She arched her brow and placed her hands on my shoulders, looking me in the eyes. "You're the best mother I know besides my own."

I sighed. "How do you think it will go over when Colt's in high school and his forty-year-old mother is a stripper?"

"You're not going to be a stripper that long."

"I'm not? What will I be doing?" I challenged, crossing my arms over my bikini clad chest and making her drop her arms.

"Um …" She looked past me as though she was thinking, and after a few moments she replied, "What do you want to do?"

"Really? You think I'd be in a bad mood if I knew what I wanted to do with my fucked-up life?"

"Your life isn't fucked up."

"Right. It's been my dream to dance on a stage topless, praying people will actually give me money for my show and not just sit there for free." That reply made me even angrier because it was true. A lot of people thought they could come in, order a drink, and get a free show, but free shows didn't pay my bills.

"Then go back to school." She smiled. "Become a nurse like me."

"Blood? Gross." I shuddered.

Melony chuckled. "Well, look online and see if anything sparks your interest. You can do a lot online, and you'll still be home with Colt."

I thought for a moment and then nodded. "Yeah, I'll look into it."

"Good. Now, unless you want to be on an episode of *Strippers Gone Wild*, I suggest you keep your mouth shut about Sommer and Sebastian."

I groaned. "She was all up in *my* business when she told me it was none of my business if she gives extras. She's a hypocrite."

"She's your friend."

I sighed. "You're right." We left the bathroom, and when I entered the dressing room, Sommer glared at me. "I'm sorry. I just have a lot on my mind."

She stood, and her glare turned into a warm smile. Wrapping her arms around me, she said, "Apology accepted. I'm sorry too."

"Thank you."

She lowered her voice. "But I want to talk to you about what you know. Come with me." She grabbed my hand and tugged me to the door I'd just entered through. I looked over my shoulder, and Melony gave me a what-the-hell look. I smiled at her before I continued through the doorway and into the bathroom again.

"What do you know?" Sommer asked as she released my hand.

I shrugged a shoulder. "About?"

She snorted. "You know."

"About you and Seb—"

"Yes."

I shrugged again. "I just saw you … on your knees in his office."

"Oh, God," she groaned. "When?"

I blinked. "When? It's been more than once?"

"Ah." She looked off to the side. "Maybe?"

I chuckled. "I only saw it once almost two months ago."

She exhaled a breath. "Good."

"But why?"

Sommer turned and leaned against the counter. "I guess it's my own fault."

"What? How?"

"I've always thought he was cute, and since I started three years ago, I flirted with him a little. It led to things."

"More than a blow job?" I whispered.

She nodded.

"Oh, wow."

"And no, he doesn't pay me."

"I guess that's good?"

Sommer chuckled. "I guess it means I'm not a whore."

"But our boss?"

"It's actually really good."

"Really?"

"If you like a no-strings-attached thing. Plus, he knows what he's doing."

The mention of no strings reminded me of Vinny. I needed to talk to him. Maybe that *would* make me feel better.

"Hey, Brent," I greeted as I crawled toward him on the stage. Like clockwork, he and his construction crew were here.

"Hey, Scarlett. How's your day going?"

I chuckled and twirled my legs around as I sat on my butt. His gaze zeroed in on my center and not my eyes when I replied, "I've had better. How was your work?" I moved, forcing his eyes to move back up to my face.

"Good. It's getting hotter out there, and I'm already dreading the summer."

"I bet." I continued to dance in front of him.

Brent stuck out a bill, and I turned my hip so he could slip it into my bottoms. "Lap dance for the road?"

I grinned. "Sure thing."

My two songs of the set ended, and I quickly started to pick up the bills that were left on the stage or had fallen out. I turned to look at Brent to tell him I'd come around to get him, but just as I did, I saw a figure in my peripheral vision up in Sebastian's office. I glanced up and saw him staring at me—again.

"Have a good night, Scarlett," Galen, one of the bouncers, said as he held the side door open for me so I could exit.

"Thank you, you too." I smiled and continued to my silver Corolla.

After I slid in and buckled my seatbelt, I cranked the engine and started to reverse out of the parking space. A car a few spaces over turned their lights on, and when I pulled out of the lot, the car turned in the same direction as I did. "Chains" by Nick Jonas blared through my speakers, and I started to dance a little, moving side to side as I sang at the top of my lungs.

Just as I was about to turn onto the street where my apartment was, I realized the car that left Red Diamond after me was still behind me. The hairs on the back of my neck stood up, and I stopped singing. Was this person following me? Who was it? I couldn't tell what kind of car it was, but it was dark—maybe black or dark blue? Instead of pulling into my complex, I kept going and turned on the next street. The car did too.

"What the hell?" I whispered, Nick still trying to serenade me.

I drove to the Strip, hoping I could lose the car in the process, but it didn't work. Even though Vegas was always hopping, people were inside partying and not driving down Las Vegas Boulevard at two in the morning. I didn't know what to do. Every turn I took, so did he— or she—or they.

Deciding to get on the freeway, I merged into the far left lane. So did they, but kept their distance as though I hadn't realized they were following me. Even though it was illegal, I pulled my phone out of my purse and called the first person I could think of, hoping and praying he'd pick up at this late hour.

"Candy?"

I balked. "Candy? Who's Candy?"

"You."

"No, I'm Tessa."

Vinny laughed. "I know this is Tessa, but did you forget that you smell like cotton candy?"

Yes, I did, because there was a murderer following me. "Right. So, um … sorry for calling this late …"

I heard him yawn. "It's okay. I'll pick up whenever you call me. What's up?"

"I just got off—"

"Is this a booty call?"

I snorted and switched lanes, wanting to get off at the next exit, which would bring me close to Fremont Street. "No, it's not a booty call."

"Damn," he muttered. "Then to what do I owe this two-in-the-morning call?"

"I think someone is following me."

"What?" Vinny boomed into my ear.

"I just got off of work, and as I was driving home, I noticed this car had been following me since the parking lot."

"Where are you?" I heard rustling on the other end.

"Near downtown."

"Come to my place."

"I need to get home to Colt. Sophia needs to go to sleep."

"Right. Colt. Meet me at the Target by your apartment. I'll be there waiting."

"And what if you're not?"

"I will be. I'll never let anything happen to you."

I took a deep breath, and instead of turning onto Fremont, I went straight, the car still following me.

ELEVEN
Vinny

I<small>T HAD BEEN ALMOST FOUR DAYS SINCE</small> I'<small>D LAST SEEN</small> T<small>ESSA</small>. F<small>OUR</small> long days. We didn't have any plans to get together, and when I glanced at my phone half asleep, I instantly smiled. But then I saw the time, and I was suddenly concerned because it wasn't like her to call me, let alone at two in the morning. Then to hear that someone was fucking following her …

It made my heart race faster than it had ever raced before and panic and fear course through my entire body.

Lucky for me, I wasn't pulled over for speeding because, as I stayed on the phone with Tessa while we both drove to the Target near her place, I wasn't paying attention to my speed. When I pulled into the lot, she wasn't there yet, thank God. I'd told her I'd beat her here, but I wasn't sure if that were possible or not because I lived twenty minutes away. I'd made it in twelve.

"I'm here," I told Tessa.

"I'm almost there."

"Is he still following you?"

There was a brief pause. "Yeah."

"I hope he stops. I'd love to find out who this fucker is."

"I hope he doesn't stop," she admitted. "But I can't even tell if it's a guy or not."

"Whoever it is will get a piece of my mind if they even pull into the lot behind you."

I heard Tessa chuckle on the other end of the phone.

"What's so funny?" I asked. I didn't think any of this was a laughing matter.

"It's not *funny*-funny. It's surreal funny."

"Surreal funny?"

"It's just that, before you, I didn't have anyone to call."

"Well, it seems as if fate has brought us together at the right time."

"Thank God," she exhaled.

"Yeah." I smiled.

A car pulled into the lot. "I'm here. Where—Oh, I see you."

"Pull in next to me and don't get out of your car."

"Okay."

I watched as she drove her silver car into the dimly lit, bare parking lot, and then pulled into the space next to my passenger side door. Once she did, I turned my attention back to the entrance, waiting to see if some fucker would follow her in. Target was closed and I'd assume there would be no reason for someone else to pull in. "How close was the car to you?"

"Just a car length or two behind me."

"Do you—" Before I could finish, a dark car pulled into the lot.

"That's them."

The car pulled in slowly. I couldn't see inside because the side windows were tinted. Wanting them to know that Tessa wasn't alone, I got out of my car. The car, which I could now tell was black, drove straight instead of turning onto our row. "Write this down."

"Write—" I read the license plate number to her.

"Shit, I don't have a piece of paper."

I hung up the phone and entered the number into my notes while sliding into her passenger side seat. "I got it."

"What are you going to do with it? They didn't do anything."

"We're calling the cops."

"Really?"

"Tess ..." I turned to face her. "Never *ever* take shit like this lightly."

"Have you been followed before?"

"Yes," I stated without hesitation.

Her blue eyes widened in the dim light. "What did you do?"

"Called the cops."

"Oh."

"It's better to document it and let them run the plates. They can take it from there. I want you to be safe."

"Okay. Can we do it from my place? I really should get home and let Sophia go to sleep."

"Yes, I'll follow you."

"Okay. Thank you. Really. I feel so much safer with you here."

I smiled warmly at her. "I would die if anything happened to you." Those eight words were one hundred percent true, even though it took me off guard that I said them. Escorting and stripping weren't dangerous jobs until situations came up like what had happened tonight. People got obsessed, and there was no telling what they'd do to have you all to themselves. Even though it had only been a few months, my life would suck without Tessa in it.

She smiled warmly back at me. "I feel the same way."

I stared at her for a beat, wondering if she meant what I assumed she meant. Before I could ask, I fucking yawned.

"We should really get to my place, and then you can go home, too."

"I'm not leaving you until we talk to the cops. You're crazy if you think otherwise."

"Vin—"

I opened the door. "I'll follow you."

"Okay."

I got out and turned, leaning inside. "Your car smells like cotton candy too." I winked, and shut the door without letting her respond, and walked back to my car.

After we both started our engines, I followed her to her place, looking in my rearview mirror for any car that might have been following us. I didn't see any that were consistent with each turn we took. Once we were there, I parked in a guest spot and jogged to where I'd seen her park. I wasn't going to let her walk anywhere alone.

"You know I work tomorrow night too, right?"

"Yeah?"

"Are you going to escort me every night?"

"If I have to," I deadpanned.

"Vin—"

"Let's just get into your apartment and call the cops and see what they say."

"Okay."

We walked to the second floor apartment, and with every other step, I looked behind us to see if a car pulled up or a person was following us. By the time we made it to her door, there was no one, and I was hopeful that fucker didn't follow us when we left the Target parking lot. Tess stuck the key into the lock, and we entered her living room, which was lit by one lamp near the couch. On the sofa was an older lady who I assumed was Sophia.

Her gaze met mine and I smiled as Tessa introduced us. "Sophia, this is my friend Vinny, who I went to L.A. with. Vinny, this is Sophia."

Sophia struggled slightly to get off the couch, but she made it by the time I moved to her to shake her hand. "It's nice to meet you. Sweet Tessa hasn't told me much about you, but I hope that changes."

I turned my head toward Tessa, and she blushed with a shrug. "Not much to tell," Tessa admitted.

"Yet," I stated.

Sophia patted my cheek like most grandmas do. "I like you already."

I smiled. "Thank you. I like you already too."

"You kids have a nice night—or early morning. This old lady needs her bed."

"Sorry I'm later than usual. I had a situation after work that Vinny is helping me with," Tessa admitted, and because she brought it up, I got the impression she looked up to this lady as either a mother figure or grandmother.

"What kind of situation?" Sophia asked, stopping just before she reached the door.

Tessa sighed and looked at me.

"Someone was following her home, and I'm helping her take care of it."

"Oh my," she gasped and walked the few feet to Tessa. "Are you okay?" She grabbed her hands.

"I am."

"It was smart calling Vinny."

Tessa's blue eyes looked at me. "I had no one else."

"I'm all you need," I stated.

Sophia grinned at me. "Listen to this boy. You need a good man in your life."

"I know," Tessa admitted and smiled at me.

"Let me walk you home," I said to Sophia and started for the door.

"Thank you. Now, Tessa, please call me if you need me."

"I will," Tessa replied.

I opened the door, and Sophia and I stepped out. "Lock it," I stated to Tessa. She nodded, and I went in the direction Sophia led me. "What are your intentions with my Tessa?"

I smiled. Definitely a mother or grandmother figure, and I liked that. I liked her. "Honestly, I'm not sure."

"What do you mean?"

"I like her, I really do, but you know what I do on the side, right?"

She stopped walking, and I looked down at her. "I actually don't know what you do for a living."

"Oh. Well, I'm actually a special ed teacher and will be Colton's kindergarten teacher this fall."

"Really?" Her eyes brightened.

I nodded. "Really. I also work as an escort."

"Oh my," she gasped.

I chuckled. "Yeah."

Sophia turned toward the door we stopped in front of and stuck a key into the lock. "I'm sure you kids will work it out if it's meant to be."

I grinned. "I hope so."

"Now, get back to our girl and do whatever needs to be done to keep her safe."

"Will do. It was nice meeting you," I stated again.

"Likewise. Have a good … morning."

I chuckled. "You too."

When I got back to Tessa's door, I knocked lightly. After a few moments, she opened it. "Did you just open the door without seeing who it was?"

"No." She frowned. "I looked through the peephole."

"Oh, okay. Now, let's call the cops." It wasn't every day I said those words, and I hoped I'd never have to again.

Tessa called the non-emergency line for Las Vegas Metro, and while we waited for them to arrive to file a report and get more information, we sat on her couch side by side, staring at a blank TV screen.

"Go to sleep if you want. It might be awhile before they get here."

"Really?"

I stretched my arm across the back of the couch, hoping she'd lean in and sleep against me. "Yeah, it's non-emergency, but they'll come eventually." I figured it would be maybe thirty minutes, but I could tell she was tired because she was yawning. Hell, I was tired, too.

"Tell me about the time you were followed."

"You really want to know?"

She turned her head toward me. "Of course I do."

I patted the top of my shoulder, silently asking her to do what I wanted, which was for her to get closer to me. She smiled and snuggled closer. I grinned to myself and held her tighter. "I've been followed twice, and both times was because a client wanted more."

"Like to date you?"

"Yeah."

"What happened?"

"First time, after I brought a date home, she followed me to my place. She didn't stop, but I made the mistake of letting her know where I lived by going home. You should *never* go home if you're being followed."

"I didn't."

"I know. That was smart."

"So, what did she do since she didn't stop?"

"Well, she started parking outside of my place a few nights a week, and then once I found her in my bed."

"What?" she shrieked and sat up.

"Naked."

"No," Tessa breathed.

"True story. Had to call the cops and got a restraining order."

"Wow, that's crazy."

"Yep. The second woman didn't follow me, but she somehow traced my phone and got my address. Showed up at my house wearing only a trench coat."

"You don't like women showing up in a trench coat? Isn't that sexy or something?"

"Yes, when both people are interested. But I don't have feelings for my clients."

"So, what did you do?" She placed her head back on my shoulder.

"Asked her to leave because I was busy, which I was."

"With another woman?"

"No." I chuckled. "A friend of mine from college was visiting, and we were engrossed in Call of Duty and drinking beer."

"What happened with the woman?"

"She apologized, but I never accepted a date with her again. Not sure what happened to her after that."

"Do you think my person is a regular?"

"Could be, or just someone who's obsessed with watching you from afar."

"My—"

There was a knock on the door. "Vegas Metro."

Tessa and I both stood. She went to the door, looked through the peephole, and opened it. For the next ten or so minutes, Tessa told the two officers everything that happened, and I gave them the license plate number. We were told they'd make a report, and when it was available, we could get a copy if we wanted it. There wasn't much they could do other than run the plates to make sure there wasn't a warrant out for their arrest, and before they left, they told Tessa to drive to a police station if it ever happened again, but I wasn't convinced that was the best plan. Most stations closed at five in the evening around here *and* weren't open on the weekends.

After the cops left, I turned to Tessa. "I better get home so you can get some sleep before Colt wakes up. I'll follow you home tomorrow night, and Sunday you're going to the range with me."

"The shooting range?"

"Yeah. Gabe and Paul teach women how to shoot guns, and we're getting you one."

"Seriously?"

"Abso-fucken-lutely."

I wasn't letting her walk alone at night without protection because when I told her I would die if anything happened to her, I fucking meant it.

And I wasn't taking that chance.

TWELVE

Tessa

WHILE COLTON TOOK HIS AFTERNOON NAP, I TOOK ONE AS WELL. I WAS used to going to bed late on Fridays and Saturdays, but not close to four in the morning—except when we'd gone to L.A. And I was certain I'd only made it through the game because I was high on the adrenaline of being at a game with a hot guy.

I was still tired by the time I made it to Red Diamond. Before I got out of my car, I looked around for the black vehicle that had followed me the night before. I didn't see it, but that didn't mean I wasn't looking over my shoulder as I walked in through the side employee door. When I turned the corner in the hall that went back to the dressing room, Galen stood in his usual spot where he made sure no one entered the club who didn't go through the front door.

"Hey, Scarlett. Have a good night last night?" He was a little taller than me, had dark red hair, a trimmed beard, and green eyes. He wasn't bad on the eyes at all.

I cocked my head slightly. "Why?"

He arched his brows. "Just making small talk like I normally do. Is that okay?"

I smiled, remembering that he did, in fact, usually ask me if my day or night was good. "Yeah, sorry. Something happened last night."

He turned to face me head on. "What happened? Are you okay?"

"Yeah, I'm fine." I took a calming breath and thought of something. "Actually, are there cameras outside?"

"What? Something happened here?"

"Someone tried to follow me home last night."

"Are you serious?"

"Yeah." I sighed.

"Of course we have cameras. The monitor and recordings are in the boss's office. You should go talk to him."

I swallowed and nodded slightly because I didn't really want to bother Sebastian. Plus, I wasn't sure what I'd walk in on if I did. "Thanks."

"No problem. What kind of car was it?"

"A black one."

"Doesn't narrow it down by much." He chuckled.

"No, it doesn't." I shook my head. "My friend got the plates though."

"And you called the cops?"

"Yeah."

"Good. Go talk to the boss. Hopefully, you can get something from the police. I doubt they will follow up, but maybe, with the plates, they can at least tell you a name."

I was hopeful they would because I didn't want to look over my shoulder every day. I was already going to change my route home. The police had told me they'd file a report and run the plates. Stalking was a crime, but the only thing I could do would be to get a restraining order, and that was only a piece of paper. A piece of paper couldn't physically protect me.

"Right. Well, thank you."

"You bet. Thank you again for telling me. I'll walk all of you ladies to your cars and make sure no one leaves behind you."

I smiled tightly up at him. "Thank you."

Instead of going to the dressing room, I took Galen's advice and went up to Sebastian's office. I figured that since it happened to me, it was happening to other girls—or would, and the boss should know about it. With each step I took up to his office, my heart pounded in my chest. What if Sommer was in there again? What if it was another girl? What if he was just busy?

When I knocked, he called out for me to come in. I opened the red door, took a deep breath, and entered.

Sebastian was alone and behind his desk that pointed toward the stage to my right. He smiled and turned to face me as I stepped inside. His dirty blond hair was styled in its usual slicked back way, and he was in a gray suit with a white button-down shirt and lavender tie. "Tessa, to what do I owe the pleasure of you coming up here?"

"Ah." I rubbed the back of my neck nervously. "I was wondering if I could look at the security feed from last night."

He set the pen he was holding down and leaned forward. "Why do you need to do that?"

"I—"

"Come in and close the door."

I still stood a few steps inside the office, so I took a deep breath and shut the door before walking to a chair in front of his dark wood desk. Before I sat down, I paused, wondering if it was the one he sat in when Sommer was on her knees. Without too much hesitation, I sat on the edge of the chair.

"So, what's going on?" he asked, resting on his elbows on the top of his desk.

I proceeded to tell him everything. "... and I hope that maybe the cameras will show me their face."

"Good thinking. The cameras are on a three day cycle, so it should be here." He pressed a button as he turned around in his chair, and a screen rose from a credenza behind him. I watched as he pulled a keyboard and mouse from a drawer and then typed some things on the keyboard and moved the mouse around, bringing up a color feed. "You left at what time last night?"

"Well, it was two this morning."

"Right." He pressed some buttons, and after a few moments, I saw myself exit the door.

"Do you see the black car?" Sebastian pulled up another view, this one of the parking lot and not the employee door. He rewound the feed until we saw the black car pull into the space. "He pulled up a little after nine."

"Nine?"

"Yep."

"And it's a guy?"

"Well ..." He zoomed in with the mouse, and I stood, getting closer so I could see better. "Yeah, it looks like a guy. Does he look familiar to you?"

I bent and got right in front of the monitor. The screen wasn't clear since it was dark with only the parking lot lights casting a glow. The guy in the car didn't look familiar at all, though it could be anyone because it was too grainy to discern any features. I sighed. "No. I don't think I've ever seen him before."

Sebastian turned his head toward me, and I looked down into his dark blue eyes. "Are you sure?"

I stood and stepped back. "I think so."

"Okay, I'll tell all my bouncers to keep an eye out for this car, and I'll talk to Honey so she can talk to all the girls."

"Thank you, Mr. Delarosa." My gaze moved to his desk, and I noticed there was a stack of money on the wood top and several small empty plastic bags with a red diamond printed on it. I had no idea what they were for because I'd never seen them before.

"Please, call me Sebastian."

My hand rested on the credenza as I turned my head and smiled slightly. "Okay."

He reached out and placed his hand on top of mine. "If you ever need anything else, please don't hesitate to come to me."

A feeling of uneasiness washed over me, and I wanted to pull my hand away, but I resisted so that I wasn't rude to my boss. "Thank you. I will."

Sebastian removed his hand and turned his chair back to his desk, looking at a desk calendar. I started to turn to leave, but he spoke again, and I stopped. "Remind me again what days you work."

"Wednesday and Thursday days, and Friday and Saturday nights."

"That's right. Are you up for making extra money?" He looked up at me.

My stomach dropped into the pit of my stomach. "Um—"

"It's not what you're thinking."

"It's not?" I asked, my brows furrowed in confusion. I wasn't sure if he remembered that I'd seen him getting his dick sucked a few months ago.

He leaned back in his chair. "Monday, I'm going to the fight at the arena, and I want you on my arm."

I balked. "What?"

He grinned. "This town is small, Tessa, and if I show up alone, I won't hear the end of it from my friends."

"Really?" He nodded. "Why me?"

"Why not you?"

I leaned my hip on the credenza, needing something to hold me up because he was talking about being one on one. One on one with my boss. Alone. "Because ..." I hesitated, not sure if I should bring up the Sommer situation or not.

"Do you want me to invite someone else?"

Yes. "I—"

He stood and moved in front of me, touching my hand again. I stared up into his eyes. He wasn't a bad looking guy, but he was my boss. Wasn't there a law or something? Probably not, but it was still weird to me.

"I'll pay you a grand."

My mouth fell open. "A grand?"

"Plus your ticket for the fight, of course."

An extra thousand dollars was tempting. I could put it away for a rainy day. "Why me?" I asked again. I didn't understand why he was asking me and not Sommer.

"Are you not grateful for the extra money?"

"It's not that. I'm just confused why you'd choose me and not one of the other girls."

He grinned and leaned a hip on the credenza, matching me, except he crossed his arms over his chest as though to get comfortable. "I'm going to be honest with you, Tessa. My friends are ruthless. They'll flirt and try to get in your pants."

"And you think I'd be okay with that?"

He smiled and shook his head. "No. That's exactly why I want it to be you and not someone else. I've already made the mistake of bringing the … easier girls, and while I don't want you to go home with me, I don't want you to go home with anyone else."

My mouth hit the floor again. "What?"

"You know how it is for bachelor parties—"

"This is for a bachelor party?"

"No. It's to be my arm candy, but I need someone who won't run their mouth about what happens here at Red Diamond."

"I don't understand. What happens here at RD that I'd talk about?"

"Just say yes, Tessa. I've always told you that if you ever need anything to come to me. That goes for your safety. I want to protect you, and I want to give you money to spend a few hours with me so I can brag to my friends that you're mine."

"But I'm not yours," I corrected.

"They won't know that."

"So, I'll be like an escort?"

His grin widened. "If that makes you feel better about this. I'm just looking to hire you to be on my arm. That's it."

"Okay," I agreed. I was going to treat it as though it was a bachelor party, but this time, I wouldn't have to take my top off or grind on someone's lap. I hoped.

"Thank you." He turned to the stack of cash on his desk. I watched as he pulled out a few hundred dollar bills and then handed them to me. "You'll need to get a nice dress to wear. Our seats are ringside."

"Wow, really?"

Sebastian smiled. "I only sit in the best seats, Tessa."

"I had the wrong idea about boxing," I admitted. I'd assumed people went in jeans and a nice shirt with heels.

"It will be the funnest way you've ever made a grand."

True to his word, Vinny was waiting for me when I got off at two. He'd texted to say he was coming and would meet me in the parking lot, but he didn't want to freak me out when I saw a man standing by the door. I'd told Galen my friend was coming and to not think he was my stalker, so when I walked outside, I saw Galen and Vinny laughing and talking like they were best friends. Vinny stopped talking and immediately turned his gaze toward me and smiled. My belly dipped. I'd never get tired of the way he made me feel when he looked at me.

"Hey," I greeted Vinny as I stopped in front of him.

"Hey, Candy." He immediately wrapped his arms around my back and pulled me to him for a hug. He'd said I smelled like cotton candy, but he equally smelled good—like citrus, mint, and a hint of lavender, which calmed me. He smelled like my Vinny.

"Ready to go?" I asked.

We broke apart. "Yep, but first ..." He dug his wallet out of his back pocket and pulled a business card out. Handing it to Galen, he said, "Call my boss, Mark, and tell him I gave you my card to look into setting up a meeting with him."

Galen took the card and smiled. "I will. Thanks, man."

"No problem."

"Keep our girl safe," Galen said.

"Always." Vinny wrapped an arm around me and started for my car.

"You gave Galen your card to become an escort?"

"Yeah. He was out here when I arrived, so I introduced myself, and we started shooting the shit. Told him about S&R and he was interested."

"Dang. You work at a place a little over a year, thinking you know everything, and then everything starts to change."

"What do you mean?"

We stopped in front of my car. "Well, it seems everyone's going to be an escort now."

His brows arched. "Really?"

"Well, kinda. My boss asked me to be his date for some boxing match on Monday. Said he'll pay me a grand."

"Holy shit."

"I know. I'm not sure why he asked me to do it."

"Because you're awesome."

I laughed, throwing my head back. "He actually said it was because I don't have a big mouth."

"Really? What does that mean?"

"I have no idea. He said something about not talking about what happens here at RD."

"He just wants to date you."

"I don't think so."

He cocked his head to the side as if to imply I was oblivious to the obvious. "Are you sure?"

"Why would he want to date me?"

Vinny reached up and brushed my hair behind my ear. "Because you're beautiful, Tess."

I stared up into his chocolate eyes. "What are we doing, Vin?"

He stared back, not saying anything for a few moments. "I don't know, but I don't want it to stop."

"Me either," I admitted.

He grinned. "Good. Now, let's get you home so tomorrow you can be awake and ready to shoot shit."

I chuckled. "You make it sound so fun."

"It should be. I heard it's a high you've never been on."

Vinny followed me home, walked me to my door, and kissed the top of my head before leaving. It was the first time his lips had touched me, and it wasn't even on my skin. I had to admit it was sweet. And the way he turned, one last time, to see I was watching him leave, made me think that he was trying to be a gentleman and take whatever we were doing slowly. There was just something in the way he looked back at me that gave me that feeling—or I hoped that was the reason. I really needed to talk to him, but not at two o'clock in the morning.

"That boy has it bad for you," Sophia stated as she came up behind me just as Vinny was out of sight.

"What makes you say that?" I asked.

"A boy who walks you to the door wants more than in your pants."

I snorted, not believing that had come from her mouth. "I think he wants that too, but I wouldn't be the only woman."

"He told me he was an escort, and while I'm not fully certain what that means, a man in love will do anything for the woman he loves."

"Even quit a job?"

"Even quit a job if it meant being with the one who's captured his heart."

"I don't think he loves me."

She frowned slightly, a look of sorrow on her face. "Then I don't think either one of you knows what love truly is."

The next morning, I thought about what Sophia said as I got ready to go to the shooting range. When I was in high school, I thought I was in love, but that was short lived. Like a lot of high school boys, he cheated on me with my then best friend. I'd never trusted anyone since because, despite my father being a good guy, that boy left a mark on my heart early on. Except now, I trusted Vinny.

Fuck.

Before I could think any more about it, there was a knock on my door. As I walked out of my room toward the door, Colton was sitting in front of the TV, baseball in hand and watching a new episode of *PAW Patrol*. We were making progress, little by little, and when he stopped obsessing over something I thought we could never shake, it amazed me. It made me wonder what the future had in store for Colton and me.

Looking through the peephole, I saw it was Sophia. "Morning," I greeted her as I opened the door.

She looked me up and down. "Are you wearing that?"

I looked down at my black Chuck Taylors, capri jeans, and Giants T-shirt—a jab at Vinny because not only did it rep the Giants, but it mentioned their number of World Series wins, which was currently higher than the Dodgers'. Plus, there was a game today. "Yeah, what's wrong with this?"

She entered and patted Colt on the head, saying hello to him before turning back to me. "You need to show your boobs."

I chuckled and closed the door. "He's seen them."

"I know that, but you need to dress better for your date."

"It's not a date."

She turned to face me. "Are you sure?"

"Who brings someone to a shooting range with his friends for a date?"

"His friends will be there?"

I smiled. "Yes. They're the ones who are going to teach me how to shoot."

"That's a shame."

"A shame that I need to protect myself?"

She shook her head slightly. "A shame he hasn't had the balls to take you on a proper date."

"Sophia!" I scolded and motioned with my head toward Colton.

She waved me off. "He's watching his program. He's not paying attention to us."

She was right. When he watched his cartoons, he was zoned out like any kid his age. Before I could say anything further, there was another knock on my door. I knew it was Vinny, and after checking in the peephole to make sure, I opened the door with a huge grin on my face.

He smiled and then looked down at my T-shirt, causing his smile to fade instantly. "All right, I see how this is going to go down. You better clear some space because Dodger blue is about to fill up your world."

I cocked my hip, resting my hand on it. "Think again. I only bleed orange and black."

THIRTEEN

Vinny

T ESSA WAS TRYING TO KILL ME.

Okay, not really, but I knew she was wearing a Giants tee to ruffle my feathers. It was sure as shit working too. The Dodgers and Giants rivalry was a big deal, but it wasn't unheard of for friends or couples to support rival teams; it made it fun. But I wanted to see Tessa in Dodger blue. Honestly, I wanted to see her in nothing.

After saying a quick hello and goodbye to Colton and Sophia, I drove Tessa to the shooting range where I had set up an hour of shooting with Gabe and Paul. They were both going to be there because Paul was training for an undercover mission or something. The guy had a nasty habit of revealing just enough to make you confused, but then telling you he couldn't tell you any more details because it was top secret—just like he did when he told me he was getting married to an FBI agent. He'd also quit S&R, and that made me take a step back when it came to Tessa and me because both Gabe and Paul had quit because of women.

The night before when I'd picked Tessa up at Red Diamond, she'd asked me what we were doing—meaning us. I wasn't sure, but I knew I wanted to keep getting to know her and not quit S&R. Saddles & Racks was more to me than just having fun with clients; it was a way to make the money I needed to live the fun life I had. Sure, I could survive on my teacher's salary, but I also loved being able to go wherever I wanted on a whim. If I only had my teacher's salary, I'd live paycheck to paycheck and have to save money to afford any vacation.

"Have you ever shot a gun?" Tessa asked as we got closer to the range.

"Nope," I replied.

"Are you going to today?"

"Yep."

"Do you think the Giants will win today?"

"Nope."

"Are you only giving me one worded answers because you're mad at me?"

"Yep."

"It's not the first time you've seen me in Giants attire."

"So?"

Tessa chuckled. I was just messing with her. I wasn't really mad or using one worded answers on purpose. It had just come out that way.

When we pulled up to the cement building, Gabe and his fiancée, Autumn, were getting out of Gabe's Yukon. Tessa started to open the passenger side door but stopped. "Is that his fiancée?" she whispered, looking over at me.

"Yep."

"Now's not the time for your one-worded answers Vincent."

"Why?"

She rolled her blue eyes. "Because you didn't tell me that I was coming to hang out with the fiancée."

"Why's that a problem? Autumn's cool."

"Do you forget how we met?" she asked, motioning with her hand between us.

A lightbulb went off in my head. "Oh. I don't think she'll care."

"Does she know?"

I shrugged. No one had said anything to me. In fact, I hadn't heard from Gabe much since the night of his bachelor party a little over two months ago. I had my class, dates a few times a week, and I was spending time with Tessa. He and Autumn were probably banging every second of every day in conjunction with planning a wedding and the arrival of their baby. The older you got, the busier you got.

"I don't want to be confronted by the fiancée, Vinny. That's not cool."

"Why do you think she'll do that?"

Tessa sighed and shook her head slightly. "Because women always blame other women when, in fact, it was the men—or in this case, the friend—who hired me."

"Autumn knows what Gabe and Paul used to do for a living—"

"Use to do? Paul doesn't anymore?"

"No. They both quit the game because of the women in their lives."

Tessa stared at me, not saying anything. Did she want me to quit? Did she want to be with me? Like, truly be with me as boyfriend and girlfriend and not friends. She was starting to become one of my best friends, but at the same time, I didn't know how to do the boyfriend thing other than pretending when I was on dates, and I just had to do that a few hours at a time.

"Let's just go inside. I'm telling you that Autumn's cool. She's also pregnant, so I doubt she'll start something with you."

"Is that supposed to make me feel better?"

I shrugged a shoulder. "Just come on, Tess. I promise not to let anything happen to you. If she starts to get upset, I'll step in and remind her it's not your fault and you were only doing your job. Plus, nothing happened." Shit, nothing had happened with us, and I'd spent more time alone with this woman than I had with any other woman in my entire life, including my ten-year *relationship* with Shelby.

"Promise?"

"Yes. Let's go. Paul's already here. That's his Jeep." I pointed at it parked on my side of the SUV.

"Okay."

Tessa finally opened her door, and I followed. We walked inside and were welcomed by my friends, plus two other people I didn't know.

"What's up, man?" Paul greeted as he gave me a bro hug consisting of a strong handshake and a pat on the back.

"Hey," I replied and then turned to Gabe and gave him the same hug. "Thanks for doing this."

"No problem," Paul stated. "Vin, this is my Joss and her best friend, Seth. They're here for—"

"Practice," Joss cut in and glared at Paul as she extended her hand toward me. I got the impression she was used to the guy not being able to keep his mouth shut.

"Nice to meet you," I replied, and we all shook hands.

I turned to Tessa. "This is Tessa. Tessa, you remember Gabe and Paul." She waved hello, and so did they. "This is Autumn, Gabe's fiancée, and like you heard, Seth and Joss." She shook hands with them too.

"Now that we got the formalities out of the way," Paul chimed in, "it's time to show this little lady how to shoot." He turned and went to the counter with Gabe, but we didn't follow.

Autumn stepped toward Tessa. "Gabe told me that you had a stalker the other night."

I looked to Gabe, wondering how he knew. He motioned his head in Paul's direction, and it clicked.

"I'm not sure if it's a stalker," Tessa replied. "But someone followed me when I left work the other night."

"Where do you work?" Joss asked. "I can maybe look into it when I'm done with the case we're working on."

"You're a cop?" Tessa asked.

"FBI actually."

"I'm a cop," Seth stated. I knew he was here to help, but I assumed he was with the FBI too.

"Thank you, but I already contacted Vegas Metro, and they're supposed to be following up," Tessa informed them.

"If they don't, or it happens again, let me know," Joss said.

Tessa smiled at her. "I will. Thank you."

"Where is it that you work?" Autumn asked again.

Tessa turned her head to look up at me, and I grinned at her. I assumed Autumn would be okay with it given she knew all about S&R and the fact that I still worked there. Shit, how was it possible that I was in a group of people that consisted of two former male escorts, an FBI agent, a cop, a stripper, a current male escort, and a—well, I didn't know what Autumn did. She used to be a housewife, but I knew that she now helped Gabe and Paul with their self-defense classes.

"Red Diamond," Tessa replied.

"The strip club?" Autumn asked.

Tessa nodded, and I placed my arm around her, letting her know I was going to live up to my promise. Paul and Gabe came back with target sheets and whatever else we needed.

"Were you the stripper from the bachelor party?" Autumn questioned.

Tessa peered up at me again. "Yes?" It came out like a question, and I knew it was because she was nervous to admit the truth.

Autumn smiled and punched Paul in the arm. "This jackass said they were only going camping. I found out when Gabe got home that they'd hired you."

"Are you mad?" I asked, stepping in.

Autumn chuckled. "No, I'm not mad. Paul has a big mouth, but not when it comes to strippers apparently."

"Good to know," Joss chimed in.

"Gorgeous, I don't need to hire strippers anymore. I've got you," Paul replied and pulled her in for a hug.

"Now that we know what everyone does for a fucking living, I'm going to go shoot some targets," Seth cut in and started to walk away after snatching a sheet out of Paul's hand.

"Me, too," Gabe agreed.

"Let's pick out a gun for you to use," Autumn said, and motioned for Tessa to follow her to the counter.

Before Tessa stepped away, I leaned down and whispered into her ear, "Told you she was cool."

"Yeah, but I have a feeling there's a joke about walking into a bar somewhere in this situation."

I laughed. "Fuck yeah, there is."

Three escorts, a stripper, a housewife, and two law enforcement officers walk into a bar ... Yep, don't see that every day.

Tessa stayed with the girls to pick out a gun, and I went into the back with the guys. Apparently, since Gabe and Paul held their classes here, the fee for the hour was put on their tab. I was cool with that. When I'd called Paul yesterday and told him the situation, he told me he'd take care of everything and he and Gabe would meet us here. Didn't know the entire gang would be here minus my boys, Brad and Nick. Like Gabe and Paul, they were ex-military. I was the odd man out in the group, but if that dude Galen called Mark and got hired, I would no longer be surrounded only by military men talking about wars. There was nothing wrong with that, but I didn't have any war stories to share. I didn't know Galen's story, other than he wanted to become a fireman. Plus, Gabe and Paul were out of the game, and we needed more in the group.

"Saturday."

"Saturday, what?" I asked, looking at Paul.

"That's the day Joss and I are getting married," he replied, clipping a target into place.

"Seriously?"

"Seriously."

"Well, shit. Now I need to change my date to Sunday."

"You're still escorting?" Gabe asked.

"Yeah. Why wouldn't I be?"

He looked at me as though he were confused. "Tessa. She's okay with that?"

I chuckled. "We're not dating."

"You aren't?"

"No."

"Vin's scared to pull the trigger," Paul stated.

"It's not like that," I corrected. "We're just friends."

"Keep telling yourself that," Gabe laughed. "See how being friends with Autumn turned out?"

I nodded. "Situation's different though."

"While not all relationships are the same, it's clear you both want each other. I can tell that just by being in the same room as you two with your dreamy looks toward each other. It will happen."

"And I'll have to quit S&R."

"Take a break," Gabe suggested. "If it doesn't work out with her, then you can go back."

"I need to talk to Tessa," I confessed.

"Then do it."

"Take her to my wedding," Paul chimed in.

"Do you three talk like this all the time?" Seth cut in.

We all turned to look at him.

"What do you mean?" Gabe asked.

"Like chicks braiding each other's fucking hair. I used to live with Joss, and she wasn't even as bad as you three."

Paul slapped him on the back and squeezed his shoulder. "It's because you haven't found your girl yet."

"I've only been in love once, and I have no desire to ever fall in love again."

"Young love is just the beginning, man," Paul stated. "Once you find the one worth fighting for, you won't give up if shit hits the fan. Look at Joss and me. She thought her past and being FBI would turn me away, and it didn't."

"Look at Autumn and me," Gabe went on. "I literally fought her husband for her."

All three of the guys turned to me, and I shrugged. "I got nothin'."

"You will," Gabe stated. "It's only a matter of time for the both of you."

"How the fuck do you know?" I asked.

Gabe chuckled and grabbed Paul's shoulder and squeezed it. "Because the night of my bachelor party, I told this fucker that someday soon some woman was going to barge into his life and he wouldn't know what to do without her. A few weeks later, Andi, aka Joss, showed up on his doorstep ordering him to let her inside."

Their stories were nothing like ours. She wasn't married or asking to move in with me. We were just doing our thing and getting closer with each passing day.

Seth and I looked at each other and chuckled. "You're so full of shit, Gabe," I stated.

"Okay." He grinned. "When something goes down with you and Tessa, you owe me a grand."

"Speaking of a grand," I said, thinking about the fact that Tessa's boss wanted her to go with him to a fight tomorrow night. "Since you're getting married on Saturday, what are we doing for a bachelor party?"

Paul shrugged. "Nothing."

"We can't do nothing," I stated.

"Yeah," Gabe agreed. "Not after you stripped me down to my boxers and made me run in the fucking woods with you all shooting paintballs at me."

Paul laughed. "That was epic."

"And I warned you that paybacks are a bitch."

"We don't have time to do anything," Paul stated back to Gabe.

"We can go to the fight tomorrow," I suggested.

"What fight?" Seth asked.

"Steven "The Predator" Williams versus George "The Thunderstorm" Campbell," I replied. So, I might have gone home after dropping Tessa off and looked into what fight she was going to. I had to admit, I was a little jealous that she was going out with another man, even if it was her boss. "At the arena. There are tickets still available."

"I'm in," Gabe agreed.

"Me, too," Seth replied.

"I'll get Nick and Brad to come, too," I said. "It will be fun."

"It's not paying you back for my shit," Gabe stated. "But going to a fight does sound like fun, and I'll have plenty of time to pay your ass back."

Paul shrugged. "All right. Let's do it."

The arena was huge, but that wasn't going to stop me from *accidentally* running into Tessa and her boss.

Watching Tessa shoot a gun was hot. There was something about watching her handle a firearm that was badass and it made me hard watching her be strong and self-reliant. I loved it. Plus, she was a decent shot, and I knew if anything were to happen, she'd be able to defend herself. But then, when we were done, she wasn't ready to purchase a gun. I understood. Guns weren't my thing either unlike all of our other friends. So, Tessa settled on getting pepper spray from Autumn, who had a supply she sold to her class.

Since Tessa had to go on a date with her boss the next night, I took her straight home after the range because she still needed to buy a dress for the fight. A high profile match brought out all the celebrities and power players, so people dressed up if they were in the decent seats where cameras might see them. Since she said she had to get a dress, I knew they had good seats.

So, that meant I had to get the boys and me good seats too.

Before I walked away from Tessa's door, I asked her to be my date for Paul's wedding. She was the only one I wanted to go with, and she was already getting along with everyone who would be there.

"Now that you're cool with Autumn and Joss, want to go to Paul and Joss's wedding with me on Saturday?"

Her blue eyes widened. "Yes!"

I grinned. "I mean as my date, Tess."

"Like a real date?"

"Like a real date."

She thought for a moment as we stared at each other and then she finally agreed. "Okay. I would love to."

"*Great. Have fun tomorrow night. The boys and I are going to get Paul fucked up.*"

She laughed. "*I can only imagine all of you drunk. I didn't get to see that.*"

"*You're lucky you didn't get to see that.*" I chuckled.

"*I bet I'll see you drunk at the wedding.*"

"*Yeah, I bet you will too.*"

Now, I was getting ready for a night at the arena with my boys so I could stalk the girl I had feelings for. All so I could make sure her boss was on his best fucking behavior because I didn't like that she was going out with him. Which meant I needed to figure my shit out with S&R and maybe take that break Gabe suggested.

Of course, that needed to be after my date with Shelby on Sunday.

FOURTEEN

Tessa

WHEN VINNY DROPPED ME OFF AFTER THE RANGE, MELONY AND I WENT shopping. I wasn't exactly sure how fancy to get for the fight because when I googled it, some celebrities dressed in thousand dollar dresses and some people wore simple cocktail dresses. Others wore jeans and a T-shirt, but I assumed the T-shirts cost at least a hundred bucks—not the kind found at Target. Plus, it seemed it was only the men who dressed down.

"Do you think it's weird that Sebastian asked me to go with him to the fight?" I asked, looking at the dresses in the department store.

"No, I've actually known a few girls who've gone."

"Really?"

"Yeah."

"Who?"

"Well, Sommer for starters."

I glared at her. "Seriously?"

"What?"

"Sommer gives him sexual favors. Do you think that's what he wants from me?"

Melony shrugged. "I don't know, but like I told you before, you don't need to do anything you don't want to."

"Well." I grinned. "I would never, but especially now that Vinny asked me on a date."

"Shut up!" she shrieked. "When?"

"To one of the S&R guys' wedding."

"The one you stripped for?"

I shook my head. *"No, the one who hired me to strip."*

"Wait. Two escorts are engaged?"

"Apparently."

"So, there's hope for you and Vinny then? Maybe he'll quit for you."

"We definitely need to talk about it."

"Finally. This whole 'you don't know what the hell you two are' thing is confusing me."

"Me, too," I admitted.

When Vinny asked me to be his date—a real date—I wanted to ask him again what we were, but Sophia was sitting in my living room, and I didn't think it was the time. So, I was going to talk to him at the wedding—hopefully. I had to. It was time to go after the person who made me smile. Made me laugh. The man who was good with Colton and cared enough about me to walk me to my door each time, and who set-up a training at the shooting range. Even though I didn't choose a gun, just the experience of having shot a gun was enough to put me at ease. If it came down to it, I wouldn't hesitate with my pepper spray.

To get ready for the night, I curled my hair and pinned the left side back with a bobby pin to give it more of a styled look. While shopping, I came across a dark navy, A-line dress with a deep V-neck and pockets, and I couldn't resist it. I fell in love with it instantly, and my silver heels went with it perfectly.

Sebastian had told me to meet him at Red Diamond, and then we would take a limo to the arena. I was okay with him not picking me up because the entire situation was still weird to me. I just kept telling myself it was an extra thousand dollars and I didn't have to get naked. I could easily do that. When I pulled into the parking lot at Red Diamond, Galen was manning the door. "Wow, Scarlett. You look amazing tonight."

"Thank you," I replied. At the mention of my stage name, I wondered if I would need to be Scarlett or Tessa tonight. Scarlett was a man-eater in a sense, and Tessa was the girl next door. What did

Sebastian need me to be in front of his friends? "I'm going to that boxing thing with Mr. Delarosa."

"Ah," he groaned. "You're lucky. There's a lot of hype about the fight. I bet on Campbell. He's the underdog."

"Is that who I should go for?" I'd never been to a boxing match before. The guys at work talked about them all the time because it was a big thing in Vegas. Apparently, they happened often, and it was a big deal when two popular men or women had a match. I knew nothing when it came to boxing.

He grinned. "If you want."

I heard a car pull into the lot, and I turned, seeing a black limo pull in. "My ride is here."

Galen whistled. "You're riding in style."

"Looks like it."

The car pulled up, and Galen opened the door. "Have a good night."

"Thank you," I replied and slid inside onto the black leather seat. He shut the door, and I turned my gaze to the front. Sebastian sat across from me in a black suit with a red button-down shirt and black tie. "Hi," I greeted him with a smile.

Sebastian handed me a flute of champagne, his gaze lowering to my chest briefly. *Scarlett then?* "Love the dress, Tessa." *Okay, Tessa then?*

"Thank you, and thank you for the money for it."

"It only seemed appropriate since I invited you to come. Have you ever been to a fight night before?"

I took a sip of the bubbly wine. "No, I haven't."

"Well." He grinned. "Your first time is going to be amazing since we have ringside seats."

"I'm looking forward to it." I assumed it would be fun and exciting to be ringside. I would kill to be in the front row behind home plate or even front row near the dugout at a baseball game, and I supposed ringside was the equivalent for people who loved boxing. "What am I supposed to do tonight?"

He arched his brow as he studied me. "What do you mean?"

"Well, you said I wouldn't need to strip, so I'm not exactly sure what I'm being hired to do."

"You're to sit by my side and watch a fight."

"That's it?"

"That's it."

"Am I Tessa or Scarlett?"

"Who do you want to be?"

I thought for a moment because I wasn't sure. I was only Scarlett at Red Diamond and when I worked bachelor parties, but I was with my boss now. Deciding I was going to stick with Scarlett for stripping, I answered, "Tessa."

Sebastian smiled, and it calmed me. "I like Tessa better."

I smiled in return. "Thank you."

We sipped our champagne as the driver drove us toward the arena. I had yet to go to anything at the T-Mobile Arena though there had been several concerts I'd wanted to attend. We pulled up to the oval building, and I looked out the window at a digital sign advertising the fight between Williams and Campbell.

"Who are you rooting for?" I asked.

"Doesn't matter."

I blinked. "Really?"

"I don't come to the fights because I like the fighters."

"Then why do you come?" The driver opened the door and extended his hand. I took it and slid out of the car. Sebastian followed.

"I come for business."

"To find girls?"

"Not exactly. Red Diamond isn't my only business."

"Really? I had no idea."

"I'm a man who loves money, and I do what I need to do to get it."

I had no idea what that meant, nor did I care. I was only here to sit with him and get my thousand dollars.

A man in a black suit with a white shirt stepped behind us, and I turned slightly to look over my shoulder at him. He nodded once. "Who's that?" I whispered.

"That is Mateo, my bodyguard."

"You have a bodyguard?"

"There's a lot you don't know about me. For one, I always have to get nachos when I come to a fight." Sebastian winked at me and then hooked his arm with mine. We took a few steps until I stopped. He looked down at me. "What is it? You don't like nachos?"

I snorted. "No, I love nachos, but I just need to know what you don't want me to say. I'm not sure what you meant the other night, and I don't want to say something I shouldn't if someone does speak to me."

"Do you seriously not know what I'm talking about?"

"I don't think so."

The wind blew, and he brushed a piece of my hair behind my ear. Something that Vinny had done too. Something I *only* wanted Vinny to do. "Then you have nothing to worry about."

"What if I do say something?"

"Tessa, I've been watching you for a while, and I can tell that you're not one to gossip. Sommer doesn't know you saw us in my office, and that's what I like about you."

Sommer *now* knew I saw them. I didn't ask any more questions because I just wanted to get my money and not stir up anything. It was bad enough Sommer and I had gotten into a fight the other day and I'd called her out on the BJ. That wasn't like me at all.

"You're right. I don't gossip." Except with Melony, but I kept that to myself.

"Good. Now, we're going to go in, sit with some of my friends, and watch a bloody fight. Are you ready?"

I nodded. "Yep."

After we got nachos and beer—something I never thought I'd see my put-together boss eating or drinking—we walked down to our seats. It was amazing to be so close. As I looked at and listened to those around us, I realized there had already been a few matches, but not the title fight. Sebastian chatted with his friends, to whom he didn't introduce me when we'd arrived, and it was clear I was here just to be arm candy. The other women seemed to be in the same boat because they too were sitting silently while their dates chatted with Sebastian.

"Do you come to these often?" I asked the redhead sitting next to me after I'd taken my last sip of beer. I didn't know her name because there had been no introductions between any of us.

The girl turned her head to look at me, and then looked up at her gray-haired date. The guys were in their own conversation and not paying attention to us. "We're not supposed to talk," she hissed.

I pulled back. "What? Why?"

"Shh. You're going to get me in trouble," she whispered.

I opened my mouth to respond but didn't. Instead, I looked up at the group of guys, wondering what she meant by getting in trouble. Did he hit her? Get mad at her and yell? Was this why Sebastian invited me to come with him? Did the other girls from Red Diamond talk and get the girls in trouble? Why did women stay with men who were abusive? Money? Fear? Because they had kids? I knew that if it were me, I would take Colton and run far away.

That thought made me think about Vinny and his group of friends. Gabe, Autumn, and Paul taught classes for self-defense. Somehow, I needed to get this chick their info, but then I didn't want her date to see it, and I couldn't talk to her again because she didn't want me to talk to her. I felt horrible for her, and as I leaned forward to get a look at the other girl, my gaze landed on the familiar brown eyes that made me smile.

Vinny smirked at me and then winked as he walked my way. I grinned and stood, but then stopped from running toward him and throwing myself into his arms since I was supposed to be on a date with Sebastian. My eyes widened, and I looked to Sebastian and then to Vinny. Vinny's eyebrows furrowed and then, as though he'd understood the look on my face, he stopped, said something to Paul, and then motioned with his head for me to come to them.

I stepped next to Sebastian. When he stopped talking and looked down at me, I said, "I'm going to use the restroom before the fight starts."

"Sure." He smiled. "Should be starting soon, so hurry back."

"I will." I took a few steps forward and felt as though someone was following me. I turned to see that it was Mateo. "You don't need to come."

With a straight face, he replied, "Boss's orders."

I scrunched my eyebrows. "Really?"

"Yes."

I wasn't sure why Sebastian would think that I needed an escort to the restroom. Was it because I'd told him about my stalker the other night? Was he just making sure I didn't get lost? I followed Vinny's group of guys up a few stairs and into a lower level where there were concessions and a bunch of people standing around chatting. I stopped walking just before the group of guys. "I see some friends. Are you supposed to report back to the boss?"

He balked. "No."

"Okay, good."

I went to Vinny and finally got the hug I was craving. "Having fun?" he asked.

I smiled up at him. "Well, I was fed nachos and beer, so I'd say that's a good start."

"You didn't go to dinner?"

I shook my head. "With my boss?"

"With your date."

"I don't think it's really like what you do."

"It better not be."

I cocked my head to the side. "What does that mean?"

"Nothing. You remember all the guys?"

"Yes." I smiled, remembering that I'd met them the night of Gabe's bachelor party, and gave all of them a hug. "What are you guys doing here?"

"Bachelor party for this guy." Nick slapped Paul on the back.

My gaze moved to Vinny. "Well, isn't that a coincidence that you'd have it here?"

He grinned. "Ain't it?"

I shook my head as I laughed. Vinny hadn't mentioned that they were coming to the fight when I told him I was, but then we didn't know until the range that Paul was getting married this coming Saturday. Had Vinny talked the guys into coming so he could keep tabs on me?

"How'd you find me anyway?" I asked.

"Not a lot of people sit ringside. You were easy to spot."

"How'd you know I was sitting there?"

He shrugged. "Lucky guess."

"Where are you guys sitting?"

"On the opposite side and up a few rows. Ringside was sold out."

"Oh." I looked at the other guys, and they were all chatting amongst themselves. "I better get back. Sebastian told me to hurry because the fight is starting soon."

"Dinner tomorrow at your place for winning the bet?" Vinny asked.

"Steak and lobster?" I beamed.

"If that's what you want."

"That's what I want."

He smiled. "I'll be at your place at five."

"Okay." I hugged him once more and took a step away, but then stopped and turned back toward him. "Just so you know, the Dodgers are only allowed on my TV when they play the Giants."

Vinny grabbed his chest as though he was having a heart attack or that I'd wounded him. "That shit will change one day. Might not be tomorrow night, but it will."

I laughed and started to walk away, calling over my shoulder. "In your dreams."

The fight went eight rounds. I didn't know if that was long or not, but in the end, Campbell did win. The arena seemed to be torn with the win because when he knocked out Williams, there were gasps, groans, and cheers, plus, a lot of shouted cuss words. It was fun to watch, but also kinda scary. How did these guys do it? I'd hate to have a job where I got punched in the face, suffered broken bones, or whatever. That was not my idea of fun. It also wasn't fun because I sat there and didn't talk to anyone. During the fight, Sebastian only talked to his friends. I had no idea why he'd invited me or wanted to pay me a grand to sit by his side.

"How was your first fight?" Sebastian asked as the limo drove us toward Red Diamond. He was again sitting across from me.

I shrugged. "It was okay."

"Didn't have fun?"

"Well, you'd said that your friends would try to flirt with me and get into my pants. They didn't even utter a word to me."

"Because I warned them not to."

"To not flirt with me or not to talk to me?"

"Both."

"Why?"

He shrugged as though it was nothing. "Because I can."

"The women didn't even speak with me," I informed him.

Sebastian leaned forward and rested his elbows on his knees. "My friends and I are all about business. They probably instructed their women to not speak because when you spend more than one night with us, you're bound to find out things. We don't like people talking, Tessa. When people talk, it can ruin our business."

"They own strip clubs too?"

"No." He shook his head. "Like I told you earlier, that's not my only business."

"What else do you do?"

He leaned back against the black leather seat. "That's a story for another day, Tessa Baby."

Tessa Baby? What the hell? "Well, I still don't understand why the girls and I couldn't have talked about our dresses, our shoes, or hell, even their names."

"Everyone has their own rules. You're lucky I let you go to the restroom."

I blinked. "Lucky you let me go to the restroom? I can go to the restroom when I feel like it. And plus, you sent me with a bodyguard."

"Didn't want you to get lost."

I snorted. "I wouldn't have gotten lost. The seats are numbered."

"That may be true, but it was easier if I sent Mateo with you. One can never be too careful."

The limo pulled into the parking lot of Red Diamond. "Well, thank you for inviting me."

Sebastian pulled out a small wad of bills and handed it to me. "Thank you for coming. What are you doing next Sunday?"

I balked. "Um, I'm actually working. I have a wedding to go to on Saturday, and I was going to work a few hours to maybe make up for the lost money." Fridays and Saturdays were the best days to make money, but I wasn't going to miss Paul's wedding. Everyone loved weddings, and I felt as though I was part of Vinny's group of friends now that I'd hung out with them for a few hours.

"I'm having a party at my house on Sunday. I'd like for you to be there."

"I really can't. I need the money."

He reached into his pocket and pulled out more bills. "Would a grand work or do you want two?"

My mouth fell open. "Seriously?"

He leaned forward again. "I like you, Tessa. I want to keep you happy so you stay working for me. A party will be fun."

"Why not Sommer? At least she'd sleep with you."

Sebastian chuckled. "Yes, that's true, and so would a lot of the other girls. Sommer will be there."

"Okay, but I won't sleep with you."

"I'm not asking you to sleep with me. I'm asking for you to come to a party at my house. What's wrong with having some fun?"

"I—but you want to pay me to come to your party," I stated.

"I want you to come to have a good time. You said you needed the money and so I'm offering you both. Think of it as a thank you for coming with me tonight."

"Really?"

"Really. There will be music, dancing, people having fun. Bring a friend if you'd like."

My first thought was Vinny, but I didn't know if he'd want to come to a party on a school night. I needed to talk to him, and I'd have to do that tomorrow night because I assumed he was getting drunk with his buddies—though it was a school night too. "Okay, I'll bring a friend."

"Great. Here." He started to count the bills in his hand, and then reached toward me with a stack. "Two thousand to make up for your missed shift."

"You don't need to pay me to come to a party."

Sebastian grinned. "I make a lot of money, Tessa. Two, three grand is nothing to me."

Two or three grand was about a week's worth of dancing for me, and he was saying it was nothing to him? What the hell was his other business, or did he make that much just from Red Diamond?

"Some of the other girls from RD will be there," he continued. "Bring whoever you want. I'm only extending an invite because I truly like you as a person."

"Okay. Thank you for inviting me tonight."

"Thank you for coming."

I smiled and said my goodbye just as the driver opened my door.

As I drove home, I wondered if making three grand for *having fun* was the start of something good or bad. It had taken a year for Sebastian to invite me to do anything. Maybe I was just the next one in line, and this was how it all started with the girls who did sexual favors.

I'd quit Red Diamond before that ever happened.

FIFTEEN

Vinny

I KNEW ONCE I TOLD THE GUYS THAT TESSA WAS AT THE FIGHT, THEY would give me shit. I didn't care. Sure, we were having a guys' night out for Paul's bachelor party, but I wanted to get close to Tessa and let her know I was there. Luckily, when she found out, she wasn't mad.

"You have it bad for her," Gabe stated as I watched Tessa walk away—with a fucking bodyguard. What the hell was that all about?

"We're just friends," I lied. We were friends, but damn it if she didn't make me hard, especially in that dress she was wearing with the deep V neckline. It was also blue, not Dodger blue, but close.

"You keep saying that, but it's not true," Gabe replied.

"Like I told you yesterday, I have shit I need to figure out before I get serious with her." Tessa walked out of sight, and I turned my attention to Gabe. The other guys were staring at me, too.

"You better not be saying what I think you're saying," Nick warned.

"He is," Paul stated.

I rolled my eyes. "I'm not quitting."

"Yet," Gabe threw in.

"I'm not quitting," I repeated.

"Yet," Gabe said again.

"I'm going to talk to her and figure out what she wants. I'm not quitting until I talk to her and even then, it would only be a break."

"She's into you," Paul affirmed. "If things get serious, your break will turn into forever."

"Well, we can stand here all night and talk about it, or we can go get drinks and get back to our seat before the fight starts," I suggested.

"Don't get all pissy. You wanted to come see your girl. You're lucky we came along." Bradley slapped me on the back and started to walk away. We all followed to get drinks before heading back to our seats just as the fight started.

The fight was fucking awesome.

The older I got, the harder it was on me the day after drinking. That was why I didn't have dates or drink on school nights anymore, except last night, and that was Paul's fault. Okay, it was my idea to go to the fight, but it was his fault we all drank like fish after the fight.

I strolled into school hungover as fuck. Hell, I didn't even remember much after leaving the fight other than we went to Commonwealth on Fremont Street. The guys and I drank and drank and drank some more. I should have known better, but Paul was getting fucking married, which meant he was getting married before Gabe, and *none* of us saw that shit coming.

Bypassing my classroom, I went straight for the teachers' lounge in search of coffee. I needed something to wake me up and help with my pounding head, and I hoped the caffeine would help.

"You look like death. Are you coming down with something?" Kandace, one of the other teachers, asked as she walked into the room.

"No." I chuckled slightly, which only made my head hurt more.

"My friend had his bachelor party last night and … Let's say I don't remember much past ten."

"You had a bachelor party on a Monday?"

"Yeah. He's getting married on Saturday." I poured the java into a mug before setting the pot back onto the burner.

"Why not have it on Saturday?"

"He just got engaged, and we didn't have time to plan a bachelor party for another night."

"It's a shotgun wedding or something?"

I laughed again and then sucked in a breath. I needed to find aspirin for my head. "Not exactly. We went to the fight last night."

"Oh, right. Heard about it. Weird it wasn't on Saturday too."

I moved to the fridge to grab the hazelnut creamer. "It wasn't a title fight. Title fights are usually Saturday."

"Oh. Well, I hope you feel better soon."

"Thanks. I should be fine after this coffee and some aspirin."

"I have some if you need it."

"You're a lifesaver. I would love two, please."

"Sure, I'll go get them."

"I'll come with." I poured creamer into the coffee and stirred it slowly for a few seconds. After putting the creamer back into the fridge, Kandace and I started to walk toward her classroom. "Can I ask you a question?"

"Sure, what's up?"

"Hypothetically speaking, if you won a bet and the prize consisted of a guy cooking you dinner, would you expect the guy to bring flowers?"

She stopped walking and looked up at me. "Are you telling me you have a date?"

"It's not a date." Or was it? Hell, I didn't know anymore what anything with Tessa was. I just knew I wanted to spend all my free time with her.

Kandace snorted. "It's a date."

"Fine, it's a date. I should bring flowers, right?"

"A girl never turns down flowers, Vincent, but it's all about which kind you buy that will tell her how you really feel about her."

I dated for a living, and I'd like to say I knew how women worked. Most of the time, I didn't even need a woman to say the words for me to know what she was thinking. Of course, that was because all the women I *dated* were into me because they'd specifically hired me. But I felt as if I was going in blind with Tessa. What kind of flowers did she like? How does she like her steak? Did she drink wine with dinner? All of those questions never needed an answer when it came to other women because I had their preferences in their client sheet at my fingertips, or it fucking didn't matter. But with Tessa, it all mattered.

"How do I know which ones to get?" I asked just as we walked into her classroom.

"Well ..." She grabbed her purse from her desk drawer. "Don't get her red roses unless you know she likes them. It's everyone's go to, and really not that thoughtful."

"Really?"

Kandace bobbed her head. "Flowers are always thoughtful I guess, but go outside the box and it will seem like you put a lot of thought into them and didn't just pick them up at the grocery store with dinner."

Damn, that was exactly what I was thinking of doing. "Do you have any suggestions?"

She handed me two pills, and I stuck them into my mouth with a swallow of coffee. "Go with whatever ones remind you of her."

I thought for a moment, bobbing my head slightly. "That's a good suggestion."

The bell rang, and I quickly thanked Kandace before dashing off to my classroom. The entire day I thought about what flower reminded me of Tessa.

I had no fucking clue.

I stared at the cooler of flowers in the grocery store for several minutes. I'd already gotten the steak, lobster, salad, garlic bread, a package of hot dogs for Colton, a bottle of wine, a bottle of Bacardi, Coca-Cola, chocolate milk for Colton, and chocolate cake, and now, I just needed the flowers. Every item I placed into my cart made me realize more and more that this *was* a date. I wasn't taking her out, but we were going to be alone, just the two of us—and Colton, who would be engrossed in his cartoons or toys—and we'd be cooking dinner like a couple. I thought the idea of doing something so domestic with a girl would be frightening, but it wasn't. I was actually looking forward to seeing a relaxed Tessa at home with Colt.

Just as I was about to grab the first bouquet of mixed flowers in front of me, a person stepped beside me and slid something into the cooler. I looked over at her, and noticed that it was someone who worked in the department. After she stepped back, I looked to see what she'd put into the fridge, and knew the moment I saw the pink and purplish flowers, they were the ones I needed for Tessa.

"Excuse me," I said, getting her attention. "What kind of flowers are those that you just put in there?" Right off the bat, I knew the pink and white ones were lilies, but I didn't know the others.

"They're oriental lilies with lavender gillies, blue irises, lavender daisies, and purple matsumoto asters."

The colors reminded me of cotton candy, and the moment I saw the flowers, I swore I could smell Tessa's sweet scent filling the air around me. "Thank you," I replied and reached for them. "They're perfect."

When Tessa opened the door, I couldn't hide my smile, even after I noticed she was wearing a Giants T-shirt again. I'd missed her, and it had been less than twenty-four hours since I'd seen her. What was wrong with me? Gabe and Paul were right. I was scared to pull the trigger.

But it was also only a matter of time.

"Your chef has arrived," I stated.

She grinned back and waved for me to come in. "Thank God, I'm starving. I had a small salad for lunch because I wanted to save myself for my surf and turf winnings."

I'd never made lobster before, but what the lady wanted, the lady would get. It couldn't be that hard. Plus, it was just the tail, and I knew how to make a bomb steak in the oven. "I've had a hangover all day," I confessed.

She chuckled as she closed the door behind us. "Really?"

"Yeah. It was a good night." I brought the flowers from behind my back and held them out to her. "These are for you."

Her blue eyes brightened. "You got me flowers?"

I grinned. "They reminded me of you."

Tessa chuckled. "Really?"

I nodded and stepped up to whisper into her ear. "Reminds me of cotton candy, and we know how I feel about cotton candy now." I winked and then moved to where Colton was sitting on the floor in front of the TV, his attention on the iPad he was holding. I set the bags down and got in front of him, cupping his ears. "Hey, buddy. Do you want chocolate cake for dessert?"

He flapped his arms excitedly, and I grinned. "Good."

"Feeding him sugar again?"

"You have to have dessert after dinner."

Tessa chuckled as I continued to talk to Colton. "I also brought you this ..." I dug into a bag and pulled out a volleyball I had brought from home. "In a few years, I'll teach you how to volley back and forth. For now, you can play with it like your baseball." He rocked back and forth in excitement, and I handed him the ball.

"You remembered," Tessa stated.

I stood and picked up the bags. As I walked toward the kitchen, I replied, "Of course I did. I'm going to teach him everything I know." I smiled and set the bags on the counter.

"So, what else did you bring besides lobster, steak, and chocolate cake?"

"I've brought a three-course meal, sweets. And hot dogs with no buns for Colt." I'd remembered at the game that Colton had a hot dog without the bun and so I figured that was the safest thing to get for him.

Tessa followed behind me. "So, now you're calling me 'sweets'?"

"Want me to call you 'candy' instead?"

She grinned. "Just not 'baby'."

"Why not 'baby'?"

Tessa groaned and leaned on the counter while I began to unpack the bags. "My boss called me that last night."

I stopped, holding the cake in my hand. "What?"

"Not like in a romantic sense—I don't think." She started to help me unpack the bags.

"Then how?"

"He called me 'Tessa Baby'."

"In what context?"

"I don't remember exactly, but something along the lines of the story of his life and then he added the 'baby' after my name."

"Why were you talking about his life?"

She shrugged and walked to the fridge and put the cake inside.

"Well, it started off by him asking me to go to a house party at his house on Sunday."

"By yourself?"

"No, other girls from Red Diamond will be there, and he said I can bring someone. So, you want to go with me?"

"On Sunday?" I asked, looking around for a knife—not to kill anyone, though the thought of her boss wanting to spend more time with her was weird and made me want to have a talk with him. "Knife?"

Tessa pointed to the cabinet above the stove, and I opened it to see the knife block was inside. "Yeah, on Sunday."

I sighed. "I'd love to go with you, but ..." I stopped and looked at her. This was it. This was the time to ask her if she wanted to try dating. I wasn't even sure if people still did that, but under the circumstances, it seemed like the only way to move our relationship forward. Luckily, I had a plan if she gave me an ultimatum about S&R.

"But?"

I placed the knife on the counter next to me and leaned against the cabinet, my butt resting on it as I faced her. She was filling a vase with water for the flowers. "This is going to sound like we're in middle school or some shit, but do you wanna be my girlfriend?"

Tessa turned off the water and slowly turned to face me, her hip resting on the sink. "As in us dating?"

"Pretty sure that's what boyfriends and girlfriends do, even though I've never had one before."

"Wait, what? You've never had a girlfriend before?"

I shook my head. "Don't get me wrong, I had plenty of hook-ups in high school and college. I was the star volleyball player, and everyone wanted to date me, so I gave the ladies what they wanted."

"Ah, you were one of *them*."

"What does that mean?"

"A player. Both on and off the field—or court, in this case."

I shrugged. "I like the term 'ladies' man' better."

She chuckled. "Okay then."

"But seriously …" I took two steps to stand in front of her, my hip resting on the sink. "I like you a lot, Tess, and I want to try—with you."

"Why me?"

"Because I like you—a lot," I repeated.

"But what about S&R?"

I swallowed. "You want me to quit?"

She sighed. "Well, I can't ask you to do that, but if we're going to date, I want to be exclusive. Even if it's for your job."

"Then we need to start dating after Sunday."

"Why?"

"Because, I have a date on Sunday with a regular, and I need to keep it so I can tell her face to face that I'm taking a break to pursue a relationship with you."

"Okay. I can wait a week. I've waited this long."

I grinned. "So, you've been wanting this for a while?"

"Maybe?" She smirked.

I brushed her hair behind her ear and leaned down to taste her lips after all this time. My lips were an inch from hers until she turned her head. I blinked, not understanding what happened until she looked down and I followed her gaze. Colton was standing next to us, patting her leg.

"What is it?" Tessa asked him. He was already worked up by the look on his face, and he started to cry as he dropped to the floor in immediate frustration. She looked up at me as though she was embarrassed for his outburst. "I'm sorr—"

"Hey, it's okay." I touched the back of her arm. "I'm used to this, remember?"

"Right."

From an outsider's perspective, one might think that Colton was having a temper tantrum when, in fact, I knew this to be an autistic meltdown because kids like him weren't able to express or communicate what they wanted like a typical child his age. When someone with autism reaches a point of sensory, emotional, and information overload, or even just too much unpredictability, it can trigger a variety of external behaviors that are similar to a tantrum. It was clear to me—

and apparently Tessa—that Colton needed something. Figuring out the what was the hard part.

"Are you hungry?" Tessa asked.

Colton laid on his back, kicking his legs out and screaming in frustration.

I looked around the small space and saw his sippy cup sitting next to the fridge, and probably just far enough back on the counter that it was hard from him to reach it—and maybe see it too. "Thirsty?" I asked, and grabbed the cup with Superman on the outside.

Colton sat up, reaching for it as he flexed both hands rapidly. He took the cup from me and instantly started to drink from it. "Just thirsty," I stated and rubbed the top of his head playfully. "I brought chocolate milk too, buddy."

"Thank you," Tessa replied.

I smiled at her. "Let's get you fed before you have a tantrum of your own." I winked at her, and she laughed.

"Yeah, you better hurry up because I've been looking forward to this for weeks."

The lobster came out perfectly, and so did the steak, and I mastered the microwaved hot dog. Tessa helped with the salad and garlic bread, and to my surprise, she went for a rum and Coke with dinner.

"I knew I liked you for a reason," I stated as I watched her take a sip of her drink. Colton sat across from Tessa, absorbed in his iPad as he ate his cut up hot dog with his free hand.

"Why's that?"

"Because you like the same drink as I do."

She shrugged. "I don't really have a drink, but I'm not much on wine unless it's champagne."

"Good to know."

"Are you okay if I stay working at Red Diamond?"

I thought about her question as I stared at her. Would I be okay with other men seeing her tits? Watching her work a pole, wishing it was their dick she was sliding on? But I knew she needed the job because that was her only source of income, unlike me. "I can't ask you to quit—at least, not yet. How about we play it by ear for a few months?"

Tessa smiled and nodded slightly. "Okay. I was also thinking that since I can't work there forever, I want to go back to school."

"Oh yeah? For what?"

She shrugged a shoulder. "I'm thinking hotel management or something in hospitality."

"We're in the right city for that."

"Hope so. I'm also hoping I can do it online so I can still work and take care of Colt."

"I bet you can," I stated and stuck a piece of lobster into my mouth. "Plus, with me taking a break from S&R, I can help."

"That means you might be with him day and night."

"Don't think that will be a problem if that also means I can crawl into bed with his mother each night." I winked.

"Okay." She grinned. "I see how your mind's working."

"Can you blame me?"

"Nope," she replied with a pop of the P.

If Colton weren't still fully awake, I'd have taken her to bed that second. I wanted not only to feel her lips pressed to mine, but also to feel her pussy finally wrapped around my dick as I thrust in and out of her, our frantic passion making the headboard slam against the wall. I didn't care that Sophia's bedroom was probably on the other side. Even if she banged on the wall, I knew I wouldn't be able to stop until Tessa came apart multiple times.

Working for S&R had taught me a few tricks, and I was ready to show Tessa how good I was.

The night went by quickly. Tessa gave Colton a bath and put him to bed, and before I knew it, she was waking me up on the couch.

"Hey, it's getting late. You should head home."

I opened my eyes to see her peering down at me. "Kicking me out? I cooked you dinner and fed you cake."

She grinned. "No, but I'm tired too. Plus, since you're passed out on my couch, I take it you had a long night last night."

I sat up and ran my hands down my face. "Not sure. Can't remember what time I made it home."

She chuckled. "Even more of a reason to go get a good night's sleep."

I wanted to tell her I could do that here, but then I didn't have clothes for school tomorrow, and I figured it might not be good for Colton to see me in his mother's bed just yet. I knew he was warming up to me because of his blinking and hums when something I'd say excited him, but it wasn't the time, especially since Tessa and I had just talked about dating, and I was going to go on a date with someone else on Sunday.

I wasn't going to sleep with Shelby. Probably wasn't even going to charge her. But since she had been my longest client, I felt the need to tell her in person. I was also going to refer her to Brad. No way in hell would I put sweet Shelby with Nick. I knew he took care of his women—at least I assumed he did since he was still in the game and getting clients—but Nick was the asshole of our group, plain and simple.

"Will I see you before Saturday?" I asked as I stood to gather my things.

"Tomorrow I'm going dress shopping with Melony. Which reminds me, since you can't come to the party on Sunday, I'm going to ask her to come with me."

"Don't go."

"I have to go."

"Why?"

She shrugged. "Because my boss asked me to, and even though I don't plan on working at RD my entire life, I don't want to get on his bad side either."

"He can't force you to go to a party." I started to walk toward the door.

"I know that, but it's better if I go. Then I won't have to lie to him and shit."

"You can just tell him you're busy."

"Well, he's paying me to go."

"What?" I spun around to face her.

"I told him I was taking Saturday off for the wedding and was planning on working Sunday to make up for it. He already gave me money to make up for the time loss."

Something wasn't sitting right with me. What boss pays an employee to go to a party at their house? And why did he want her there that badly? It was on the tip of my tongue to tell her not to go, that I would pay her to stay home, but then I realized that I couldn't do that either. I didn't want to control her.

"He said a few people from RD will be there," Tessa continued. "It just sounds like he invited his favorites or something."

Or something. "Okay. Well, if I don't see you before Saturday, I'll pick you up at four."

"Are you in the wedding?"

"Yeah."

"Then are you sure you can pick me up?"

"I'm picking you up either way, sweets. I'm not letting you drive home at night by yourself."

"Right, the stalker situation."

"It might have only been a guy from the club, but I don't want to take any chances. Call tomorrow and follow-up with the cops, okay?"

"Yeah, I will."

"Good. Now, I'm going to fucking kiss you, and I'm not stopping until I'm good and fucking ready. Not even if there's a fucking fire."

Tessa bit her lip. "I won't stop you."

I took two large strides, cupping her cheeks, and finally sealed her lips with mine. Her back hit the closed door, and I pressed into her, not wanting any air between us while I stole her breath.

Her mouth was perfect.

It tasted of rum and chocolate, and unlike any other mouth I'd ever kissed before. Kissing Tessa—hearing her moans, her whimpers, her need—was different, and I realized I would never get enough of her no matter how long our tongues swirled together. I poured every interrupted kiss into my movements, wanting Tessa to feel what my mouth was capable of. Wanting Tessa to ache for me when we were apart like I knew I would be aching for her. The longer I kissed her up against her door, the more I realized that all the kisses I'd had before this one were fake and Tessa was the real thing.

SIXTEEN

Tessa

IF I HAD KNOWN KISSING VINNY WAS GOING TO BE LIKE THAT, I WOULD have done it sooner. Never in my entire life had a man almost brought me to my knees with a kiss. I was seconds away from turning into a pile of mush when he broke our kiss and leaned his forehead against mine.

"When I get home, and I'm in the shower, I'm going to remember that kiss. When I'm lying in bed, I'm going to remember how soft your lips are and imagine them wrapped around my dick. And when I dream of you tonight, it's going to be filled with the sounds you make when you're thirsty for more."

I *was* thirsty for more. I wanted all of him, but there was a thought in the back of my mind that Colton would either walk in on us or have a meltdown because he couldn't get into my room if he needed to. So, when Vinny opened the front door, I stepped to the side so he could leave.

"Sweet dreams, sweets." He kissed my lips softly and then turned and walked to the stairs before disappearing.

I closed and locked the door, my pussy aching with the need to come. Sure, I'd gotten wet from a man's kiss before, but never to the point where I literally ached to have an orgasm.

After turning off all the lights, I walked into my bathroom and turned on the shower. The water was warm as I stepped in, and without hesitation, I propped my leg on the edge of the tub, leaned my head on my forearm, which I pressed against the tiled wall, and sent the other hand straight to my clit. The water beat onto my back as I rubbed the nub, needing to come faster than I'd ever come before. Images of Vinny's smile flashed through my mind, and images of his hard body pressed against mine sent tingles down my spine as I rubbed my clit over and over until I was gasping, my body bucking, as the orgasm raced down my legs and back up. I knew it wasn't going to take long, and even after my body stopped pulsing, I knew I needed more.

I hurried and bathed myself before jumping out of the shower and running to my room still dripping water from barely drying myself off. I climbed into my bed naked, and as I replayed our kiss over again in my head, I brought myself to another orgasm.

Once again, Melony and I had found the perfect dress for me. This one was the color of red wine with an off-the-shoulder neckline and went to the middle of my calves. It was cute, simple, and perfect for keeping me cool at the outdoor wedding.

Vinny and I hadn't seen each other since the night of our dinner and kiss because he had to do groomsman things after school and I was busy with Colt or working, but we'd spoken on the phone during his lunch break each day. He'd told me the wedding was being held at his boss's house. Learning that information put me at ease when it came to going to a party at Sebastian's. It was essentially the same except one was to witness a wedding and the other … Well, I wasn't sure yet, but it wasn't unheard of to go to a party at a boss's house. I didn't think so, at least.

This would actually be my first time to attend a wedding, and I

was excited. Plus, Paul and Joss were perfect for each other. I'd realized that in the few hours I'd spent with them at the range. At the
time, with every kiss they shared, and with every touch, I'd wished it
was Vinny and me. But, I'd finally gotten my kiss, and I was hoping to
get many more tonight—and in the foreseeable future.

At 3:30, Sophia came over so she could watch Colton while I went
to the wedding. The moment she saw me in my dress, she said, "In the
year and a half I've known you, I haven't seen you this happy."

I closed the door and sighed with a smile on my face, thinking
about Vinny. "I am happy."

"No, sweetie. You're glowing. That's more than just happy."

I leaned against the door where Vinny had kissed me and exhaled
a breath. "Vinny kissed me."

"It's about time that boy stepped up to the plate." Sophia moved to
Colton and compressed his ears. "Hey, honey. Want spaghetti and
meatballs for dinner?"

His little hands flapped excitedly.

My grin widened, still thinking about the kiss. "I know. I'm more
than just happy."

"If I need to sleep on your couch tonight, just call. I don't mind
staying over if you need to have alone time." She wiggled her brows,
causing me to laugh.

"I'm not going home with him. He has … uh, work tomorrow, and
he needs to deal with that before we can take the next step."

She sat on my couch. "He will. I've already told you that he has it
bad for you. He'll quit his nighttime job. Just call if you won't
be home."

"That won't happen. Colt would freak if I wasn't here in the
morning."

"That may be true, but just in case, you have my number." She
grinned, and I got the impression she really wanted me to go home
with Vinny. Maybe it was because I was happy and Vinny made me
that way. If I didn't have Colt, I *would* probably go home with him, but
I did have Colt and I needed to be home when he woke. He had

routines, rituals and a specific schedule to keep, and I wasn't ready to change or upset his little world for my pleasure.

"Also, just a reminder that I have that thing at my boss's house tomorrow, and Melony is going with me."

"I remember. It's not a problem."

There was a knock on my door behind me. My grin instantly widened, and I leaned off of the door and peeked in the peephole. I opened the door to see the man who took my breath away standing in khaki shorts and a dark blue tee that hugged him all the right places. "You're wearing that to the wedding?"

He chuckled. "We're getting ready at the house."

"Oh. Well, let me get my purse, and then I'm ready to go." I walked to my kitchen table, which was still in view of the living room.

Vinny stepped inside and waved at Sophia before walking to where she sat on the couch and leaned down to hug her. "Sophia, are you aging in reverse?"

"Stop." She blushed and waved him off as they broke apart. "I'm not the one you need to compliment."

Vinny turned toward me and grinned. "The problem with that, Sophia, is the way I want to compliment our Tessa isn't PG."

I stopped mid-step as I was walking toward Colton to say good-bye, and bit my lip as I looked at Vinny. No words were spoken. I took a deep breath and knelt beside Colton, kissing him and saying good-bye. Vinny said goodbye to Colt before grabbing my hand and leading me out the door.

"You kids have fun," Sophia called out as she stood to lock the door behind us.

"We will," Vinny replied.

We walked down to his SUV, hand in hand. Just before he opened the passenger side door to let me slide inside, he turned me so my back was against the car. Without a word, his mouth met mine, and like the other night, we kissed as though we were starving for each other. After several moments, we broke apart, and Vinny opened the door. Still, no words were spoken as I slid inside and he shut the door.

He got in, cranked the engine, and grabbed my hand, lacing our fingers together before pulling out of my complex.

"Who all are coming?" I asked as we pulled onto the freeway.

"All the guys plus a few of the S&R girls—"

"Really?"

"Yeah. One of our own is getting married."

"No, I know. I'm just excited to meet female escorts."

"Why?"

I shrugged. "Just to pick their brains."

"You want to join S&R?"

I snorted. "No, of course not."

"So, you want to get the lowdown on Duane Wood?"

"Maybe." I smirked.

"Do you think Scarlett and Duane would have hotter sex than Tessa and Vinny?"

I bit my bottom lip, thinking. "I guess there's no way to know for sure until they've all had a chance."

"I like your thinking, sweets."

We drove to a beautiful, contemporary house on the outskirts of Vegas overlooking the desert mountains. It was a two-story, flat roof, stucco home I'd kill to own one day. It was stunning.

"I'm not sure of the exact plan, but you can hang with me and the guys until the others get here."

"Sure, whatever." Before I could get out of the SUV, Vinny ran around and opened the door for me. "Do you do this for all your dates?"

He shrugged. "Habit."

"It's a good one to have." I leaned up and pressed my lips to his softly because I could. I could, after all this time, do what I'd wanted to do since the night I'd met him.

We walked hand in hand to the front door. Just before he knocked, Vinny brushed a piece of my hair that had come loose from my chignon knot behind my ear, and I sighed, loving when he did it. "This may be Joss's day, but to me, you're the most beautiful woman who will be here tonight."

"How do you know?" I whispered as I looked up into his chocolate eyes.

"I could tell you all the sappy lines you've heard before, or what I've told my dates, but those are all lines I've used to make a woman feel good about herself and make her think she is the only one in my life. The truth is, you're the only one in my life, Tess. I've never done this before, but I'm trying, and I remembered that I forgot to tell you that you look beautiful tonight, so I needed to so before things get crazy."

As I listened to him speak, I felt a lump form in my throat, and I knew hat I was starting to fall hard for him—if I hadn't already fallen. "You're the only one for me, too."

Vinny grinned. "Good." He kissed my lips once more and then knocked twice before entering the house.

Just as we stepped inside, I took in the modern-contemporary home, which was sleek and stunning and mostly white. Somehow the whiteness made the space elegant and not boring.

"I'm getting married!" Paul exclaimed as he came into the foyer.

Vinny stepped toward him and gave him a hug. "Congrats, dude."

They broke apart, and I stepped forward, giving Paul a hug as well. "Yeah, congrats."

"Thanks for coming, Tessa. I know Joss is looking forward to getting to know you better," Paul stated.

"Likewise."

"She and Autumn should be here soon. Also," he stepped forward and lowered his voice, "Joss's childhood friend, Cat, will be here too. I think she and Seth had a thing because whenever she's mentioned, I swear he stops breathing."

Vinny and I looked at each other and shrugged. "All right, what's the plan?" Vinny asked Paul.

"Time for shots and getting dressed," Paul replied.

"Did someone say shots?"

I turned to see Nick and Bradley coming in from the backyard.

"Who else is here?" Vinny asked.

"Just us and Mark," Bradley replied.

Vinny turned to me. "Do you want to hang with us or ...?"

I looked to the guys and then back to Vinny. "I'll just go look around." I didn't want to impose on whatever guys did as they got ready for a wedding. Paul needed his friends, and even though I was hopefully becoming a friend, I didn't feel like they needed a woman present.

"The caterers are setting up the bar. I'm sure they'll pour you a drink," Bradley stated.

"Are you sure you'll be okay?" Vinny asked.

"Of course." I smiled up at him.

"Are you two a thing or what?" Paul questioned.

"We're something." Vinny kissed the side of my head as he brought me against his side, and I blushed.

"It's about fucking time." I turned to see Gabe walking in from the backyard.

Paul slapped Vinny on the back. "Well, I'm glad you finally pulled the trigger, but this is my day, and it's time to get me ready so I can marry the love of my life."

Vinny looked down at me, and I shooed him away. "Go. I'll be fine."

He kissed me quickly, and then he and the guys went up the stairs. Once they were out of sight, I turned and went toward the backyard, assuming that was where the wedding would take place.

When I got outside, I gasped as I took in the pool that looked as though it went on for miles and miles into the desert. People dressed in black pants and black polo shirts were placing flowers and floating candles in the L-shaped infinity pool, and I added that look to my mental wedding wish list most women had. From what I understood, Paul and Joss hadn't had long to prepare for the wedding, but as I looked at everything being set-up, it seemed as though it was going to be gorgeous. Strands of white lights criss-crossed over the pool and adjacent dance floor. Just beyond, two large sections of chiavari chairs stood in neat rows on either side of a white runner. White roses hung at the end of each row, flanking the aisle as it approached an arbor covered in more white roses.

The mountains in the background made the whole scene breathtaking.

"Bride or groom?"

I jumped slightly at the man's voice and looked up to meet his eyes.

"Sorry, didn't mean to scare you."

"No worries. I was just fantasizing about my wedding." I smiled. "And *groom*, I guess."

"You guess?"

"Well, I know them both, but I've known Paul longer."

"Ah. Oh, where are my manners? I'm Mark, Paul's—well, I was his boss." He chuckled and stuck out his hand.

I grinned again and stuck my hand out as well. "Tessa, Vinny's—"

His brows furrowed. "Vinny's?"

We shook. "I'm not exactly sure. We're friends for sure."

Mark placed his hands on his hips and eyed me curiously. "Are you and Vin serious?"

It was my turn to furrow my brows. "Why do you ask?"

"Because it seems as though they're dropping like flies around here, and I have a business to run, so I'd like to know with more notice than what Gabe and Paul gave me. It seems I might need to talk to the ladies in their lives and find out what's really going on since they keep me in the dark."

"Oh," I chuckled. "I'd suggest talking to Vinny actually."

"Because you don't know, or because he's quitting?"

"I don't think he's quitting."

"Okay, good." I wasn't going to tell him Vinny had said he was going to take a break. That was for Vinny to talk to Mark about, not me. "Well, Tessa, it was nice to meet you. Guests should be arriving any minute now, and I need to make sure the boys are dressed and ready to be escor—ushers. And please, have a drink."

"I will. Thank you."

Mark walked back into the house, and I went to the bar as suggested. I wasn't sure what I was in the mood for, but after I scanned the bottles behind the bartender, my gaze landed on the bottle of Bacardi. I smiled and ordered a rum and Coke. I would never be able to look at rum again without thinking about Vinny. The night of our dinner we each drank a couple, and when we kissed, he tasted of rum and the sweetness of Coke—a perfect combination.

Just as the bartender placed my drink in front of me, two couples stepped up to the bar. "Two beers, two vodka cranberries." I turned to glance at the man who'd ordered, and he smiled a smile that instantly dampened my panties. *What the fuck? How did that happen just by looking at this guy's smile?* "Bride or groom?" he asked.

"Groom," I replied, and looked to his group. The guy he was with looked as though he could be his brother. One of the women was brunette and gorgeous, and the other was blonde and equally as pretty.

"Us too." The guy stuck out his hand. "I'm Brandon. This is my wife, Spencer, my brother, Blake, and his friend, Sarah."

"I'm Tessa. My … um, boyfriend worked with Paul."

"Oh yeah?" Blake asked. "Your boyfriend's an escort?"

"I guess he is."

"You guess?" Spencer asked and took a sip of her drink the bartender placed on the bar.

"It's new," I clarified.

"Who is it?" Brandon questioned.

"Vin—I mean, Duane."

"Vinny?" Blake boomed. "Seriously?"

"Um, yeah?"

"No shit?" Blake continued.

"Those boys are droppin' like flies," Brandon stated.

Spencer hooked her arm with mine and started to guide me toward the seats. "I've actually never met any of the guys, but they go to the gym we own. I just came to get out of the house. We live in San Francisco—well, Brandon and I live in San Francisco. We just had a baby not too long ago, and I needed a vacay."

"I'm from San Francisco too," I gushed.

"Really?"

"Yeah, moved here about eighteen months ago."

"Small world."

"I guess so." The two of us walked to a row of seats, and I realized Sarah had stayed with the guys. "Totally random, but are you a Giants fan?"

Spencer's eyes lit up. "Of course I am."

"Oh, phew."

"Why do you ask?"

"Vinny's a Dodgers fan."

She sucked in a breath. "And you're still dating him?"

I laughed. "I know, right?"

"He must be something for you to date a rival."

I smiled. "He is."

At that moment, something told me to turn around. Vinny and the guys walked into the backyard, all of them dressed in black and white tuxes, and all of them looked hotter than the last time I'd seen them only thirty or so minutes prior—especially Vinny. Good lord, he could fill out a tux like nobody's business.

"Are those …" Spencer trailed off.

"Yep," I answered, knowing she was wondering if they were all men of Saddles & Racks.

"Who's who?"

"Well, left to right is, Bradley, Gabe, Paul, Vinny, and Nick."

"My best friend, Ryan, is going to die when she finds out I hung out with hot male escorts."

"Aren't you married to Brandon?"

"Yep, but that doesn't mean I can't make my best friend jealous."

I grinned. "Totally understandable."

"And I have to admit Vinny is the hottest Dodgers fan I've ever seen. I totally get it."

We both laughed just as Vinny's gaze met mine. He walked over to us. "Sweets." He kissed my lips. "I see you've made a friend. I'm—"

"Vinny," Spencer interjected. "And I'm Spencer."

"Brandon's wife?"

"How many female Spencers do you know?"

"True."

"But we can't be friends."

Vinny balked. "And why not?"

The next three words out of Spencer's mouth sealed our friendship.

"Fuck the Dodgers."

Vinny's mouth dropped open, and his gaze moved to me. "Seriously?"

I shrugged. "Fuck the Dodgers."

"Do you want to walk home?" he teased.

I grinned. "You know I can never root for the Dodgers, and you know you'd never let me walk home."

He leaned down and pressed his lips to mine again. "You're lucky you're cute."

"Everyone," Mark called out, "the bride has arrived."

SEVENTEEN

Vinny

ONE OF MY BEST FRIENDS WAS MARRIED.

Holy shit, how did that happen? Watching my friends love their women, made me recognize that I wanted that in my life. I'd never realized it before, but I was lonely. That, of course, was before Tessa walked into my life. Now, she was all I ever thought about. Was that what happened to Gabe and Paul? Did Autumn and Joss consume their world so much that it made them want to settle down? It had to be, and honestly, it scared me, but I was going to see where things went with Tessa because I couldn't imagine my life without her.

It all moved so fast, but what was fast? My group of friends seemed to be settling down at lightning speed, but I guess if you know, you know. Tessa and I hadn't done anything beyond kissing, but that didn't stop my desire for some kind of future with her. Everything was there. We got along, laughed together, had amazing chemistry, and the sexual tension was off the charts. I could feel it with every look, and I'd never had that connection before.

I knew she was a little hesitant at first because of Colton, but I had the knowledge, the skill, and the personality to help her with him, and I hoped she realized that, because I felt as though I was on the lightning speed roller coaster just like my friends.

"Your boss asked me if you were quitting," Tessa stated as we were eating dinner in Mark's backyard.

My fork stopped at my mouth as I looked over at her. "He was asking you?"

She shrugged. "I guess since you brought a date to the wedding and that's not normal? And also because Gabe and Paul quit?"

"Well, I plan to talk to him on Monday about taking time off."

"Okay." She smiled. "Want to make dinner at my place on Monday too?"

I grinned. "You bet your sweet ass I do." I wanted to have dinner at her place every night. "But, the Dodgers are playing the Padres, so ..."

"I already told you they won't ever be on my TV. Plus, the Giants are playing the Diamondbacks."

"So, you're telling me I need to bring over my own TV?"

Tessa laughed. "Yeah, if you want to watch your team. Otherwise, Colt and I will be watching the Giants."

"You're killing me," I teased.

"Speaking of killing ..." my brows furrowed at her change of subject. "I followed up with Metro, and they gave me the report. Apparently, the guy who followed me home is a regular at the club."

"Really?"

Tessa nodded and took a bite of her fish. "He's actually been coming to the club for as long as I've worked there. Not sure if this was the first time he had followed me or not though."

I dropped my fork and turned my body to face her. "What did the cops say?"

"When I saw the name, I realized who it was, and they said to get a restraining order if I wanted."

"A restraining order's not going to do shit. You better tell Galen and all the other bouncers. Fuck, we're changing your locks too."

"Change my locks?" she asked. "You really think that's necessary?"

"You think I want to take a chance on something happening to you? I bet you could ask every single one of these people who work at S&R if they've had a stalker, and they would all answer yes. I'm not going to take this lightly."

"Okay," she replied.

"Sorry, to interrupt," Spencer cut in. "Did you say you have a stalker?"

Tessa nodded. "Yeah. I work at a strip club, and this guy tried to follow me home one night."

Spencer looked at Brandon briefly and then back to Tessa. "You probably don't know my story, but Brandon's ex tried to kill me, and his college classmate kidnapped me. If something seems off, you need to take every precaution there is."

"Oh my god," Tessa gasped. "You almost died *and* someone kidnapped you?"

My gaze flicked to Brandon's, and he gave me a tight smile with a nod. As I listened to Spencer tell Tessa her story, it solidified the fact that the world we lived in was dangerous and you never knew what lay beneath the exterior of a person.

"… so, move if you need to," Spencer finished.

Tessa turned her head back to me. "I don't want to move. Sophia is there for Colt whenever I need her, and Melony lives a few doors down. I'm happy there."

I kissed the side of her head. "We'll figure this out. Even if I need to get Seth to pay the guy a visit."

Seth wasn't Metro, and as far as I knew he was moving back to D.C. when the case he and Joss were working on ended. But, if I needed to scare the guy stalking Tessa, I would. Hell, if I needed to spend every night at her place, I would. I already followed her home each night she worked. Last night, I wasn't able to, but I got Seth to do it, which she didn't know about.

Which also meant she wasn't good at making sure someone wasn't following her.

I introduced Tessa to everyone I knew. She loved Leah and Nina, who both wanted to recruit Tessa to join S&R. That, in turn, made me tell them I was taking a break.

"You too?" Leah asked.

I shrugged and brought Tessa to my side, wrapping my arm around her shoulder. "We're gonna see what happens."

Leah turned to Nina. "We should make a bet on who's next."

Nina's eyes became wide. "Yes!"

"I've got Bradley," Leah stated.

Nina thought for a moment as she looked over at the guys doing shots. "Okay, I'll take Nick, but it's going to need to be a strong woman to take that boy down."

I had a feeling Leah was going to win the bet. I didn't know how, and I didn't know when, but out of the two, Brad was for sure the one who'd get attached to a woman before Nick would. Or hell, Nick might surprise me and be the one to settle down first. Only a few months ago, I assumed I'd never settle down, and now I was thinking about cooking dinner every night at Tessa's.

"Come on, sweets. I wanna show you something." I took Tessa's hand and led her toward the stairs that led to the roof. Before we could get there, I saw Seth walking with Joss's childhood friend, Cat. Even from where I stood, I could tell he was a man on a mission and Paul must have been correct when he said something was going on. Then it hit me: Seth had said he'd only been in love once, and I'd bet my next paycheck that Cat was the one he loved. And from the looks of it, I'd say was still in love.

"Where are we going?" Tessa asked, bringing me out of my thoughts.

"Oh, well, I was going to take you up to the roof, but seems we're too late."

"The roof?"

"Mark's wife turned it into a garden. She reads up there. It's like an oasis."

"Really?"

"Yeah. I'll show you another time, but now, I want to be alone with you."

"What time does the wedding end?"

"Not sure, but let's go."

"Go where?"

I looked toward the house and remembered the room where the guys and I had gotten dressed in, and then I remembered the bathroom. "I want to show you one of the reasons I'm still escorting."

"Still?"

"Well, why I'm hesitant to leave S&R."

"I don't understand."

I grabbed her hand, lacing our fingers together, and started for the house. The music was bumping, and I figured no one would know we slipped away. "Don't worry. After tomorrow, I'm still taking a break, but maybe you'll understand why it's hard for me to walk away."

"Okay ..."

I stopped walking just before we got to the stairs. "I'm not saying I'm only going to take a break. If we work out, of course I'll quit."

"I understand."

"I'm not sure you do. It's not because I like fucking for a living, sweets."

"It's not?"

"No." I chuckled. "I like the money."

"Who doesn't?"

I grinned. "Exactly."

"So, you're going to show me a pile of money or something?"

We started up the stairs, and I brought her into Mark's bedroom. At least I assumed it was his bedroom. "Not exactly." We walked down the hall and into the last door.

"Holy crap. This bedroom is bigger than my apartment," Tessa stated in awe.

"I don't think it's that big, but wait until you see the bathroom."

I led Tessa into the adjacent room that had what I assumed was marble floors, at least a six-person glass shower with multiple rain shower heads, a step up sunken tub perfect for two people with a fire-place to the side of it, and beige granite encasing the tub and counters.

"Holy crap," Tessa breathed.

"Right?"

"It's amazing," she gushed as she ran her hand along the side where the tub was.

"Right?" I repeated.

She turned to me. "How is this why you don't quit S&R?"

I sat on the ledge near the tub and reached for her, bringing her between my legs as I wrapped my arms around her waist. "Because one day, sweets, I want to own a place like this, and working for S&R gives me the means to be able to save for it. Granted, each year I tend to go on trips and spend some of the money, but one day I will own a place like this one."

"You make that much going on dates?" She wrapped her arms around my neck.

"That and my teacher's salary, which isn't nearly enough on its own."

"So, you don't want to quit?"

"I'm not saying that. I'm telling you why it took me so long to pull the trigger, so to speak."

Tessa looked around the room. "So if you quit, you won't ever be able to afford a place like this?"

I shrugged. "Just means it will take a little longer than planned."

"Are you sure? You're making it sound as though I'm crushing your dreams by asking you to stop escorting if we start dating."

I kissed her lips softly, loving that I was now able to do it. "My mom used to tell me that once in a lifetime you meet someone who will change everything. And you, sweets, are changing everything in my life, and honestly, I'm diggin' it."

She stared at me with her blue eyes. "How is it that you've never had a girlfriend before? You know all the right things to say."

"It's the job, but with you, it's everything. I want you to be my actual girlfriend."

She smiled. "I want to be your girlfriend."

"Good. Now, we're all alone up here. Kiss me like you mean it."

She licked her lips and tilted her head down, brushing her lips against mine before I took over, deepening the kiss and making her moan like she did with our first one.

"Tess ..."

"Hmm?" she asked against my mouth.

"I want you."

"You have me."

"All of you," I clarified.

She broke her mouth from mine. "It's been a long time."

"How long?"

"Over five years."

I balked. "That's—"

Tessa sighed. "I haven't had sex since the night Colt was conceived."

"Damn, sweets," I breathed. "That's a long time."

"I know."

I stared into her blue eyes. "That's a lot of sex we're going to have to make up for."

She stared back and grinned. "Okay."

"Starting now?"

Tessa started to nod, and I didn't need more of a green light. I stood, picking her up in the process, and turned her so that she sat on the counter next to us. Pulling her legs, I brought her to the edge and slid my hands up her thighs until they were under her dress. The moment my fingers brushed against her pussy, I felt how wet she was.

"We're about to find out the answer."

"What answer?" she asked.

"If you taste like cotton candy."

I tugged on her panties, bringing them down her legs and dropping the black lace to the floor. She stared down at me as I got onto my knees, pushing her dress up past her hips. This moment had been played in my head on repeat since the night I met Tessa—even when I thought we'd only be friends. I'd stroke my dick, imagining it was her, wishing it was her, wanting it to be her. But now ...

Now it wasn't going to be my fucking imagination.

It was going to be real.

The moment my tongue took its first swipe up her slit, she moaned and I groaned. I felt like a starving man despite the fact that we'd just had dinner. Her pussy was sweet on my tongue as I licked and sucked and made her moan over and over. Replacing my mouth with my hand, I pumped my finger inside of her. She was tight and wet and fuckable, so fucking fuckable, but given that it had been years since she last had a dick inside of her, I knew she needed more time.

When she was ready, I stuck another finger in. "I have my answer," I stated.

"What is it?" she panted.

"You don't taste like cotton candy, sweets."

"I don't?"

"You taste fucking better."

She moaned at my words. "Let me see. Kiss me."

I didn't hesitate as I stood, my fingers still inside of her, and crashed my mouth against hers, letting her taste her arousal coating my lips. My fingers pumped deep inside of her as she leaned back against the mirror and started to ride my fingers as I worked her, our tongues still dancing together.

"I'm close," she gasped against my lips.

Pumping my fingers harder and faster, I worked her deep, making sure to hook my fingers, which caused her hips to buck. "That's it," I coaxed, breaking our kiss so I could look at her face. I wanted to see her come. Wanted to watch as the pleasure raced through her body. Wanted to know what she looked like when she came apart so I could use that memory when I jerked off.

And then Tessa shattered, her body jerking as she climaxed around my fingers. The scent of her arousal filled the air, and I groaned, aching to be inside of her. Needing to be inside of her. Wanting to feel her pussy clench my dick and not just my fingers.

I couldn't wait any longer to be inside of her, so while she came down from her orgasm, I worked my pants and freed my cock.

Spreading her wide, I stepped forward, aligning my shaft to her pussy, and inched in slowly.

"Fuck, Tess. You're so fucking tight."

"Just fuck me already," she demanded, reaching around my back and pulling my ass forward. I slid inside of her, her pussy clenching at the intrusion. She hissed. "Fuck."

"Greedy are we?"

"Yes," she panted. "It's been too long."

"Then you better hold on because once I get going, I'm not going to be able to stop until we're both spent."

Tessa's hips began to move, and I followed, taking that as my cue to fuck her.

And fuck her I did.

I spread her legs out, my fists holding onto her ankles. She was spread wide, her pussy on display as I rocked into her. She pulsed as I drove into her as deep as I could go with each thrust. Her gaze met mine, and the look of pleasure radiating off of her was enough to make me tip over the edge.

"I've got you. Let go." Our eyes stayed locked, and I picked her up off the counter and carried her to the ledge near the tub, the entire time staying inside of her.

After placing her down with her back against the granite, I laced her fingers with mine above her head and continued my rhythm. We slid against the hard surface, and I second guessed where I'd chosen to bring her. But then she was climbing again, her pussy pulsing as I pushed into her over and over.

"You feel so good," I groaned, increasing the speed of my pumps.

"Yes," Tessa panted. "So good. I'm gonna come again."

Reaching between us, I rubbed her clit, my hips still working inside of her. She moaned, her back arching off the smooth surface, and I groaned as I came as well. We were spent—at least I was—and I collapsed, spinning us so she was laying on top of me and I wasn't crushing her.

Her head rested on my chest as our breathing returned to normal.

After several moments, Tessa leaned up and looked into my eyes. "That was ..."

"Worth the wait?"

She grinned. "Yeah."

I leaned up and pressed my lips to hers. "Not gonna be the last time either."

"Good."

I faintly heard the DJ announce it was the final dance. "We better get cleaned up and say our goodbyes to the bride and groom."

"I'm not sure I can walk." She grinned.

I chuckled. "What every man wants to hear after they've fucked a beautiful lady." I sat up. "While I would love to sit here all night with my dick inside of you, it's not my house, and we have to go say goodbye."

Tessa's eyes widened, and she scurried off of my lap. "Oh shit. You're right. We just fucked in your boss's bathroom."

I brushed a piece of hair behind her ear. "Trust me, he won't care. He runs an escort service." I started to stand so I could right my pants when Tessa gasped.

"What?" I asked.

"We didn't use a condom," she groaned, running toward the toilet and grabbing toilet paper to clean herself.

"Oh fuck. I'm so sorry, Tess. I've never gone without before. I swear. I'm clean."

"I'm clean too, obviously, but I'm not on birth control."

My eyes were the ones to widen this time. "You're not?"

"I wasn't getting laid, remember?"

"Right." I ran my hand on the back of my neck. "Whatever happens, we'll figure it out."

"I can't believe this," she stated, snatching her panties off the floor.

"Hey." I moved to her and wrapped her in my arms. "It will be okay. You've managed to have Colton on your own, and this time, you won't be alone if you do get pregnant."

"I can't think about this right now."

"Okay. Let's go say goodbye, and then after Paul and Joss leave, I'll take you home."

"Okay." She stepped into her underwear. "I can't believe this happened again."

"Well." I smirked. "In your defense, I'm pretty irresistible," I teased.

Tessa's gaze cut to me and she chuckled, shaking her head. "You are, but that's no excuse."

I buttoned my pants and then wrapped her in my arms again as I tried to comfort her. "It will be okay. We're adults, and adults have babies all the time. Plus, we don't even know if you will get pregnant."

"I know. I'm just mad at myself because I let it happen again."

"We'll be okay."

I meant every word. I wasn't ready to be a father, but I loved kids —it's why I became a teacher. Besides, I truly believed things happened for a reason. There was a reason Tessa was the stripper for Gabe's bachelor party. There was a reason I couldn't get her out of my head. There was a reason I was going to be Colton's teacher. And there was a reason, after all the sex I'd had in my life, that Tessa was the one to make me lose my mind and forget to use a condom.

We made it down to the backyard just as Paul and Joss were saying their goodbyes. Afterward, with the party winding down, I drove Tessa back to her apartment. We didn't say much as I made the drive, and when I pulled up to her complex, she hesitated before getting out.

"You know I'm not mad at you, right?"

No, I didn't know that. I assumed she was. "You're not?"

"I'm disappointed in myself."

I grabbed her hand and kissed the back of it. "I promise you everything will turn out fine. Let's not worry until we know for sure."

She smiled tightly at me. "You're right."

"Good. Now, let's go let Sophia go home."

"Okay."

We both got out of my SUV, and I grabbed her hand as we walked up to her apartment. After Tessa used her key to get in, we stepped inside to see Sophia sleeping as she sat on the couch, a book resting on her chest. When the door clicked shut, she started.

"You're home."

"We are," Tessa stated. "Thank you so much for watching Colt."

Sophia stood. "You know I would, anytime. I love you both."

"Thank you," Tessa replied.

"I'll see you tomorrow." Sophia turned and looked at me. "I'm starting to love you too."

I stepped to her and kissed her cheek. "Feeling's mutual."

She patted my cheek and then turned and opened the door before saying goodbye and leaving. I turned to Tessa, ready to tell her goodnight, but she stepped over to me and shut the door.

"Stay?"

"Are you sure?"

She nodded. "Yes."

"Okay," I agreed.

Tessa locked the door behind me and then took my hand. "Melony gave me condoms."

"Did she now?"

She shrugged and turned off the lamp by the couch. "She wanted me to be prepared. I didn't realize I'd need them at the wedding."

"Sweets, we're going to need them every fucking day."

But, I was wrong.

Because the next morning would be the last time I'd see Tessa until her wedding day *to someone else*.

EIGHTEEN

Tessa

SOMETHING TOLD ME TO NOT LET VINNY GO HOME.

Maybe it was because after hearing Spencer's story, I realized life was dangerous and I needed to take more precautions to stay safe. Or maybe it was because I freaked out after sex with Vinny. The sex was amazing, but I'd once again had unprotected sex, and this time, I wasn't even drunk. I was so wrapped up in the fact that this hot guy—who was now my boyfriend—took charge and made me feel things I'd never felt before. And I wasn't only talking about down below. He made me feel special, cared for. *Safe.*

I didn't want him to go home after Sophia left for the night. I wanted to know what it would feel like going to sleep wrapped in his arms and wake up just the same. Though, when I woke up the next morning, he wasn't in my bed, and there was a slight moment of sadness that washed through me until I smelled bacon.

Walking down the hall, I peeked into Colton's room and noticed he wasn't in there. When I rounded the corner into the living room, I assumed he'd be in front of the TV, *PAW Patrol* playing. He wasn't. No, Colton was sitting at the dining room table, iPad in hand, a plate with a waffle covered in strawberry jam cut into triangles in front of him.

"You made him breakfast?" I asked Vinny, eyeing him in his boxers and the undershirt he'd had on under his tux.

"A boy's gotta eat."

My heart swelled as I walked over to give Colton a kiss on the top of his head. For so long I'd always assumed that no man would want my baggage. And while Colton wasn't necessarily baggage, he still required a lot of my time. I moved to Vinny and wrapped my arms around his waist, resting my head against his back. "Thank you."

"You're welcome."

"Are we having waffles too?"

"And bacon."

"And coffee?"

"And whatever you want. I have a few hours before I need to head out."

"Right." I sighed and turned to the cabinet to grab a coffee mug.

"Hey." Vinny stepped to me and brushed my hair behind my shoulder. "Don't worry. I'm going to go meet with my client, tell her that I'm taking time off, and give her Brad's name. In fact, I'm going to reimburse her for the date."

"You can do that?"

"Of course, minus Mark's fee."

"Okay."

"And then, how about I go home, grab a change of clothes and my toothbrush, and meet you back here tonight?"

"I'd like that."

"Good." Vinny kissed my temple. "Now, bacon is almost ready, and I'm starving for more than just food, sweets."

"Then you should have stayed in bed."

He laughed and moved back to the stove. "I should have, but when I woke up, I heard cartoons and knew Colt was up. I wanted to give you more time to rest."

I poured myself a cup of coffee. "Plus, I'm sore."

"Then take some aspirin. Because before I leave, I'm *eating* again."

As soon as Colton was down for his morning nap, Vinny led me to my bedroom. "Aspirin kick in yet?" I nodded, and he spun me then nudged me to sit on the side of the bed. "Good because I need dessert."

"Dessert after breakfast?" I chuckled.

He shrugged and started to remove his clothes. "We're adults. We can have dessert whenever we want."

"Is that so?" I was grinning like a fool, but honestly, I couldn't stop myself. This man had that effect on me.

"Yeah, sweets. Now lay back and let me have my candy."

I did as instructed. After removing my pajama bottoms, Vinny spread me open and feasted on me until I was using a pillow to swallow my moans. When I finally pulled the pillow away after coming down from my high, he was standing before me, a condom on his impressive, hard length.

"On your stomach," he ordered.

Without hesitation, I threw my top off. I flipped over and moved into the center of the bed. The mattress dipped, and the warmth of his body radiated against my back as he leaned against me, kissing my back with his soft lips.

"While I love your tits, I'm going to fuck you from behind so deep that you'll feel me in your belly."

I swallowed, my pussy clenching at the picture he was painting.

"And I'm not going to stop until you're screaming into the pillow again."

I nodded and grabbed the pillow by my head, getting it ready once again so we didn't wake Colt. Vinny's lips returned to my back, kissing down it as his hard length slid across my skin until he was nudging my legs apart, lifting my hips slightly and then sinking into me. He started to pump, his cock hitting the spot that caused a warm sensation to race through my body.

"Oh, God," I moaned.

Vinny's thrusts increased in speed, and he leaned across my back and captured my mouth with his. Our tongues dueled, and once again I was getting closer and closer to tipping over the edge. Our mouths broke apart, and he went harder, the bed hitting the wall with each drive of his hips. All the years didn't have sex were now being made up for by this man. He knew just the right angle to work, and I was lucky I was finally able to have him.

It didn't take long before my body came apart again, my face pressed into a pillow as I moaned my release. I expected Vinny to follow, but instead, he continued his slow drives for a few more thrusts. Once my climax had subsided, he rose, hooked his arm under my belly and lifted me so my back was curved against his front. We were both on our knees as he held me and drove up into me. His hands caressed my breasts, his teeth nipped at my bare shoulder, and I was enjoying the ride.

"You gonna give me three?" he challenged.

I nodded even though I wasn't sure if I could, but I'd give this man anything if he kept making my body feel as amazing as it did.

"Yeah, you are. Your tight pussy feels incredible around my dick, sweets. And when you can't walk tonight at that party, all the guys are going to know you were fucked good."

I moaned my response, not able to form a word as his cock pounded into me.

"And then, when we get back here tonight, we're going to do it all over again."

Vinny's mouth found mine again before I could respond—even though I likely couldn't being so lost for words—and we kissed. His hands roamed my body, and once again I chased the orgasm on the brink of exploding inside of me. Never, and I mean *never*, had I ever had three orgasms given to me by someone else, but it was happening.

With a few more hard and deep thrusts, I was coming, my moans swallowed by Vinny's kiss, and then he was groaning his own release. I sagged against him, not able to move.

"Now, *I* need a nap," he admitted as he kissed my shoulder.

"Me, too."

"But," he sighed, "I don't have time to do that."

I turned to face him as he pulled out of me. "Lay with me until you need to leave?"

Vinny kissed me quickly and grinned. "Be right back."

After he discarded the condom, we laid under the covers and kissed until he had to leave to go on a date with someone else.

Hopefully for the last time.

I wasn't sure what to wear to Sebastian's gathering. Melony told me she had never attended one of his get-togethers before, but some of the other girls had and said it was more or less a cocktail party, so I pulled a little black dress out of the closet that I had for moments like this. I also wore my red heels and curled my long, brown hair.

After saying our goodbyes to Colton and Sophia, Melony and I walked down to get into the Uber Melony had ordered.

"Will there be food?" I asked Melony as we headed toward the address Sebastian had given me.

"I have no idea," she replied.

"I thought you knew about these parties?"

"I just heard that they're fun."

"Well, I hope there's food." I looked out the window as we made our way out of the city.

"We'll just raid Sebastian's fridge if not," she joked.

"I still hope there's food, or we're stopping at Raising Cane's on the way home."

"Why are you so hungry?"

I shrugged.

Melony gasped. "Oh my God. You got laid."

My gaze flicked to the rearview mirror to see the driver make eye contact with me. I broke the stare and turned to face Melony. "Why do you think that?"

"Because you dance for a living, and I can see you go all shift without eating. But now it's like you're starving. They don't call it 'working up an appetite' for nothing."

I rolled my eyes and grinned. "And so what if I did?"

"Shut up!" She slapped my arm. "Tell me everything."

"I'm not telling you shit."

"Come on. I wouldn't care if he didn't fuck for a living."

My gaze met the driver's again, and I sighed. "Can we not talk about this now?"

"Please." She waved me off then hooked her thumb toward the driver. "We'll never see this guy again."

I huffed. "Fine. We had sex, he spent the night, cooked me breakfast, and had sex again. I had to take four aspirins because I could barely walk afterward."

"Holy shit. I want to screw a male escort now."

I snorted. "I don't think I fucked Duane though."

"You think they bang differently?"

I chuckled, thinking about how we were talking about one person as though he were two. Maybe he was. He did ask if I thought Duane and Scarlett would have hotter sex than Vinny and Tessa. Maybe it was like role playing? I knew when I was Scarlett, I was acting. "Maybe." I shrugged.

"You better tell me when you find out."

"Maybe I will, or maybe I will keep that shit to myself."

"You better not. I'm your best friend, and I need to know how the men of S&R are."

"I'm only sleeping with one of them," I reminded her.

"But if they are all still employed, they must all know what they're doing."

"Maybe you should hire one and find out for yourself," I suggested.

Melony grinned. "Maybe I will. Who's left?"

"Well, assuming I've met them all, Bradley and Nick."

She thought for a moment, tapping her finger against her lips as the driver gave our name at the gate that led into a subdivision. "Maybe I'll test drive both."

We both started to laugh, and a few minutes later, the driver stopped. "We're here."

I looked out the window at the house we pulled up to. It was a three-story, stone mansion with a fountain in the center of the walkway that led to the front door. "Is this really his house?" I asked, looking back at Melony.

"I guess so."

"Holy crap," I breathed and opened the door, stepping out. Melony followed, and the car drove off. "I assumed he had money, but I wasn't expecting this."

"Let's go check out the inside." Melony started to walk up the stone walkway, past the lush landscape, and I followed.

The closer we got, the louder the bass of the music grew. Two men guarded the door, and when we approached, they opened the brown, French double doors. If I'd never gone to the fight with Sebastian and known he had a bodyguard, I'd think having security at the door would be weird. I still didn't understand why he had security.

Melony and I walked into something out of a magazine when we entered the house. Marble floors spanned a massive space to a stone fireplace in the open living room that sat adjacent to an enormous kitchen with all the bells and whistles. Everything was brown and beige and the complete opposite of what I assumed Sebastian would live in. In my head, I'd pictured his house to be red like the club. Brown and beige weren't anywhere close to red, but it was stunning.

There were a ton of people mingling, dancing, and—*eating?* I didn't see anyone actually eating, but servers walked around, carrying trays of something. I couldn't tell what, but I assumed it was appetizers.

"There's food," I stated to Melony.

"Yes!" she exclaimed. "Let's get a drink and then grab some food."

We found the bar that was located outside by the pool. In the distance, you could see the Strip as it glowed against the setting sun. The pool wasn't an infinity pool like Mark had, but it still looked inviting. Thoughts of what Vinny had said the night before floated to my head, and while he said he hoped to have a house like Mark's one day—the bathroom especially—I wanted to have a backyard like Sebastian's.

"Let's sit by the fire pit and wait for a server to come to us," Melony suggested.

We took the drinks we'd ordered and made our way to the cushioned seats that circled the fire. I hadn't recognized anyone who worked at Red Diamond, and I was glad that Melony came with me. I hadn't even seen Sebastian yet.

As we sipped our cocktails, a server finally came toward us. Melony and I stood, ready to grab whatever they had on their tray, but I stopped when saw nothing except lines of white powder and rolls of bills. I snapped my head toward Melony, my mouth hanging open. She waved the server off and then turned to me.

"Did you know drugs would be here?" I whispered.

She shrugged and sat back down. I followed. "I assumed so, given that Sebastian's a drug dealer."

"Wait, what?"

"You didn't know?"

"How would I know that?"

Melony took a sip of her vodka cranberry. "How do you *not* know that?"

"Again, how would I know?"

"Tessa," she turned and faced me. "Most of the girls sell for him."

"Really?"

"How do you not know this?"

"Because I go in, do my shit, and leave. I don't have time to know what shit goes on at the club."

"You've never seen any of them selling on the floor?"

I thought for a moment. "When I'm on the floor, I pay attention to the clients. I need to make money, not gossip."

"Wow," she breathed. "I can't believe you've never known."

"Why do you still work there if you've known about the shady shit?" I asked. "You don't sell for him, do you?"

"Of course not."

I lowered my voice. "Then why not turn him in?"

"Because it's none of my business, Tessa. I need the money for school and rent. I don't care what other people do with their time or money, and as long as they pay me to dance and give them lap dances, I'm cool."

I took a sip of the rum and Coke I'd ordered, and like always—and the reason I got it—it reminded me of Vinny. It reminded me that we were dating, and his friend was now married to an FBI agent, and Vinny was also friends with a cop. What would happen if they found out I danced in a club that was some sort of front for cocaine dealing? I felt stupid for not knowing, but honestly, what I'd said to Melony was true. I went in, did my shit, and went home. It was better that way —clearly. But then, if Vinny could be friends with an FBI agent and a cop, did that mean they didn't care about him sleeping with his clients? Did they not know? Joss had to know since she was under-cover for S&R. Maybe they only cared about the cases they worked? Should I tell Vinny? So many thoughts ran through my head as I sipped my drink, letting everything sink in.

I looked around at the vast backyard that was covered in pavers and lush greenery. Then I really looked. People were dancing and laughing and snorting from the trays that were being walked around. Was this what Sebastian meant the night of the fight about me talking about what went on at Red Diamond? Who were the guys who sat with us at the fight? Who were the women? Knowing what I just learned made me wish I would have helped the girls. I didn't know what, but something wasn't right. I should have listened to my instincts.

My clutch buzzed on my lap, and I opened it, pulling out my cell phone.

Vinny: *I'm on my way home. Meet at your place in an hour?*

I typed back right away: *Let me check with Mel. The party blows.*

I rolled my eyes, realizing what I'd typed. "Hey, do you want to stay?" I asked her.

"You want to leave already? We just got here."

"I know, but—"

Melony looked down at the phone in my lap. "But Vinny's texting you, and you want to go to your man."

I grinned. "Yeah."

"Shouldn't we at least let Sebastian know we're here?"

"Shit," I sighed. He'd given me money to come, and now I was going to leave without letting him know I was here. No matter how I felt about the way he made money, he'd still shown me compassion on a few occasions. Like when he told me to come to him if I ever needed anything, or when he helped me try to figure out who was stalking me. I needed to tell him about the regular who stalked me now that I knew his name.

"You're right."

I texted Vinny back: *Make it two hours. I'll text you when we're leaving.*

"Let's go see if we can find Sebastian and then we can leave."

"Okay." Melony took a big sip of her drink, finishing it. "Let's get another drink too since it's free alcohol."

I nodded and stood, sticking my phone back into my purse. As we walked toward the bar, I finished my rum and Coke. Once we were at the bar, we ordered our drinks and then turned to walk away.

"Maybe he's in the house?" I suggested, walking toward the open entry that was more like a garage door opening than your standard sliding glass door. Just then, Sebastian walked out, Mateo behind him and the two guys from the fight next to him. Sebastian's gaze met mine, and he smiled.

"Scarlett, Crystal." He nodded a greeting.

Okay, so I was Scarlett tonight, and Melony was her stripper alias too. "Thanks for having us," I stated.

He grinned. "Please, make yourself at home. The other girls are upstairs."

Doing what? "They are?"

"I have a game room, and I've been told there's a high stakes pool tournament happening."

"Oh." I blinked. "Want to go check it out?" I turned to Melony.

"Sure," she replied.

I turned back to Sebastian. "Thanks again for having us."

"Before you go, let me introduce you to my friends." Sebastian turned slightly to the men next to him. "Tony, Xavier, this is Scarlett and Crystal. They work for me."

Tony, the man with gray hair, stepped forward with an outreached hand. I extended my hand and he took it, and kissed the back. "Scarlett, my apologies for not meeting you properly the other night. It's good to see you again."

Xavier stepped forward. "Yes, our apologies."

I eyed Sebastian, wondering what he'd said to his friends to make them apologize.

Tony looked at Sebastian and then back to me. "If you two ever want to make real money, give me a call."

"That's enough." Sebastian chuckled. "You know my girls are off-limits."

I looked at Melony, and she shrugged.

"That's a shame," Tony went on. "We could get a lot—"

"Have fun, ladies. *Everything's* on me tonight," Sebastian cut Tony off, stepping between Tony and me.

"Thanks but—" I started.

"Thanks. We'll go find the pool table." Melony grabbed my arm, tugging me away from Sebastian and his friends and into the house.

"Why'd you do that?"

"Because you were about to tell him we don't snort coke."

"So?"

"He might think you're a narc or something."

"What?" I rolled my eyes. "He won't think that. He took me to a fight because I keep my mouth shut." Though keeping my mouth shut about something I had no clue about was easy.

"Well, whatever. Just pretend you don't know or something. His friends give me creepy vibes."

"Me too, but I don't think I can just forget he's a drug dealer now," I stated as a server passed me with a tray.

"I don't want you to get mixed up in anything because you have Colt."

We started up a curved staircase. "I don't want to get mixed up in anything either."

"Good. Turn a blind eye like I do."

The stairs led to a loft type area that overlooked the downstairs on one side and a hallway that led to what I assumed were bedrooms and bathrooms on the other side. Sure enough, there was a group of people hanging around a pool table, laughing and drinking and probably high. I was totally out of my element. The Vegas skyline shined behind a foosball table that sat in front of a large window, a bar was next to the pool table, and there was a large TV hanging on the wall. It was larger and more well-equipped than my living room.

"Crystal! Scarlett!" I turned to see Sommer standing next to Ginger, waving us over. I grinned, and Melony and I started for them, each of us greeting the other with a hug. "I'm so glad you both came."

"Does Sommer sell too?" I whispered into Melony's ear.

"Of course."

"Of course what?" Ginger asked.

Melony leaned in and spoke low. "Scar just found out about the other—dealings."

"Oh." Her green eyes flicked to me. "It's about time."

I rolled my eyes. "Not my thing."

"The money's great," Ginger stated.

"Then why still dance?" I asked.

"Because doing both will make it so I can quit both sooner than I'd planned," Ginger replied.

There was no way I could sell cocaine, even if the money was good. I already wanted to quit Red Diamond, and getting mixed up in the *extras* wasn't in the cards. I wanted to do everything legit, make a good living the legal way. Now that Vinny and I were together, it made me want to start school for hospitality management sooner rather than later. The shitty part though, was that classes didn't start until the fall and it was just now the middle of May.

"Are you two playing?" I asked, changing the subject.

"No, we're just watching."

The girls and I watched the people play a few games. At one point, Melony went to get us another round of drinks at the bar was next to the pool table. I wanted to leave, but since she seemed to be having a good time—laughing and chatting with Sommer and Ginger—I made myself do the same. Though the later it got, I knew that Vinny had school in the morning, and I really wanted to fall asleep in his arms again.

After I finished my third drink, I leaned close to Melony and spoke into her ear over the loud music. "I'm going to go find a bathroom. Are you okay if we leave?"

"Sure. I'll get us an Uber."

I didn't realize I'd lived in my own bubble until I saw everyone around me snorting coke, but it was easier that way because I had Colt and my priority was him. The problem with that was I was oblivious to my surroundings most of the time. If one's head was stuck in the ground so to speak, how could they see what was about to happen?

As I walked down the hall in search of a bathroom, a thought popped into my head. I wanted to see what Sebastian's bathroom looked like in comparison to Mark's. If it was better, I could tell Vinny, and we could make a list of what we'd want in a bathroom. I couldn't believe I was thinking about us having a list of wants for a house. We'd barely started dating, but it was fun to think about all the possibilities because I really liked Vinny, maybe even loved him. I knew that not only did I want to fall asleep in his arms each night, but I also wanted the dinners, the TV time, the *alone* time.

Opening doors, none of them were what I'd consider the master bedroom or bath. So, I kept walking until I got to the end of the hall. There was no way one of the bedrooms I'd seen was the master. They were on the smaller side, and this house wasn't small by any means. There was one more door to try, so I did. It opened, and just down a short hall were more stairs. That was when I remembered this was a three-story house, so it made sense that the master would be on the top floor.

I hurried up the stairs so I could get a quick look at the bathroom before I was caught, except when I got to the top, I stopped dead in my tracks, my eyes widening in instant fear. Sebastian had a gun pointed at a guy who was sitting bound to a chair in front of a dark wood desk. Sebastian's friends stood behind him, Mateo behind them, and a few other guys I didn't recognize.

"Please just give me one more chance," the guy in the chair begged.

"No," Sebastian simply stated and then I heard a loud pop.

I screamed.

Sebastian's gaze met mine, and I turned around, running back down the stairs as fast as I could go in my heels.

"Get her!" I heard from behind me.

Before I could get to the door that led to the second floor hall, a hand wrapped around my arm and yanked me back against a hard body. I screamed, only for it to be muffled as a hand went over my mouth. Tears pricked my eye as I struggled and struggled and struggled to break free, my clutch falling to the floor.

"Let me go," I mumbled against the hand, kicking my legs as I tried to get away. I heard a chair drag against the floor behind me, and then

I was thrown down onto it. Mateo rested his hand on my shoulder, keeping me in place. "Please?" I begged, looking at Sebastian as tears ran down my cheeks.

He closed his eyes briefly and shook his head slowly. "Fucking hell, Tessa."

"I thought her name was Scarlett?" Tony asked.

"Stage name," Sebastian clarified. "Tessa here is my angel."

"Your angel?" Xavier asked.

"My pure, sweet Tessa." Sebastian ran his hand over my cheek, and I swallowed.

"Please just let me go," I begged again, looking up into his dark blue eyes.

"I can't do that," Sebastian answered and stepped back, running his hands through his perfectly styled hair, and began to pace.

"Why not?" I looked at the dead body next to me. "I won't tell anyone. You know that."

Sebastian moved in front of me and bent at the knees. "While that may be true, I can't take the chance. Murder will cost me more than a drug charge, Tessa Baby."

My stomach coiled at the name. "Please? Melony and I will just leave. I won't tell her or anyone."

He stood and looked at Mateo. "Get rid of Melony."

"No!" I screamed.

"I'm not going to kill her, Tessa," Sebastian stated, and then looked back at Mateo. "Get her in a car and have her leave."

I kept my mouth shut, hoping and praying she wouldn't question why she was leaving without me. Hoping and praying she'd actually leave and hoping and praying I wasn't a dead woman.

Mateo left, and Tony took his place, placing a hand on my shoulder. His grip was firmer as he pressed down, actually restraining me. Mateo had simply placed his hand on my shoulder. This was harder, and I didn't like it. I didn't like any of it, and I just wanted to go home and wake up from the nightmare.

"Please!" I begged again. "Just let me go."

"I can't do that," Sebastian repeated and started to pace again. "But

I'm not exactly sure what to do with you."

"Just kill her and get it over with," Tony suggested.

"No!" I shouted. "Please, I have a son."

Sebastian stopped in front of me. "How did I not know you have a son?"

"Because I go to work, dance, and leave. I don't gossip, and I keep to myself. Melony only knows I have a son because ..." I stopped myself from reminding him she was my neighbor because I feared he would still do something to her.

"Because why?" he asked.

"Because she's my best friend."

"She's the one who got you the job at Red Diamond, right?" Sebastian questioned.

I nodded.

He bobbed his head. "That's right. Makes sense that the two girls who don't do extras are best friends."

"Please, just let me go. I swear I'll never tell anyone."

"I can't do that," Sebastian affirmed. "I'm not a stupid man, Tessa."

I sniffed, my tears still streaming down my face. I *was* fucking stupid. Why had I gone into an area alone in a drug dealer's house? I'd seen enough TV to tell me that was senseless, and yet I fucking did it. All because I wanted to see a bathroom? God, I was an idiot.

"You know what women are for," Tony cut in. "Use that to your advantage."

I looked up at him, confused by what he meant.

"Yeah, keep her up here and fuck her," Xavier chimed in. "I bet her pussy just might send you to heaven."

"No, please!" I shouted and tried to struggle against Tony's hold on me. He held my shoulder tighter, and then placed a hand on the other, forcing me down harder.

"Will everyone shut the fuck up so I can think?" Sebastian bellowed.

"I'll take her," Tony stated. "I have an entire warehouse of whores ready for Mexico."

Sebastian stepped forward, getting in Tony's face, finger pointed at him. "You are *not* taking her. She's mine. Do you fucking understand?"

"Fine, but you have a house full of people, and now two bodies on your hands—one of them dead, so you better figure your shit out before someone else walks in here."

"Please," I begged again, this time as a whisper. "My son's autistic and he needs me."

Mateo walked back into the room.

"The girl leave?" Sebastian asked.

Mateo nodded. "Took some coercing, but yes. Told the driver to take the long way home, too."

"Good. See, Tessa," Sebastian cupped my cheek, "Mel's fine."

"But I'm not," I whispered.

"You'll be fine, Tessa Baby."

"Will I?"

Sebastian smiled tightly. "I hope so."

I closed my eyes and took a deep breath. "Please, just let me go."

He sighed. "No can do."

I looked up at him. "But my son."

He thought for a moment then stepped back, barking orders. "Mateo, get the car. You two," he pointed at two guys, "clean this shit up."

"Where are you going?" Tony asked.

Sebastian looked at me and smiled. "To get Tessa's son."

"No!" I shrieked.

He brushed my hair behind my shoulder, and I tried to shrug him off. "Don't worry. You're going too. Mi casa es tu casa."

"What?" I whispered.

"My house is your house."

"I know what you said, but I don't understand."

"I can't let you go, so that means we're getting your son and you're moving in here."

I stared up at him. "For how long?"

"Indefinitely."

"No." I started to sob harder.

"Don't worry, Tessa Baby. I'm going to take good care of you."

NINETEEN
Vinny

ONE HOUR TURNED INTO TWO.

Then two became three, and by the fourth hour, I still hadn't heard from Tessa. I'd texted her a few times with no text back. No call. Nothing. I didn't have Melony's number, didn't have Sophia's either. But knowing that Tessa had a stalker made me worry. Did something happen to her and Melony on their way home? Tessa had said she'd text me when they were leaving her boss's house. Were they still there? I never thought I would be driving to my girlfriend's place at midnight to see if she was home, worried she was kidnapped, or hell, just blowing me off.

When I got to Tessa's, I noticed the living room light that usually shined through the window by the front door was off. I knocked. There was no answer. I knocked again. Nothing. I tried calling Tessa's phone again, hoping to at least hear her phone inside so that I'd know she was okay and probably passed out drunk, but I didn't hear anything. I knocked again, this time harder. Still nothing.

"Vinny!" I heard my name, looking over to see Melony rushing out of her apartment.

"Hey," I replied. "Where's Tessa?" As Melony ran to me, I noticed that she'd been crying. "What's wrong?"

"Tessa—"

"Where is she?" I asked, placing my hands on Melony's shoulders and looking down into her tear-stained eyes.

"I don't know," she whispered.

"What do you mean you don't know?"

"Sebastian's bodyguard—"

"Who's Sebastian?"

"Our boss."

"Right. I saw his bodyguard the night of the fight."

Melony nodded. "Yeah, and he made me leave. Made me leave without Tessa."

"Why?"

"I don't know," she cried.

"Where's Colton?"

"Sophia said that Tessa came and got him before I got back."

"Really?"

"I don't know what's going on. The driver took forever to get me here, and then when I arrived, I stopped by Tessa's, and no one was there. I went to Sophia's, and she said that Tessa came and took Colton. Why would Tessa take Colton somewhere at this hour?"

"Where's Sophia?" There was no reason for Tessa to take Colton anywhere at this hour unless he was sick. I needed to check with Sophia.

She pointed at Sophia's apartment. "Home."

I walked to Sophia's door and knocked, not caring that it was midnight. Sophia watched Colton until two-thirty in the morning on Friday and Saturdays, and I was hoping she was still awake.

When she answered the door a few moments later, her eyes widened. "Vinny!"

"Hey, Sophia. Do you know where Tessa went?"

She shook her head. "No. She came in with a guy—"

"A guy?" I asked, raising my voice in concern—and anger.

She nodded slightly. "A man I'd never seen before. She also looked like she'd been crying."

"What?" I bellowed.

"She took clothes with her."

I looked over at Melony. "What the fuck is going on?"

She shrugged. "I don't know. She went to the bathroom at the party and never came back."

I dug my wallet out, pulled out my S&R business card, and handed it to Sophia. "If she comes back, call me. If you hear anything, call me."

"Do you think she's in danger?" she asked.

I closed my eyes and sighed. "I hope not. Call me if you hear anything."

Sophia nodded, and I stepped back as she closed her door.

"What are we going to do?" Melony asked.

I took another deep breath. "I don't know."

"I don't understand what's happening," she cried.

"Me either," I admitted. I'd thought Tessa and I were good—moving forward. Now I wasn't so sure. But, it didn't make sense. Why would she stay and Melony leave when they went together? Why was she crying? Why did she take Colton? I had too many questions and no answers.

"Can I give you my number in case you hear anything from her? I'm really worried."

"Yeah, I'll give you mine too." I pulled out my phone, and we exchanged numbers. "Do you think he kidnapped her?"

Melony blinked and then motioned for me to go inside her place. "Want to go inside?"

"Yeah." I walked inside, and she closed the door as I sat on her couch.

"Sorry, I don't want the neighbors to hear anything else."

I chuckled sarcastically. "Besides someone being kidnapped?"

She sat in the chair beside the couch. "Our boss doesn't just own Red Diamond. He's also a drug dealer."

"Of course he is," I stated and rolled my eyes. In the years I'd been escorting—especially in Vegas—I'd seen it all, or at least I assumed I had. I didn't do drugs or any of that shit, but some of my clients were into Molly or whatever else they needed to get high to have a good time and relax. I'd also been to my share of strip clubs in my day, and seen drug deals go down.

"What do you mean?"

"Most strip clubs are fronts for drugs and shit."

"I wouldn't know any of that. This is my first club to dance at."

"Then how do you know he deals?"

"Because some of the girls do too."

"Does Tess?"

"No! We only dance. Tessa apparently didn't know about the drugs before tonight."

"Then why the fuck did she get Colt and go back to your boss's house?"

"Maybe she didn't?"

"Then where would she go? Who was she with?"

"I don't know." She sighed. "She got uncomfortable when she found out tonight about the drugs and the fact that Sebastian's a drug dealer."

I looked off, staring at the TV that was off. I needed to find Tessa. Something wasn't right, and I was worried. We had plans. She wouldn't make plans and then go with another guy. She didn't even like when her boss called her Tessa Baby and now she was ...

She was what? Spending the night? There was no way.

"Is the party still going on?"

"Yeah, I think so."

"Let's go there."

"Really?"

"If something's going on, I want to know."

"What if he's dangerous?"

I took another long breath and leaned back on the couch, thinking. "Actually," I shot up, "I know the FBI."

"What?"

"My buddy just married an FBI agent. We'll get them involved."

"Okay."

"Fuck," I groaned, rubbing my hands down my face. "They're on their honeymoon."

"Shit."

"But," I snapped my fingers, "her friend is here, and he's a cop."

"Okay."

"Though, he's not Metro." I sighed. "Should we call Metro?"

"I don't know, Vinny. I've never dealt with this shit before."

"Neither have I."

"What if she did it on her own?"

"Did what?"

Melony shrugged. "I don't know. Decided to stay the night?"

"We had plans," I informed her. "I was supposed to stay the night. Plus, Sophia said she looked like she had been crying."

"Right. She mentioned that."

"So, she's not doing this on her own," I stated. "Something's not right."

"You think he kidnapped her?"

I shook my head slowly, thinking with a long sigh. "It's the only explanation."

"But why? He has an entire house full of people. It doesn't make sense."

"Tell me exactly what happened." I sat back down on the couch and leaned forward, my elbows resting on my knees.

"Nothing happened. We showed up, got a few drinks, saw Sebastian for a minute while he introduced us to his friends he was walking with. Then we went to watch a pool tournament, saw our friends from Red Diamond, and hung out for a while. Tessa wanted to leave, and so did I, so she told me to get an Uber while she went to the bathroom. I was standing outside when this guy came up and told me to leave."

"Told you to leave?"

Melony shrugged. "He was nice about it, but I told him I was waiting for Tessa. He said that she wasn't coming, and when I questioned why I had to leave, he just told me that I needed to leave *now*."

"So you did? Just like that?"

"No, of course not. I told him I wasn't leaving without Tessa, but then the Uber arrived and next thing I knew, I was being picked up and put into the car. Physically picked up by this guy and put into the backseat. Then the driver left and went the long fucking way home. I tried calling Tessa over and over, but she never answered, and I didn't have your number."

"Something must have happened. That's the only thing that makes sense."

"What would have happened? We were drinking and watching pool."

"I have no fucking clue."

"So, what do we do?"

"I'm going to go talk to my friend Seth." We weren't close, but I'd hung out with him at the fight and while we got ready for Paul's wedding. Plus, I didn't know what else to do. If I called Metro, what would I say? My girlfriend came home, got some clothes and I assumed went back to her boss's house? From everything I'd seen on TV and the movies, once a person was kidnapped, they stayed hidden. They didn't go home to get an overnight bag.

"I'm coming with you."

"No. Stay here in case she comes back."

"Right." She sighed. "This is too surreal."

I grabbed her shoulders and looked straight into her eyes. "I know, but I'm going to fucking find her. I'll be damned if the first woman I fall in love with disappears."

She smiled slowly. "You love her?"

I blinked, not realizing I'd actually said the L word. I'd never been in love before, but what I felt for Tessa had to be love. Thinking about her hurt, kidnapped, or dead made my heart fucking ache and I didn't fucking like it. I wanted those butterflies girls talked about. I wanted to laugh with Tessa, hold her, kiss her, make love to her again. I wanted to cook breakfast and dinner for her and Colton, and everything in between.

I wanted them.

I wanted them *back*.

"Yeah, I do," I admitted. "I love them both."

Her smile widened. "I can't wait for you to tell her."

I stared into her blue eyes. "Me, too."

I wasn't going to think about the fact that I might never get to tell her. I was going to think positively. I knew a fucking FBI agent for Christ's sake, and if that didn't count for something, I didn't know what would. I needed to find them and tell them, maybe get their help and advice. Or I could walk into a drug dealer's house and find Tessa myself.

That was going to be plan B.

I dropped my hands and moved to the door. "Call me if you hear from her."

"You, too."

"I will."

As I walked down the stairs toward my SUV, I dialed Gabe. I didn't know where Paul lived anymore. When he quit S&R, he moved out of the house he and Gabe had shared when they transferred to Vegas from L.A.

"Vin?" Gabe answered, groggy.

"I need your help." I slid into my car.

"At this hour?"

"Tessa's missing."

"What do you mean Tessa's missing?"

I cranked the engine, and after a few moments, the call transferred to my car speakers. "It's a long story, but I need to find Joss or Seth."

"Not possible."

I put my car in reverse and pulled out of the space. "Why not? I know Paul and Joss are on their honey—"

"Yes, but ..." He paused for a moment. "Shit. Look, tomorrow afternoon the mission starts."

"Their undercover mission?" I asked, turning onto the street in the direction of Gabe's because that was the only place I knew.

"Yeah."

"So? That's not tonight. I need their help *tonight*."

"I don't know where they are. Paul just told me that Monday the mission starts and he'd be off the grid until it was over. He couldn't give me any details."

"Fuck!" I slammed my hand against the steering wheel. "What do I do?"

"Tell me why you think she's missing." I told him what I knew as I continued to drive to his house and his first reply was, "Go to the cops."

"Yeah." I sighed. "Seems that's my only option."

"Keep me posted. I'm here to help if you need me."

"All right." I hung up and pulled over. A Google searched confirmed no local police stations were open at this hour. How was that possible? Where did the calls go? I was about to find out. I texted Melony, got Sebastian's address, and then dialed 9-1-1. Maybe I should have called the non-emergency line, but something wasn't sitting right, and I needed them to act fast.

"9-1-1, what's your emergency?"

"I think my girlfriend's been kidnapped by her boss."

"Why do you think that?" she asked. I told the dispatcher everything I knew. "It sounds like she went on her own."

I sighed. "She didn't go on her own."

"You said—"

"I know what I said," I snapped. "Can you help or not?"

"The only thing I can do is send a call for a welfare check."

"Do that then." Something was better than nothing.

"What's the address of the location?" I told her. "I'll send someone to check on her, but if she went on her own—"

"She didn't go on her own."

"Whatever the case, we'll call you back when we have word on her well-being."

"Thank you." I hung up, typed Sebastian's address into my GPS, and drove toward his house. I wasn't going to sit back and wait. Time was ticking, and there was no telling what was happening to my girl. When I arrived close to the address, I had to stop at a security gate.

"Address?" I gave the guy the address. "Name?" I gave him my name. "You're not on the list."

"There's a list?"

"Yes."

"Oh. Well, I'm here to pick up my girlfriend."

He smiled. "Sorry. Can't let you through. You'll need to have her meet you at the gate."

Of course this asshole would live in a gated community. "Look, man. My girl went to a party at this house, and I haven't heard from her in several hours. I just need to check on her."

"Sorry. I still can't let you in."

"The cops are on their way," I stated.

"Why?"

"Because my girlfriend went to a party at that address and I haven't heard from her in hours."

"That's no reason to call the cops."

I didn't want to tell this guy any more detail than I needed to. "I have my reasons."

"Then pull over to the side and wait for them. I can't let you in."

I groaned. "Fine."

I pulled over to the side and waited for Metro to show. It took them almost two hours to arrive, so it was well after three in the morning. I was running on adrenaline, but I couldn't close my eyes for even a second.

When the cop car arrived, I watched him pull up to the gate. "You're the one who called?" he asked as he stepped out to talk to me.

I nodded. "Yes, sir."

"Tell me what's going on." I did—again. "All right. Stay here, and I'll go check it out."

"I can't come with you?"

"It's better if you stay here."

I sighed. "Fine."

As I waited for the cop to come back, I felt as though everything was stacked against me and I didn't like it. How was this happening? Just yesterday—hell, this morning—Tessa and I were happy and laughing and fucking. She'd told me she hadn't been with anyone in five years and now—and now, it was as if it was all a lie. I couldn't believe that, though. Tessa wasn't that type of person. Even if she didn't want to be with me, she wouldn't have left Melony like she did. In a matter of hours, I'd gone from high on life to confused as fuck.

Time seemed to crawl as I waited twenty minutes for the cop to come back. "Well?" I asked the moment he stepped up to my car.

"She said she's fine."

I balked. "What? You saw her?"

"Yes, her and her little boy. Said she came on her own."

"She told you she took her four-year-old son to a house party?"

"There's no party."

I sighed. Of course there wasn't. Whatever had happened caused this fucker to cover his tracks. But why was Tessa saying she was okay?

Was it all a lie?

TWENTY

Tessa

I WAS SCARED, TERRIFIED, PETRIFIED, THAT IF I DIDN'T DO WHAT Sebastian told me to do, he'd kill me, too.

After I begged and pleaded over and over to no avail, Mateo drove Sebastian and me to my apartment so I could get Colton, as though Sebastian thought it was better for me to subject my son to this danger. I'd only mentioned Colt because I was begging for my life. Now, I felt as though it had backfired on me because I didn't know what was in store for us. Would he hurt us? Hurt me? Kill us? If he were going to kill me, he'd have done it already.

Right?

When I walked into my apartment, I tried to hide my fear from Sophia. I couldn't let her know something was wrong because I didn't want to involve her. I couldn't think about Vinny either, because if he got tangled up in this, he'd be in danger too. So, I told Sophia to go home, and when she left, I packed bags for Colton and me. I made sure to grab his essentials: his nightlight, iPad, baseball and fidget spinners, and after I grabbed what I could in a hurry—per Sebastian's orders—Mateo carried the bags, and I carried Colt to the car. I was shaking and crying, and all while I was trying not to wake Colton. I held him while Mateo drove us back to Sebastian's. There was no car seat, nothing to keep Colton safe except my arms, and I wasn't letting him go. I didn't know what was going to happen to me, but when we came back to Sebastian's, the house was empty, and that made me even more nervous.

"What are you going to do to us?" I asked as I held a sleeping

Colton tightly in my arms in what I assumed was the living room. When Melony and I had arrived, I thought it looked like a hotel. Now, as I stood in the empty room, it looked like a prison.

"I don't know," Sebastian replied.

"Then just let us go back home." I'd stopped crying and was hoping to talk to Sebastian in a reasonable manner.

"Can't do that," he responded, moving to what I assumed was a bar and pulling out a decanter of caramel colored alcohol.

"Why not?" I started to bounce slightly, hoping Colton would stay asleep. It also helped calm my nerves in a way.

Sebastian frowned. "You know why. Don't play dumb with me now."

"So, you're just going to keep us locked up in your mansion?"

He closed his eyes briefly, and then took a sip of the alcohol he'd poured himself. "For now."

"He has school, therapy."

"Therapy for what?"

"He has special needs, Sebastian. You can't just keep us locked up."

He stepped around the bar. "I didn't ask you to go snooping in my house, Tessa. This is as much your fault as it is mine."

I blinked. "It's my fault you killed a guy?"

"No, he had it coming, but what I do is my business and *you*," he pointed at me, "interfered."

"Please let us go. I won't say anything, just like I never said anything before."

He sighed and responded in a stern voice, "For the last fucking time, no. Now, Valentina will show you to your room." An older, Hispanic lady stepped into the room from the kitchen. "It's late, and we all need sleep."

"Colton has school in the morning."

"He'll be absent."

"Sebastian, please," I pleaded. "His schooling is more than drawing and taking naps and whatever you might think he does in pre-k. He has special needs and therapy."

"Then I'll hire someone."

"What?" I breathed.

He walked the few feet to me and cupped my cheek. I moved my face away, not wanting him to touch me. He smirked. "This little game is going to be fun."

"Fun?" I questioned.

"I've had my eye on you for a while, Tessa Baby. Now that I have you, you're mine."

"I'll never be yours."

"You're wrong. I always get what I want, and I want you."

Never.

I stared up at the ceiling covered with blue waves as Colton laid next to me in the strange bed. He hadn't woken up for more than a few seconds when I put him down in the guest room. After I changed into my pajamas, I got into bed and replayed everything over and over in my head.

Arguing with Sebastian hadn't got me anywhere. I needed to think. I needed to come up with a plan. I *needed* to escape. I wasn't sure where Colt and I would go now that Sebastian knew where we lived, but I couldn't stay with a man who had essentially kidnapped my son and me.

And then it hit me—like *really* hit me. I'd been kidnapped.

By my boss.

By a drug dealer.

By a murderer.

The tears started to fall again. How was this happening? *Why* was this happening? And how was I going to get Colton and myself out of the situation? Colton needed extra care, and being trapped in a house wasn't going to be good for him. But I didn't know what to do. I'd dropped my purse when I was running, and I had no way of calling anyone. No way to tell Melony what had happened. No way to call for help. Maybe I could sneak back into the room where I saw Sebastian kill the guy? That seemed like an office of sorts. Maybe I could find a computer and send an email to Melony. Maybe there was a phone in there. Maybe…

"Get up!" Sebastian came into the room without knocking and turned on the light.

I scurried up against the headboard, covering myself with the blankets. I wasn't naked, but I didn't want him seeing me in my pajamas either. "Can you be a little quieter?" I whispered. "My son's asleep."

"You're getting feisty. Didn't think you'd have it in you, my angel."

I rolled my eyes. "What do you want?"

"Cops are here."

My heart started to race. "Really?"

He grinned. "They're not taking you, Tessa."

"Then why are they here?"

"Welfare check."

"Yeah?" I glared. "Well, you fucking kidnapped me and my son. We're not doing too well are we?" I mocked.

Sebastian shrugged. "You're fine. I haven't hurt you, and we're not going to keep going around and around about this."

I got out of the bed. "Then I'll tell the police *everything*," I hissed.

He laughed. "Tell them." I started for the door, and then stopped and looked back at Colton. "Don't worry. I don't hurt children."

"No, you just kidnap them," I sneered and turned back around to leave. When I stepped into the hallway, I stopped when I noticed a person standing just outside the door. It was Mateo. He nodded, and I walked down the hall toward the stairs. How was Sebastian letting me tell the police I was kidnapped? He acted as though it was no big deal.

Just as I was about to take the first step down, a hand wrapped around my upper arm and pulled me back into a hard body.

"Whatever you tell Officer Cameron won't matter. He's on my payroll," Sebastian stated into my ear.

I closed my eyes, a lump forming in my throat. Now it made sense why he didn't care if I told the police what had happened. "Who are you?" I whispered. I worked for this man for a year and knew nothing about him. We were never close, never spoke more than a few words to each other except for the night of the fight and when I went to him about my stalker. I thought he was a decent guy—a perv, but decent.

"I'm the man who's going to take care of you for the rest of your life."

"Excuse me?"

He spun me around so that I was looking him in the eyes. "I get plenty of women in my bed, Tessa, but now I won't have to worry about them going to a cop who's not on my payroll. You've seen the worst, and if you tell anyone, I *will* kill you. I won't hesitate again."

"Just do it." I regretted the words as they left my mouth. Not because I didn't want him to kill me and end my misery, but because I was scared of what he'd do to Colton once I was gone.

He grinned. "Where's the fun in that?"

I stared at him, confused. "What fun?"

Sebastian leaned in, and before I knew it, his lips were on mine. I resisted as his tongue tried to break the seam of my lips. It only made him smirk wider when he pulled back. "I'm letting you sleep in the guest room tonight, but that changes tomorrow."

"What?" I thought I knew what he meant, but I didn't want to believe I was right. Though when he answered me, I realized I wasn't only kidnapped and held hostage in a mansion that once looked like paradise to me. Now it was a cage.

"You're going to sleep in *my* bed, and do whatever I ask of you, whenever I ask you to."

I swallowed. "And if I don't?"

"You don't want to piss me off," he warned.

"Because you'll kill me?"

"No." He shook his head. "I will *make* you."

I glared at him. "So, you'll rape me?"

"Call it whatever you want, but one way or another, you will be in my bed pleasing me tomorrow night. I'm letting you have tonight for your son. Tomorrow, you're mine."

"Why are you doing this?" I cried, the tears no longer at bay. "Just let us go. I promise I won't tell."

Sebastian finally released my arm. "If you say that one more time, I won't give you tonight in the guest bedroom. Now, go downstairs, tell Officer Cameron you're fine—not that it matters—and go to sleep. You're going to need your energy tomorrow."

When I walked down the stairs, I was no longer Tessa. I was Scarlett. Scarlett could get through this. She knew how to fake it and faking it was what I needed to do until I figured out how to leave.

Because one day, I was leaving.

When I told the cop I was at Sebastian's by my own volition, he shrugged and told Sebastian he was sorry he to come by so late. When I asked him who had called it in, he didn't answer me. Was it Sophia? Melony? Vinny? Melony was the only one who knew Sebastian's address because she was the one who had called us a car when we went to the party. Did she tell Sophia what had happened? Tell Vinny? What did Melony even think?

I was tired of all the questions I had swimming in my head. They didn't stop when I tried to fall asleep either. It was as though Satan was coming in the morning and not Santa as I tossed and turned thinking about everything on repeat. It was nowhere near Christmas, but that was the only thing I could think of because like a kid waiting for Santa, I was restless. I wished Santa was coming. I wished I was at home with Vinny. I didn't need a big bathroom, didn't need anything except Vinny, and I'd lost him.

But Santa, of course, didn't come.

The next morning, I showered, gave Colton a bath, and when we walked downstairs in search of food, I came to a stop when I noticed a woman sitting on the couch. "You must be Tessa," she said as she stood and reached her hand out as she moved closer to me.

I took her hand. "And you are?"

She smiled warmly. "Mr. Delarosa hired me to teach Colton." She bent at the knees and got in front of Colt. "Hi, Colton, I'm Joanna."

He didn't respond. Instead, he stared at his iPad.

"What do you mean that Mr. Delarosa hired you to teach Colton?"

She stood and faced me. "I got a call this morning that Colton needed to be homeschooled."

I rolled my eyes and crossed my arms over my chest. "Do you know how to teach a child with autism?"

She blinked. "Autism?"

I sighed and started for the front door, hoping this lady would follow me. "I'm sorry for the confusion, but Mr. Delarosa doesn't know what my son needs."

"I—"

"You can go." I opened the door and waited for her to move. It took her a few moments before she did. "Sorry again."

"He owes me for today," she stated as she walked outside.

"I'll tell him." I shut the door in her face. It wasn't like me to be rude, but I was tired, scared, pissed off, and frustrated. Plus, Scarlett didn't take anyone's shit. That was how it worked at the club when I was using the persona, and I needed to keep the front up, even if Sebastian wasn't in the same room.

Valentina walked into the room. "Ms. Tessa, I made breakfast for you and Colton."

"You did?"

"Si." She nodded.

"Why?"

She blinked. "Because you need to eat."

That was true, but I didn't understand why she took the liberty to make us food. "I can make us breakfast."

She smiled. "It's my job, Ms. Tessa."

The night before, I hadn't thought to ask what her role was when she showed me to the guest bedroom. I didn't care, and I was still terrified of what was to come. But, I guess it made sense. "You're Sebastian's maid?"

"Housekeeper," she clarified.

"And the difference?"

"I do more than clean, Ms. Tessa. I take care of the house."

"Cook, clean, and?"

"Whatever you need."

"Do you know why I'm here?" I crossed my arms over my chest again.

Valentina smiled warmly at me. "Yes."

"And you're okay with that?"

She grabbed my hands, bringing my crossed arms down. "Mr. Delarosa's a good man."

I sorted and stepped closer before lowering my voice. "Right. He won't let me leave and he will *rape* me tonight."

"No, cariño. He will provide for you and Colton."

"I don't need him to provide for us."

"You may think that, but he will take care of you."

"I don't want him to take care of us."

"You should. He saved me from Colombia. He's a good man."

"How did he save you?"

"Come," she motioned for me to follow, "I will tell you while you and Colton eat."

"He only eats waffles with strawberry jam for breakfast."

"I will make for him. Come."

I picked up Colton—who was still engrossed in his iPad—and followed her into the kitchen. Two plates with bacon, eggs, and toast sat at the breakfast bar. Valentina took one of the plates away, and I put Colton down in the chair. "Do you have apple juice?"

"Si." She opened the fridge and grabbed a jug then poured Colton a cup.

"Coffee?" I asked.

"Yes, of course, cariño."

I slid off the stool. "I will make myself a cup while you do the waffles. Okay?"

"Si. Colton must be starving."

"I'm sure at any minute he will make a fuss. He's usually had breakfast by now." I was actually really surprised he hadn't had a tantrum. He'd woken up in a strange bed, in a strange house. It just showed me that he was making progress with his therapy, but now, I felt as though that was all about to change. I didn't want to be in this position to see how much more resilient he would have to be to get through this change.

"I'll be quick. I went to the store this morning and bought everything I thought he'd eat. They just need to be heated in the toaster."

"You went to the store this early?" It was barely eight in the morning.

She pointed to a Keurig. "Si," she replied and handed me a mug. "I knew he would be hungry. My sons were always hungry when they woke up."

I smiled. "You have kids?"

"Had." Valentina paused and gave a sad smile, then resumed opening the box of waffles.

"Oh," I breathed. I put a pod in the coffeemaker and pressed the brew button. "I'm sorry."

She stuck a waffle into the toaster and turned to me. "Mr. Delarosa saved me."

"He saved you?"

She nodded. "Si. Bad men came into my town and killed everyone I loved."

"Sebastian?"

"No." Valentina shook her head. "He took care of the bad men and gave my small town money to get back on our feet."

"And how did you come to Vegas?" I moved to the fridge, looking for creamer. I didn't care that this wasn't my house. I had no respect for Sebastian anymore.

Mi casa es tu casa.

Valentina replied, "He'd just lost his father and was hurting. He needed someone to take care of him, and since I had no one, I offered to help him. He brought me here because my country is dangerous."

"What?" I asked. "He lost his father and then went on a killing spree and gave your town money?"

"No, cariño." She cupped my cheek. I didn't recoil because the longer I spoke with Valentina, the more she reminded me of Sophia. "Mr. Delarosa lost his father after he helped my town. He'd always come to check on us, give us money, food, whatever we needed. After his padre died, he was sad, grieving. I was sad too, and he offered to bring me to America. I told him I would if he let me take care of him because I missed providing for my family."

"But how can you think a murderer is a good man?"

The toaster popped the waffle up, and Valentina moved back to get the waffle for Colton. "Because he only kills bad men."

"How do you know?"

She shrugged and then pulled a jar of strawberry jam from a cabinet. "I don't know, but I hope. He has a good heart."

"Valentina." I moved to stand next to her and lowered my voice.

"He won't let me leave. That's kidnapping. *And*, he is making me ... sleep in his bed tonight. You have to know that's not okay."

"It's not my place, cariño. I do as he says because I can't go back to my country. It's not safe."

"Help me escape."

She shook her head. "I can't. He has men who will stop you."

I rolled my eyes and grabbed a knife from the butcher block to cut Colt's waffle into triangles. "What drug dealer has all these men working for him?"

"He's not just any drug dealer, Ms. Tessa. He's El Diamante Rojo."

"El Diamante Rojo?"

"Si. The Red Diamond of Colombia. He's the drug lord between Las Vegas and my country of Colombia."

TWENTY-ONE

Vinny

I DIDN'T SLEEP A WINK. HOW COULD I?

When I got home, I carried my cell phone with me as I paced around the house. Tessa never called, and that made me even more worried about her as I laid in bed, waiting and staring up at the ceiling. What was Tessa doing at that moment? Was she okay? Scared? How was Colton? I didn't care that the cop had said she went back to her boss's house on her own. I knew better. At first, I thought that maybe she was playing me and really liked this guy, but the more I thought about it, she wouldn't leave her best friend out of the loop and worried too. She wouldn't have made Sophia concerned either.

As soon as the sun came up, I called in sick to work. There were only a few weeks left of school, and it wasn't like me to take this much time off, but there was no way I'd be focused enough to interact with my students. I was determined to get to the bottom of why Tessa was at her boss's house. Determined to save her because I felt as though she needed saving. Nothing was adding up. Nothing.

After I took a shower, I called Melony to see if she'd heard from Tessa. She hadn't, and since the cops weren't going to be any help, I needed to find Joss and Seth. So, a little after nine, I went to Gabe's. I knocked on the door and waited. Finally, it opened. It was Autumn.

"Hey, is Gabe here?"

"Yeah, he's in the shower."

I stepped inside the two-story home.

"He told me about Tessa. Have you heard from her?"

I shook my head. "Nothing."

"I'm sorry. That's crazy."

"Yeah." I sighed. "Nothing makes sense."

"Want some coffee?"

"I'd love some." I followed Autumn into the kitchen.

"I didn't get to talk to Tessa much at the wedding, but she did amazing at the range. I think she'll be able to take care of herself."

"She has no gun, and I'm pretty sure she didn't take her pepper spray with her."

"Really?" She poured a cup of coffee and slid it to me where I sat at the kitchen table.

"Well, I'm assuming so."

"Maybe she did?"

"Then why isn't she home? Her friend checked this morning already."

Autumn sat across from me. "Well, I don't know much about Tessa, but I have hope she'll be okay. She'll call you."

"Hope so."

Gabe walked into the kitchen. "Hey, heard from her?"

"Nope."

"Fuck, man. I'm sorry." Gabe kissed Autumn and sat next to her at the table.

"Cops were no help."

"What'd they say?"

"They did a welfare check and reported Tessa said she went on her own."

"Really?" Autumn questioned.

"I know differently. There's no way. We had plans."

"What are you going to do?" Gabe asked.

"I came to get Paul's address." I took a sip of the coffee.

"Like I told you when you called, the mission started. We can't get ahold of them."

"Just give me the address, and I'll wait until it's over."

"I don't know when it will be over. Could be a while," Gabe responded.

"I can't believe Paul is undercover with the FBI."

Gabe chuckled. "Me either, but I have faith in him. He saved my ass numerous times in combat."

"Do you know what the case is about?"

"Nope."

"What are you going to do now?" Autumn asked. "I don't think we'll be much help."

I sighed and closed my eyes, wanting to go back twenty-four hours so I could go with Tessa to the party. Hell, I wouldn't even let her go. I would make up an excuse, cook us dinner, hang with her and Colt. I would cancel my date with Shelby.

When I told Shelby I was taking a break from S&R, she was okay with it. She said she'd wanted to try a different guy for a while now, but hadn't wanted to hurt my feelings. It wasn't because I sucked, but because it felt as though we were in a relationship. In a sense, we were, but I totally understood. Everything worked out perfectly.

Until it didn't.

"What can I do? He lives in a gated community, and the cops won't help since Tessa said she went on her own. Something's not right." I knew I was repeating myself, but it was all I had.

"Want to go to Red Diamond and talk to her boss?" Gabe suggested. "Is he there now?" Gabe asked me.

I shrugged. "I don't know."

Autumn smiled. "Go find Tessa."

Fuck, I hoped we did.

On the way to Red Diamond, I told Gabe everything that

happened the night before. Even things I'd already told him. He agreed that everything wasn't making any sense.

"I don't know man," he'd said. *"Seeing you two together, I was certain she had it bad for you."*

"We just made it official. There's no way she'd jump ship."

"Let's talk to this fucker and see what he says."

I now knew why Tessa didn't work Mondays, or mornings for that matter. When Gabe and I walked into Red Diamond, it was dead. There were still dancers on rotation, but besides him and me in the seats, there was only one other guy. I wasn't sure how I was going to talk to the boss. Galen wasn't at the doors when we arrived—it was some other dude—and when I asked where he was, we were told he only worked nights. I had no one on the inside that I knew. No Tessa, no Melony, and no Galen.

"Now what?" Gabe asked.

I looked over at him. "Fuck if I know."

"Are we just going to sit here and wait and see if we spot the owner?"

"Yep." We saw the guy at the fight, and I was certain if I saw him again I'd know it was him.

"He has to have an office, right? Let's go there."

I looked around the dark, red room, looking for a door or something. I spotted stairs behind us and then looked up. There was a glass wall that overlooked the stage. "I bet he's up there." I pointed.

"Let's go."

"We're just going to walk up there?"

It probably wasn't a good idea to go barging into this guy's office because from what I knew or assumed of drug dealers, they had a gun on them at all times. I was certain that wasn't only in movies because drugs were a good moneymaker and no drug dealer would want to lose their shit or get robbed.

"I don't think we should just barge in." I looked around. "Let me talk to the bartender and see if we can get the okay."

"Yeah. I'll wait here."

I stood and moved to the bar, thinking about what I was going to say. Just as I stepped up, an idea popped into my head.

"What can I getcha?"

I leaned on the wood top. "Actually, I work for Saddles & Racks, and I have this client who wants a woman to come with us on our date."

The guy grinned. "Really?"

I smiled back. "She doesn't want any of the women we have at S&R, so I thought I'd come here and see if any of the girls would want to make some extra money."

"I'm sure they would."

"Great. Mind if I talk to your boss about it?"

"Yeah, let me buzz him and tell him you're here."

"Perfect."

I watched the guy grab a phone and then speak into it. I couldn't hear what was said, but after a minute he came back.

"He said to go on up."

"Thanks, man." I turned to go back to Gabe. "We're in."

Gabe stood. "Really?"

"Told the guy that I have a client who wants a girl to join our date and that I want to check with his boss about it."

"Smart."

I grinned. "Yeah, man. Now, let's go find out where the fuck Tessa is."

I started to walk away, but Gabe grabbed my arm, stopping me. "You're just going to go in there asking where she is?"

"Yeah."

"Play it cool. He thinks you're asking about girls for S&R. You want answers, so don't go in there guns blazing. You won't get any info."

I sighed. "You're right, but how can I go in there, look this fucker in the eye, and not want to beat his face in until he tells me where she is?"

"You do know where she is, but you need his approval to get past his gate. Take this slow."

"Yeah," I sighed. "I'll try."

We walked up the stairs, and I knocked on the open door. The man I'd seen at the fight was sitting behind a heavy wood desk. "Yes, come in. Have a seat." He motioned for me to sit. "Oh, I thought it was only one of you."

"I'm just along for the ride," Gabe stated.

We sat in the red, wingback chairs, and I had to hold onto the armrests to prevent myself from flying across the desk and pinning him to the wall. There were no handshakes given, and I was certain that if I touched him, it wouldn't be pleasant.

"How can I help you two?"

I rubbed the back of my neck. "I work for Saddles & Racks, an escort service. I have a client who wants to—how should I say—have a lady present."

Sebastian grinned. "You mean a threesome?"

I smiled back, though it was fake. "I can't confirm that."

He chuckled. "We all know what really happens."

I shrugged. "Can't confirm that either."

He leaned back in his chair. "Then what can you confirm?"

I looked to Gabe briefly, and then back to Sebastian. "That I need a girl for a date with a woman client."

"Saddles & Racks doesn't have women escorts? Surely they do?"

"They do," I stated.

"Then why do you need one of my girls?"

"Actually, I have a girl in mind."

"Oh yeah? Which one?"

"Scarlett."

He balked. "Scarlett?"

"Yeah. I've been in a few times, and I think she'd be exactly what my client would want."

Sebastian shook his head. "She's not available."

"Oh?" I furrowed my brows. "Why not?"

"What'd you say your name was again?" he asked.

"I didn't," I stated.

We stared at each other, my blood starting to boil.

"Do we have a problem here?" he questioned.

"Yes," I stated. I was done beating around the bush. This was Tessa —my Tessa—and he was preventing me from seeing her.

"And what would that be?"

I leaned forward in my chair. "I'm the one who called the cops last night."

His eyes cut to Gabe, and then back to me. "I think you should leave."

"I'm not leaving until you tell me what I want to know."

He leaned forward, only a few feet separating our faces. "And what is that?"

"Why you're holding her hostage."

Sebastian chuckled and leaned back in his chair again. "She came to me. She wants *me*."

"Bullshit!" I stood, slamming my hand on the top of the desk.

He stood, straightening his gray suit jacket. "It's time you two leave."

"No," I growled.

Calmly he said, "If you don't, I will have you two thrown out."

"Let's just go." Gabe grabbed my arm.

I shrugged him off. "No."

Sebastian leaned his hands on his desk, getting within a foot of my face again. "She's mine now."

I lunged forward and grabbed his lapel, then dragged him across the desk and onto the floor. Before I could land a punch, multiple hands were pulling me off of him. I didn't know where they came from, but he was lucky they did because I was seconds away from knocking him out.

"Come on, man," I heard Gabe say. "We're done here."

Arms dragged me back, and I shrugged them off, glaring at Sebastian as he got off the floor. "You haven't seen the last of me."

"Maybe not, but who's bed will she be in tonight?"

I started to reach for him again, but the arms grabbed me and dragged me out the door. I hadn't seen Sebastian call for help, but he was lucky he did because I was ready to kill him.

After Gabe and I left Red Diamond—or should I say, after I was thrown out—Gabe got a call from Paul that he was needed for the undercover mission.

"Talk to Joss," I pleaded.

"I will if I can. I have no idea what Paul needs from me. He's coming over to my place this afternoon," Gabe replied.

After I dropped Gabe off at his house, I had no idea what I was going to do with myself. I needed help. So, I went to Club 24 where I knew Blake Montgomery would be working. While he had no experience with this situation, I knew his brother did because Brandon's wife, Spencer, had been kidnapped.

When I showed up, Blake wasn't there, and I didn't have Brandon's phone number, so I went on the Club 24 website and got Brandon's e-mail address.

Hey, it's Vinny from Vegas. We met at Gabe's bachelor party. I need your help. Can you call me when you get this message?
Thanks,
Vin.

I left him my phone number and waited. Not knowing what else to do, I drove to Melony and Sophia's. I figured they hadn't heard anything because I was certain they would have called me. I stopped at Sophia's first and knocked.

"Vincent," she greeted after opening the door.

"Hey, Sophia. Mind if I come in?"

"Not at all." She stepped to the side, allowing me to enter. "Have you heard from Tessa?"

I shook my head. "No. Have you?"

"No." She closed the door, and I sat on her couch. "I hope she's okay."

"Me, too."

She sat in a reclining chair to the side of the couch, and we were silent for a few moments.

"Mind if I stay here for a while?"

"You can stay here for as long as you'd like. You don't mind Court TV, do you?"

I grinned. "No, that's fine." We were silent again. "Do you know how to get in touch with Tessa's parents?"

Sophia smiled tightly. "No, I don't."

"Shit," I muttered. "They should know."

"Tessa's never given me their number or anything."

"Do you—" My phone started to ring in my pocket, and I hurried and fished it out. It was a number I didn't recognize, but it said it was coming from San Francisco. "I need to take this." I stood and went outside as I answered. "Hello?"

"Vinny, it's Brandon."

"Thank you for calling me." I closed the door behind me.

"What's up?"

I sighed and leaned against the wall. "Tessa's been kidnapped."

"What?"

I told him everything. "So, I was hoping you might have some recommendations on what I can do."

"Our situation was different. Even though I knew where Spencer was—like you know where Tessa is—when the cops went in, she wasn't okay."

"Tessa's not okay."

"But they said she went on her own?"

"Yeah." I nodded. "It's bullshit though."

"Fuck, dude. Either she went on her own, this guy is holding her hostage, or the cops are on his payroll. I honestly don't know what to tell you."

I knew in my soul that she didn't go on her own, but the other two options? In a world of confusion, they were the only two plausible conclusions that made sense.

TWENTY-TWO
Tessa

A LITTLE BEFORE NOON, SEBASTIAN CAME STORMING INTO THE HOUSE through the garage door. "Come. Now," he ordered.

I looked at Colton, who was playing on his iPad on the couch, and then to Sebastian who was walking toward the stairs. "We're about to have lunch."

He stopped and turned around. "It's not the time to test me, Tessa."

"I'm not testing you. I'm telling you that we're about to eat lunch."

"Where's the teacher?" he asked and looked at Valentina who was dusting the fireplace mantel.

"Ms. Tess—"

"I sent her away," I interjected.

"Why would you do that?" Sebastian asked.

"Because she doesn't know how to teach my son."

"She's qualified," he replied.

"No, she isn't." I sighed. "He has special needs—a different way of learning—a different way of communicating."

"When does school end?"

"It doesn't."

"What do you mean it doesn't?"

"The school year will end in a month, but he will start an extended school year a week later."

"Why?"

"Because he can't take a break. He needs continued education and therapy, at least at this age."

"What's wrong with him?"

"Nothing's wrong with him," I spat.

"Something's wrong with him if he needs therapy."

"*You* need therapy," I countered.

Sebastian chuckled and moved to where I stood in front of the couch. He tried to cup my cheek, but I hit his hand away. "I have to admit, Tessa, I really like this feisty side of you."

"Fuck. You," I hissed.

"You will. Tonight. But first, I need you in my office."

"Why?"

"Get your ass up to my office, or I will carry you."

We stared at each other until Valentina spoke, "It's okay, Ms. Tessa. I can watch Colton. What will he eat for lunch?"

"Grilled cheese," I answered, not looking away from Sebastian.

"I make for him," she stated.

"Now," Sebastian ordered and pointed toward the stairs.

I sighed and rolled my eyes before I started to walk. Then I stopped and turned around. "I don't even know where your office is."

"You didn't have a hard time finding it last night."

I didn't respond. Instead, I turned around and went up the curved staircase and down the hall to the door that would forever haunt me.

"Go on," Sebastian said from behind me.

I sighed and opened the door, and then took the stairs one at a time. When I got to the top, I stopped and looked around. There was no evidence of a murder taking place the night before. The chairs in front of his desk were turned around, and it looked like an office. The sun shined through the windows framing the desert mountains in the distance. In front of them was his desk that looked to be solid wood. The room was masculine, with brown leathered chairs on the right with a table and lamp between them. A floor to ceiling bookshelf sat behind them, and instead of death, the room smelled like tobacco. Across from the chairs was a closed door.

"I had a visitor this morning at Red Diamond." Sebastian moved to sit behind his desk in the high-back leather chair.

"And I care because?" I asked, crossing my arms over my chest.

"He was from the escort company, Saddles & Racks."

My heart stopped. Vinny? Did he come looking for me? Of course he would. We had plans for him to stay the night and I'd vanished. Did that mean he talked to Melony? What had she said? "Okay?"

"You're not surprised?"

I wasn't sure how I was supposed to play his game. I wanted Sebastian to tell me what he knew before I offered any information. "Why would I be?"

"He asked for you."

"And?"

"Wanted to hire you to go on a date with him and a client."

"And? When's the date?" I was hoping this was my way out, and that Vinny was trying to get me back.

Sebastian chuckled. "I'm not stupid, Tessa."

"Okay. So why are you telling me this?"

He leaned forward and rested his elbows on the dark wood. "I know it was your boyfriend. So the question is, what am I going to do about him?"

I stared at him as I stood in the middle of the room. "And?"

"And you're going to call him, tell him that you came here on your own."

"And if I don't?"

"I will kill him," he stated without hesitation.

"I hate you," I seethed.

"You'll grow to love me." He smirked.

"Never."

"We'll see about that." He picked up the phone on his desk and held out the receiver for me. "Now, call him."

"I don't know his number. It's in my cell phone."

"Not a problem." He unlocked a desk drawer and pulled out my clutch that I'd dropped in the struggle with Mateo. "What's your password?"

"Just give me the phone, and I'll call him."

"Tell me your password."

I glared at him again. I didn't want him to go through my phone.

There wasn't much on it, but I felt as though he'd have a piece of me if he looked at my pictures, my texts, my emails, whatever.

"Now," he ordered.

"442687."

He punched the numbers in, not bothering to ask me why that was the code. I wasn't stupid enough to use Colton's name as my code, but the numbers did have a meaning. "And his name?"

"You don't know?"

He smirked. "Never got the pleasure before I had him thrown out."

I stared at him again. I didn't want to tell him Vinny's name because I feared if Sebastian knew his real name, he would hurt him.

He spoke as he pressed buttons on the screen of my cell phone. "We can either do this the easy way or the hard way, Tessa Baby. The easy way is for you tell me his name, and I—" He stopped talking, and my heart stopped too. "Never mind—found it. So, you did have plans with him last night." His blue eyes met mine. "Lucky for me, you're nosy."

"Just hand me my phone, and I'll call him." I reached my hand out.

He started to do just that but stopped. "When Vinny answers the phone, you will say that you're here with me on your own. You will tell him everything he *doesn't* want to hear. You will make sure he stops trying to get to you, or I will send Mateo to find him and pick him up so I can kill him."

"You don't need to kill him."

"Then you better fucking convince him."

Sebastian handed me my phone, and I hesitated. What was I going to say to Vinny? I hated having to lie to him, but I did this to myself, and I had never wanted to rewind time more than right now.

"Do it," he ordered.

"I'm going," I hissed.

"On speaker."

I sighed and pressed the call button and then the speaker button as I silently prayed that Vinny wouldn't answer. But of course, he did.

"Tessa! Oh my God. Are you okay?"

"Yes, I'm fine."

"Really?"

My gaze moved to Sebastian. "Yes."

"Where are you?"

"My boss's house."

"Why?"

I hesitated, and Sebastian cocked his head to the side as he glared at me. "Because I want to be."

"Really?"

No. "Yes."

"Tessa." Vinny sighed on the other end. "What the fuck is going on?"

I sighed too. "Look, Vinny. It was nice while it lasted—"

"While it lasted?" he yelled. "We barely got started."

"I know. It was a mistake."

"Bull-fucking-shit, Tessa. Just tell me what's going on."

I can't. "I'm sorry. We'll always have the Dodgers."

Sebastian ripped the phone out of my hand and pressed the end button before Vinny could reply. "You'll always have the Dodgers?"

I shrugged. "We both like the Dodgers." Vinny would know differently, and hopefully, he'd realize something was wrong. I wasn't sure how he could help me, but I had to try something.

"Go eat, take care of your son. I have work to do, but remember that tonight, you're in there." He pointed at the closed door.

"What's in there?"

"My bedroom."

That night, I was in his bed.

I tried to tell him Colton needed me, but that only lasted until Colt was asleep. Then I was ordered to strip, get down on my knees, and pleasure Sebastian in his brown walled room with a king-sized bed. At first, I hesitated, but then he wrapped his hand in my hair and forced me to lower my mouth onto his cock. The entire time I was on my knees, I thought about Sommer doing this exact thing. Why couldn't it have been her? She was my friend, but she had done this before. I wanted to kick, scream, bite him, but I knew that if I did anything other than what he asked, he would hurt me. He hadn't yet, but something told me he would, and I didn't want to take that chance.

After Sebastian came in my mouth, he ordered me to get on the bed brown comforter on all fours. I did. I had no other choice. Maybe if Colton weren't here, I'd try to run, but there was no way for me to leave with Colt, and I would die before I left without him. So, while Sebastian took me from behind, I closed my eyes and thought about Vinny, praying he would know what I'd said was a lie.

Once Sebastian was done, I cleaned myself up in the bathroom and I cried. I cried because this wasn't how my life was supposed to be. I cried because my boss had raped me. And I cried because he hadn't used a condom.

TWENTY-THREE

Vinny

"WE'LL ALWAYS HAVE THE DODGERS."

What the fuck? I stared at my phone in my hands, confused because we didn't have the Dodgers. *I* had the Dodgers, and Tessa hated them. I replayed the short conversation over and over in my head.

"Look, Vinny. It was nice while it lasted—"

"While it lasted?" I'd yelled. *"We barely got started."*

"I know. It was a mistake."

"Bull-fucking-shit, Tessa. Just tell me what's going on."

"I'm sorry. We'll always have the Dodgers."

The more I thought about everything, the more my chest hurt—or I suppose it was my heart. But she was alive, and because of that, there was still hope. I needed Joss. I felt as though she was the only one who would be able to help me.

It took two days until I was able to track down Joss. Their undercover mission was over, and Gabe finally gave me Paul's address. But when I arrived at the house, she asked me to go shopping with her.

"You want me to go shopping with you?" I asked as she walked to her car.

"Yes. Ride with me. I need to get Cat some clothes."

When I'd arrived, Paul had mentioned something had happened to Cat, Joss and Seth's ... Well, she was Joss's friend, but I wasn't sure what Cat was to Seth because at Paul and Joss's wedding only a few days ago, there seemed to be tension there.

"Oh, okay." We got into her car, leaving Paul, Seth, and Cat behind.

"Gabe texted Paul you were on your way and you needed to speak with me privately?" she asked as she put the car into reverse and pulled out of the driveway.

I nodded. "Yeah, I guess it needs to be private, though I'm not sure."

"What's up?" We started down the road. I had no idea where we were going, but I told her everything as she drove us to her destination. "Local PD said she went on her own?" Joss asked.

"Yeah." I bobbed my head. That was the only thing I knew for sure—though I felt it was a lie.

"And she called you and told you she was dumping you for her boss and moving in with the guy?"

"Yep."

"Huh," she breathed as though she was thinking everything over. "From what I could tell at the range and my wedding, she really liked you."

"I thought so too. We'd just made it official the night before your wedding, and the night she went to the party, we had plans for me to stay the night."

"And you're sure he's a drug dealer?"

"Pretty sure. That's what her friend Melony told me."

"And how does she know?"

"She said the girls at the club sell for him."

We were silent for a bit while she thought about everything. "The case from last night was personal."

"Okay?" I asked, confused about why she was bringing it up. It didn't involve Tessa.

"I've spent my entire life hating the man who was taken down last night."

"Yeah? And this has to do with Tessa?" I turned more toward Joss in my seat.

"No," Joss replied. "I'm bringing it up because the bust happened and we essentially got the guy, but there's more to it than that."

"Okay?"

"A lot of my time has been spent working on this case, and it still will be while the investigation is pending."

"What are you getting at?"

"While I care for you because you're my husband's friend, and I like Tessa, I'm not going to be able to spend a lot of time on this until that case is over."

"And you don't know how long that will be?"

Joss shook her head. "No. It's not your average case."

"So, what are you telling me?"

"I'll put some feelers out and get in contact with the DEA, but I can't make any promises. If there's no evidence she's not there by her own choice, then I can't barge in and save her."

"Can you at least talk to her?"

"I will when I can. It has to be on my own time because if local PD already did their welfare check, I won't have any cause to go check on her."

"She's your friend. There has to be a way."

"Let me look into it. The case we're working on is my top priority. I'm sorry, Vinny, but give me some time."

Hearing her say those words, made me think I wouldn't know anything for a long time.

TWENTY-FOUR

Tessa

Forty-Five Days Later ...

I wasn't sure how many days had passed because the weeks were running into each other, and I didn't have my phone or a calendar to remind me what day it was.

Sebastian was able to find a teacher with special education qualifications, and Monday through Friday we had class. I watched while Colton and Mrs. Porter did their daily schooling. I had nothing else to do, and there was no way I was leaving Colt alone with anyone who was employed by Sebastian.

And most nights, he ordered me to be in his bed.

A few days after we moved in, Sebastian's people went and got more of my clothes and pictures and things. I wasn't able to tell them what I wanted, and I wasn't sure happened with my apartment. I didn't ask. Deep down I knew Sebastian got rid of all of my furniture and somehow got me out of my lease.

About the same time, I deduced that something happened to his friend Tony because a few days after I was held here, Sebastian became stressed, needing me to let off steam or something. He wasn't rough with me, but he also didn't try to make me feel good—it never was good anyway. He used me, and I never questioned Sebastian about what was going on, but I'd overheard him say to Mateo that Tony's bust wasn't going to be good for him because they were friends and the Feds could link them. Link them in what? I had no clue.

Every night, I would cry after Sebastian used me, and every morning, I'd put a smile on my face so Colton wouldn't know something was wrong. But, something *was* wrong because the more time passed, the more I realized I wasn't getting my period.

And I wanted my period.

I wanted the week break from Sebastian. I wanted to not have to cry after he was done with me. I wanted to not have to wonder every day if he'd want me to pleasure him when he came home. I wanted to escape.

But my period never came, and that caused me to become more depressed. What if I was pregnant with Sebastian's baby? I'd be tied to him forever, and when I thought about looking at an imaginary child whom I had conceived with him, I feared I would always remember what Sebastian made me repeatedly do.

Every time he ordered me into his bedroom, I was Scarlett. I had to be. I put on a façade, pretended to not care, but I never enjoyed it. I never came, never had that shot of pleasure run through my body no matter what Sebastian did to it. I refused to let him win. He might think he had my body, but he'd never have all of it. There was only one man who would forever have my body, my heart, my love, and I'd told him what we had was essentially a lie.

"Helen," I called to Mrs. Porter. "Can you remind me of the date?"

"It's June twenty-ninth."

"Right." I smiled. I calculated the time and realized that I'd been with Sebastian for over a month and a half. A month and a half without my period. Panic started to set in. I couldn't let Colton see me break down. Even though he was in his own world, so to speak, and also learning from Helen, I couldn't let him see the worry on my face because even though children on the spectrum may seem as though they aren't paying attention, they are.

I stood and walked into the open kitchen where Valentina was making dinner. In the time I'd been here, she'd become a friend, the only person I talked to. I didn't think I could care about anyone associated with Sebastian, but I truly realized she worked for him because she thought he was a good man for rebuilding her town and getting her out of danger.

He'd never be a good man.

"Valentina," I whispered as I stopped and stood next to her.

"Yes, Ms. Tessa?"

"Can you keep a secret?"

She stared at me for a beat. "If it's about—"

"It's not about Mr. Delarosa."

Well, that wasn't true because if I were pregnant, it would be his. Or was it? Vinny and I had had sex without a condom before Sebastian and me. But I'd never know. I wouldn't give Sebastian any more reason to want to harm Vinny.

I thought about Vinny daily. Thought about his smile, his laugh, the way he was with Colton. I thought about how I might never see him again. I hoped he was happy. Maybe he went back to S&R and was living the life he'd had before he met me. While I hated to think of him still escorting, I had to realize it was for the best. There was no telling what Sebastian would do to him if he were still trying to get me back.

Every day while I thought of ways to get out, I thought about Melony and Sophia too. There was nothing Sophia could do, but had Melony talked to Sebastian? Asked where I was? Or was everyone really thinking I would want to be with this monster?

"Oh? Then yes. Yes, I can keep secret." Valentina smiled.

"It's a huge secret," I told her.

"Okay. Tell me." Her grin widened.

I lowered my voice. Sebastian wasn't home, but he always had guards around. I figured they were here in case I tried to escape. Mateo was the one who went with him whenever Sebastian left the house, but I didn't know the names of the ones who were paid to watch me. It was weird because I'd never seen Mateo at Red Diamond when I was there before, but when Sebastian left, so did Mateo.

"When you go to the store tomorrow can you get me something?"

"Si. Whatever you want. Mr. Delarosa has told me to make sure you have what you need."

"Right, but this is something he can't know about."

"Oh?" she questioned, scrunching her brows.

"Not until I know for sure."

"What do you need me to get you?"

I sighed and turned so that my back was to Helen, not wanting her to eavesdrop. She was showing Colton shapes, but I couldn't take the chance that she was listening too. "A pregnancy test," I whispered.

Valentina's brown eyes widened, and she grinned as though I was her daughter telling her I was making her a grandmother. "You're pregnant?"

"Shh," I scolded. "Please don't say anything. I want to make sure before I tell Sebastian."

"Si, of course. I can go right now if you'd like. The meat is marinating."

"Okay, yes. Please go now."

Her smile hadn't faded. "I go and be right back."

When Valentina came back thirty minutes later, she motioned for me to follow her up the stairs. At the top, she handed me a brown paper bag.

"Thank you," I said. "Can you keep an eye on Colt?"

"Si. Hurry because Mr. Delarosa will be home very soon and if I need to make him a cake for the good news—"

"It won't be good news," I told her.

"Si, it will, cariño. A baby will bring Mr. Delarosa so much joy."

I didn't respond as I took the bag into the bathroom. How could she think this was okay? She had to know I didn't want a baby, especially with Sebastian. Especially with the man who wouldn't let me go outside except to swim in his backyard.

After I nervously peed on the applicator, I waited and waited and waited. I couldn't time the wait because I had no watch, no phone, nothing in the bathroom and I didn't want to leave until I knew for sure. So, I waited some more, and it killed me. It was worse than the first time I took a pregnancy test after my night with Scott. Then, my only worry had been finding Scott to tell him I was pregnant. But now, how would I raise a child with a drug dealer? How would it turn out? How was Colton going to turn out if I didn't find a way to escape? Would Sebastian force them into the drug business?

Finally, I thought enough time had passed. I picked the test up off the counter and took a deep breath before I focused on the two lines on the screen. In an instant, my world stood still, the silence of the small room echoing in my ears. This wasn't happening. This wasn't happening *again*. This wasn't happening with a drug dealing murderer who took pleasure from unwilling participants.

But it was.

And since I chugged a bunch of water while I'd waited for Valentina to get back from the store, I was able to take all three tests that came in the three pack she'd bought. They were all positive. After I read the third one, I crumpled to the floor and cried and cried and cried until I couldn't breathe. I cried until there was a knock on the door.

"Cariño, it's me."

I didn't respond as more tears escaped my eyes.

"Ms. Tessa, are you okay?"

No, I wasn't. I'd never be okay again. It was hard enough being a single parent, but I knew I was raising Colton right. I might not have had the *normal* job of most mothers, but we were good. Now we were mixed up in drugs, and if I didn't find a way to escape, both of my children would grow up in this life. The only saving grace would be if they didn't follow in Sebastian's footsteps, but I knew that if we stayed, they would.

"Please, cariño. I help you."

Even though Valentina spoke broken English, I could still hear the sincerity in her voice. I got up off the tiled floor and unlocked the door. I handed the last test to her. "I'm pregnant."

Her face brightened. "This makes me so happy."

"I'm not." I sniffed.

"Cariño, the Lord works in mysterious ways. He puts children on this earth for a reason."

"Don't you see I'm hurting? That I don't want this?"

"Si, but Mr. Delarosa will make sure you and your children never go without."

I crossed my arms over my chest and leaned against the doorframe. "Why?"

She blinked. "Because he takes care of what's his."

"And you're okay with him *owning* us?" There was no other way to put it. I was no longer a person. I was a prisoner, a slave, a hostage. And while Sebastian hadn't hit me or anything, the emotional pain I felt outweighed any bodily pain I'd ever felt in my life.

"Without him, I would be homeless."

"I wouldn't be."

"Yes, you would. He gave you a job. You danced for him."

I stared at her while her words sunk in. Yes, he was my boss. He allowed me to dance and make money, but did that mean that, in turn, I owed him because I'd been able to provide for my small family? In what world was that okay? "If I had known it would turn out like this, I would've danced somewhere else."

"That may be true, cariño, but you didn't."

"So, are you saying that all the girls at the club owe him?"

"I'm saying that all the girls, including you, are lucky to have worked for a man who wants to do good in the world."

"How is dealing drugs good for the world?"

"It's not. The money he gets from the drugs help the world, help my country."

Everything always came back to money. As I stared at her again, I finally understood ...

Money held all the power.

After I washed my face, I went back downstairs and resumed my place in the lounge chair while Colton finished his schooling. As soon as Helen left for the day, Valentina came into the living room.

"Mr. Delarosa called. He wants me to take Colton to the park."

I drew my head back. "What? Why?"

"He didn't say, but he wants him out of the house."

Panic instantly flooded my body. "Why?"

"I do not know, but I do as he says."

"I'm not letting you take my son," I argued. "He's only been to the park once, and it didn't go so well."

"Please, cariño. He will be okay."

"How do you know?"

"Mr. Delarosa said he is coming with business to take care of, and he wants me to get Colton out of the house for a while."

"No, you're not taking my son."

"Please—" Valentina started to beg but stopped when Sebastian walked in through the door. He looked at me then Valentina. "I'm sorry, she will not let me take him."

He turned back to me. "Tessa, I'm doing this for your own good."

"How is taking my son for my own good?"

He cupped my cheek. In the last month and a half, I'd slowly begun to let him. Not because I wanted the affection from him, but because I wanted him to think he didn't sicken me. I felt as though if I did what he asked, there would be some sort of gap—an escape—that I could take at my first opportunity to get out.

"I have a surprise for you."

"I don't like surprises," I lied. Everyone liked surprises, but I wasn't sure what Sebastian considered a surprise.

"You will like this one, Tessa Baby. I promise."

"Why does Colt need to go away?"

"Because you won't want him to see or hear what's about to happen."

"What's about to happen?"

He grinned. "Payback." Sebastian snapped his fingers and Valentina moved to Colton, picked him up and took him to the door. "Don't worry, he'll be fine."

But would he come back?

"He likes the swing," I called to Valentina as she and a guard walked out the door.

She turned and smiled. "Okay."

I turned back toward Sebastian and hissed low, "If something happens to him, I will kill you."

"If something happens to him, I will kill whoever harms him."

Our gazes stayed locked, and before I realized it, I heard the clicking of the front door and Colton and Valentina were gone. Did I just let him take my son so he could kill me? Did I just let him take my son so he could kidnap him—again? Did I just let him take my son so he could kill *him*?

"Don't hurt him," I whispered.

"He's going to the park, Tessa. He'll have fun."

I wasn't sure if he would because while he loved to swing on the swing, I didn't know if Valentina could get him to do it. He wouldn't run off and do his own thing in the sandbox either, but maybe that was my saving grace? Maybe he'd have a meltdown, and she'd have to come right back?

A few seconds later, Mateo came in with another guy. A guy I knew. Brent came to the club most days. He was the same guy who police told me was the owner of the car that had followed me. I'd never told Sebastian I knew who it was, and I never got the chance to do anything about it because two days after I found out it was him, Sebastian took me hostage.

I eyed Brent as I watched him walk closer. He didn't have a scratch on him and I wondered how Sebastian and Mateo were able to get him to come here. I assumed Mateo carried a gun and forced Brent into a car or something. Though as he stopped in front of me and his gaze met mine, I saw the fear in his eyes.

My gaze turned back to Sebastian. "Told you I brought you a present," he stated.

"What are you going to do to him?" I asked. I didn't know what I wanted Sebastian to do to Brent. Did someone need to die because they were stalking someone? Was that what Sebastian wanted to do to him?

"First, we're going to talk in my office."

"And then?"

"And then *we'll* decide his fate."

"We?"

"Yes, my love. We."

I blinked, shaking my head at the new term of endearment. He'd never called me his love before. "Your love?" I questioned.

He grinned. "Don't play coy. Brent needs to know who holds your heart."

Sebastian didn't hold my heart. He never would. I didn't care if this was some grand gesture to win me over. I wasn't okay with it. I wasn't okay with anything Sebastian did. But then, this was a way to win Sebastian over. To make him think I was all in before I made my escape.

"Okay, lead the way."

He stepped forward and whispered into my ear, "You go up first so I can watch your ass. I want to claim that ass tonight."

I swallowed, not able to respond, and with one more glance at Brent, I turned and walked up the stairs. Once we were in Sebastian's office, Mateo led Brent to a seat that Sebastian had turned around. The same seat I assumed was used when I'd witnessed him killing that guy before. I wasn't sure what to do, so I waited for Sebastian to speak.

"Now, Brent. How long did you stalk my Scarlett?"

"I—" he started to respond, but I spoke first.

"Are you sure it's him?" I questioned. I knew it was him, but there was no way I would be okay with him killing Brent. Call the cops? Yes. Beat him up? I could probably live with that. But never murder. Brent had never laid a hand on me, and while Vinny had told me not to take stalking lightly, I still didn't think it warranted death.

"Yes," Sebastian confirmed. "Mateo was able to find the car in the parking lot, and when he came back today, we had a little chat."

"What did you talk about?"

"Seems Brent thinks he's a good liar because he denies it was him, but as you know, Scar, I have cameras."

"Okay, and you're sure?"

"100% positive, baby. Now, what do you want to do?"

I wanted to let him go because I hoped that this situation would scare Brent and it would be the end of it. If he went to Metro, I hoped that he wouldn't get a cop on Sebastian's payroll and they'd show up so I could beg them to take Colton and me with them.

"How long were you following me?" I asked, not sure where else to start.

"I—I wasn't."

Without hesitation, Sebastian hit Brent with the butt of a gun I hadn't seen him holding. "Don't fucking lie to her."

Brent's green eyes pleaded with me to stop this, but I couldn't because as I stared back, watching blood seep from his split cheek, I realized he was the reason I was mixed up with Sebastian in the first place. While he wasn't the one who forced me up the stairs, he was the one who followed me home that night, which caused me to go to Sebastian's office to view the video tapes. He was the one who made it possible for Sebastian to invite me to the fight that night. And because I went to the fight, Brent was the one who made it possible for Sebastian to invite me to the party.

"A few times," Brent stated.

I balked. "A few times?" I thought it was only that one time.

"I'm sorry. You're hot, and I wanted to see where you lived."

"She doesn't live there anymore," Sebastian cut in.

"That's fine. I get it, man. Just let me go."

"Should we let him go?" Sebastian asked me.

I opened my mouth to respond, but nothing came out.

"Yeah, just let me go. We're cool. I won't do it again."

"You see, Brent," Sebastian said as he circled him like a shark. "You know where I live, and we took you not of your own free will. Do you think I can let you go now?"

Oh God.

"Yeah, I won't say anything. I won't even go back to Red Diamond ever again. We're cool."

"You know," Sebastian snapped his fingers, "I've almost heard those exact words before." His gaze met mine, and I swallowed, unsure what he was going to do. "And the last person who said that to me didn't get to go home because I don't take chances."

"I won't say anything!" Brent pleaded.

"There's only one way to make sure that doesn't happen." Sebastian aimed the gun at Brent.

"No!" I screamed.

Sebastian's gaze moved back to me. "You think I can let him go? He needs to pay for what he did to you."

"He only followed me a few times," I replied as though that was okay. I couldn't see another person get shot again, and Brent didn't deserve to die because of it.

Sebastian turned to me, running the gun down my cheek. "You should know I can't let him go."

"There has to be another way," I pleaded.

"What? You want him to live here? Fill your pussy at night too?"

"No." I shook my head. "But I don't want him to die."

"He has to." He turned again and aimed the gun at Brent.

"No!" I screamed again. Brent was shaking, I was shaking, and I just wanted Sebastian to stop. "Please don't."

"And why not?" Sebastian asked, still pointing the gun at Brent. "Why should I not shoot him in the head?"

I stared at Sebastian, trying to come up with what to say to him.

Trying to think of how I could change his mind. "Because I don't want the father of my unborn baby to have more blood on his hands."

Sebastian lowered the gun and turned back to me. "You're pregnant?"

I smiled, trying to make it as genuine as I could. "Yes. I took three tests before you got home."

"Show me."

"They're in the bathroom on the second floor."

Without looking at Brent again, Sebastian took my hand, laced our fingers and started for the stairs. "Mateo, make sure he disappears."

My gaze met Brent's before Sebastian and I took a step down. Even though Sebastian wasn't going to kill him, Mateo would.

TWENTY-FIVE

Vinny

I HADN'T HEARD FROM TESSA IN ALMOST TWO MONTHS. I HADN'T HEARD from Joss either. When I would see Paul, he told me she was busy with her case. I felt as though my friends didn't care. If this were Autumn or Joss, Paul and Gabe would be going in with guns blazing. But that wasn't me, and they weren't helping.

I understood why Gabe wouldn't go, and that was because Autumn was pregnant. He didn't want to take a chance of getting killed or going to jail. But Paul? His wife wouldn't help me even though she worked for the FBI. Seth had gone back to D.C. or some shit, and that left me ...

Alone.

TWENTY-SIX

Tessa

When I showed Sebastian the three pregnancy tests, he was ecstatic. A part of me felt as though he would be pissed that he was going to be tied to a child for eighteen years, but he wasn't.

"Are these real?" he asked.

"Of course they are."

"These," he waved the tests in front of my face, "are proof that we're meant to be together."

It was on the tip of my tongue to tell him that he was wrong. Rape every night without a condom wasn't fate. Sebastian was delusional. "Yeah," I agreed and smiled tightly, trying to show that I did agree with him when, in reality, I was faking it.

"Good." He kissed my lips. "Valentina will help you get a room ready and whatever you need."

"I need to go to the doctor."

"When?"

"Well, I'm not sure when I got pregnant, but usually around eight weeks should be the first appointment."

"I'll make a call."

"And do what?"

"Have them come here."

"Don't be ridiculous. They need to examine me in an actual exam room." As Sebastian thought about what I'd said, I prayed he'd agree with me. I knew he would send a guard with me, maybe even go himself, but he wouldn't be permitted into the room. At least I hoped not.

"Do you have a doctor?"

"Yes."

"Okay. Make an appointment, and we'll go."

I knew from previous exams that they asked questions about abuse or if your life was in danger when you filled out an intake form. I didn't know what would happen if I checked the box.

But I was hoping to find out.

While I waited on the couch for Valentina and Colton to get back from the park, Sebastian made himself a celebratory drink.

"I'm really happy about this, Tessa Baby."

I didn't respond.

"You'll see," he stated as he sat next to me on the couch. "I've always wanted to be a father, and now I will be. I won't fuck this up."

I didn't know how, but I was going to find a way out before that *ever* happened.

A few minutes later, Valentina and Colton walked in through the front door, and I instantly ran to him. "Did you have fun at the park, Slugger?"

"He was such a good boy," Valentina stated. "He deserves ice cream for dessert."

"If you eat all your dinner, do you want chocolate ice cream for dessert?"

He started to flap his little hands, and a thought washed over me as I wondered if I should be happy or sad that he was going to be a big brother.

It had been two weeks since I found out I was pregnant. Two weeks since Mateo killed Brent. Two weeks since I decided to fake being happy with Sebastian.

It was all I could do to survive in a world I wanted nothing to do with. Maybe in another universe, things could have been different.

Every night, Sebastian ignored Colton. Maybe it was because he wasn't able to play with him in the sense of playing with someone who was interacting with you. That was why I loved Vinny with Colton. Vinny understood. Vinny cared. Vinny was good with Colt. And I still thought about him often.

But Vinny was gone.

He was probably on a beach somewhere, drinking rum and Cokes because it was, of course, summer break. Would we still be together if I hadn't disappeared? Would he love me? I loved him, and after all this time apart, I still wanted to tell him. I wanted to rush into his arms and never leave.

But I couldn't.

"Are you ready to go?" Sebastian asked as he came into his bathroom where I was getting ready to go to my doctor's appointment. The bathroom was nothing compared to the one in Mark's house. It was a decent size, had granite countertops, and a huge shower, but it wasn't special given the circumstances I was in.

"Almost."

"We don't want to be late."

"We?" I asked as I brushed my long brown hair.

"Of course. I'm going with you, Tessa. I'm going to go to every appointment. This is my child."

I nodded and sat the brush down. "Then let's go."

Just as I tried to cross over the threshold, he grabbed my wrist and spun me around to face him. "I'm glad you've come to terms with our arrangement."

Still faking it, I replied, "You're growing on me."

He grinned and kissed my lips. "If I would have known you'd be this good, I would have pursued you sooner."

I smiled softly at him. "Things happen for a reason, right?"

"They sure do."

As we walked down the stairs, Sebastian's phone rang. "I need to take this."

I nodded and kept walking. When I got downstairs, Colton was playing on his iPad. I turned to Valentina. "We're about to leave. Are you sure you'll be okay with him?"

"Si, of course. I raised four boys." Four boys who had apparently died in some sort of drug-related incident. I'd never gotten the entire story from her, but it made sense to me if a drug lord helped her town that they'd died from something drug related.

"But he won't tell you what he wants or needs, so if he fusses, you'll have to figure it out on your own."

"I know, cariño. I will take him to the park. He loves the park."

He did love the park. He loved to swing, and I was thankful that Valentina took him to the park a few times a week. I still wasn't allowed outside.

"Change of plans," Sebastian stated as he came into the room.

"I can't—"

"Mateo will take you to the appointment."

"You're not going?" I asked.

He caressed my cheek. "Business calls. I need to stay here and handle some things."

"Okay," I responded, knowing not to question him, and also knowing it had to do with cocaine and not Red Diamond.

Sebastian kissed my lips softly and then walked back up the stairs. I was surprised Mateo was leaving his side. Maybe it was because he was Sebastian's right-hand man, the one he could trust to keep an eye on me—as if I'd run and leave Colton behind.

I kissed Colton on the head and then followed Mateo into the garage. This would be the first time I would ride in a car since the night I arrived in captivity. It would be the first time I set foot on the street since that night. It would be the first time I would get a chance to run.

But, I wouldn't run. And while Mateo drove me to the doctor's office, I realized I couldn't check the box on the intake form indicating I was in danger because Sebastian had ordered Colt to stay with Valentina. It proved Sebastian was smart, but one day, I'd be smarter.

Or dead.

Mateo stayed in the waiting room when I was called back. I didn't expect him to go inside the room with me, but I wasn't sure what Sebastian would have ordered him to do. A part of me thought he would pretend to be my boyfriend so he could go into the exam room, but he didn't. He sat quietly reading a magazine, and when I was called back, he didn't even look up.

After I went through all the standard procedures with the nurse, I was taken into an exam room.

"Why are you here today?" she asked.

Apparently she hadn't read my intake form. Or maybe they were required to ask? "I think I'm pregnant."

"Congratulations," she gushed.

We went over some things like when my last period was so she could make notes for the doctor. When she left, I stripped my shorts off, covered myself with the blue disposable sheet, and waited for the doctor. On the back of the door was a poster asking if I was in an abusive relationship. Asking if I was in danger. It didn't ask if I was being held hostage, raped most nights. I had no idea what would happen if I told them I was. Would the cops storm in, want to whisk me off to a safe house or something? I couldn't do that because Colton wasn't with me. If he were, I wouldn't hesitate.

After some time, Dr. Peirce came in. "Hi, Teresa. How are you?"

I smiled warmly. "I'm good." I wasn't, but it was how I was used to replying.

She moved to the computer, pressed some keys and said, "I see you think you're pregnant."

"I took three tests."

"Well, let's examine you, see how far along you are. I'll also do some blood work to test your blood sugar and check for any abnormalities, and then have you meet with my obstetrics nurse so you can go over follow-up care and whatever questions you may have."

"Sure."

I lay back, spread my legs and waited. Every woman hated this, and I hated it even more given my current circumstance. The wand entered me, and I waited some more as I looked at the screen. There wasn't much to see, but I saw it. I saw the gummy-bear-like shape.

Dr. Pierce clicked some buttons.

"Looks like you're about eight weeks along."

There was a flicker of hope inside of me at the news that this might not be Sebastian's baby. "Okay, great," I replied.

"You don't seem too happy," she observed.

"Just—shocked."

"Not planned?"

"Nope."

"Do—"

"It's okay. I did it once, and I'll do it again. Things happen for a reason."

"They do, but if there's something you need to tell me ..."

My heart ached and I wanted to tell her there was. I wanted to break down and cry, tell her everything, but I was scared of the consequences. If I told her, and the cops showed up, there would be a chance they were on Sebastian's payroll, and then they would tell him, and I wasn't sure what he'd do to me. Or Colton. But, there was also the chance they wouldn't be. In the end, I decided I wouldn't tell her this time. And next time—at my next appointment—I would make sure Colton was with me and take the chance that the cops who were called weren't driven by money.

"Nope," I replied. "The father is really happy and will take care of me and the baby."

"Okay. Let me get some blood so we can run some tests, and then I will let you get dressed before you meet with the nurse."

The appointment was long. After I spoke with the nurse, I scheduled my next appointment. I walked out into the waiting room where Mateo sat. He looked up, set the magazine down, and waited for me to walk completely through the door. When I did, I looked to my left and noticed Autumn sitting in the waiting room. She was reading on her e-reader, and I wanted to rush to her, wrap my arms around her and beg for help. I knew she'd dealt with abuse before because when I was at the range with everyone, she'd briefly told me why she taught self-defense. Now, I felt as though I was living in the same hell she used to live in.

"One second," I stated to Mateo. "They have a bathroom in there, and I just realized I can't hold it. I'll be just a moment." He nodded, and I walked back through the doors to a nurse's station. "Do you have a piece of paper and a pen I could use?" I asked when the nurse looked up.

She smiled and slid a sticky note pad and pen in front of me. "Does this work?"

"Perfect. Thank you."

I hurried and wrote Autumn a note:

Kidnapped by my boss. Send Joss. Can't trust local PD.

I folded the yellow sticky note in half and handed the pen back to the nurse. "Thank you again."

When I walked out the door again, Mateo was standing, waiting. I smiled up at him.

"Ready?" he asked.

"Yes," I replied and started walking. Autumn was so engrossed in her book that she didn't notice me. As I passed her, I tossed the note onto her screen. She quickly looked up. Our eyes met as I walked out of the office, and I prayed this would work.

TWENTY-SEVEN

Vinny

Two months.

It had been two fucking months since I'd last seen Tessa, and I felt that shit in my heart every fucking day. This was why I didn't do love. I guess a part of me had always feared my heart would break if I ever let someone in, though I didn't think it would be under these circumstances.

Since I hadn't heard from Joss, I stayed away from all my so-called friends. They obviously didn't care about me. And fuck, I didn't care about them. Who was I kidding? I fucking loved those people, but in my time of need, they did nothing. Sure, Joss told me she needed time before she could look into it, but what if Joss were kidnapped? She'd want to be rescued. It made me sick to my stomach to think of what was happening to Tessa every day. Was she abused? Sexually assaulted? Or just enjoying life in some gated community with rich people?

Why couldn't Joss go to the house? Talk to Tessa? Get Tessa? I didn't care that Tessa had told me she went on her own. I knew better, and Joss was FBI. Couldn't they help? Couldn't Joss work on this on her own time and just find out if Tessa was all right? Apparently the answers were all a big fat negative.

Fuck. Them.

I was having my nightly pity party with my Bacardi when there was a knock at my door. I moved to it, and after I saw who was on the other side through the peephole, I said, "What do you want?"

"Open the door," Paul demanded. "We have news."

I flung the door open so fast I thought I was about to rip it off the fucking hinges. "What news?"

"Sit down," he stated. He and Joss walked in, and Paul closed the door behind him.

"Just tell me." I leaned a hand on the wall, waiting.

Joss spoke. "Autumn saw Tessa at the doctor's office."

"The doctor's? Is she okay?"

"We think she might be pregnant since it was the gynecologist."

My mouth fell open. "What did you say?"

"Autumn was there for her weekly check-up because her baby is due any day now. When Tessa was leaving, she threw a note to Autumn."

"What did it say?"

"'Kidnapped by my boss. Send Joss. Can't trust local PD.'"

"I fucking told you," I pointed at her, rage coursing through my body.

"I know, and I've been looking into it."

I chuckled sarcastically and crossed my arms over my broad chest. "Looking into it? What the fuck does that mean?"

"I've run a background check on Sebastian Delarosa, the man who owns Red Diamond."

"And?"

"All I can tell you is that he has associations with some people from another case working on and it's not good. I'll dig into him more."

"Dig into him more? It's been two fucking months, Joss."

She wrapped an arm around my shoulders. "I know. This is going to take priority, but I can't just go up to his door and knock."

"Why not?"

"Like I told you before, Vegas Metro has jurisdiction, but what I found can give me cause to get in the door."

"Why do they have jurisdiction? You're FBI. Doesn't that trump a city cop?"

"Because Metro already made a report saying she was there on her own accord. There's no evidence that she was kidnapped, and I have to listen to the police."

"She *was* kidnapped," I stated.

"While we know that—especially from the note—I can't go to my boss and say we need to listen to a person's boyfriend. There needs to be more."

"The note's not enough?"

She shook her head. "No proof it was from Tessa."

"But it was, and what more do you want besides he's a drug dealer? That should be enough."

"While it may be, it takes time to get an investigation started."

"Tessa and her son need to come home," I muttered.

"Just let me do my job. I hope to have her home in a few weeks."

"A few weeks? That's fucking forever."

"Have faith. I take this shit seriously, but Paul and I are going to Italy tomorrow for a week."

"You're going on vacation while *our* friend is kidnapped?"

"While I'm gone, my partner will be working on it. I promise we will get Tessa back."

"Not soon enough."

"It will be okay," Joss assured me.

When Joss and Paul left, I realized Joss had said they thought Tessa was pregnant. That little tidbit had escaped me when Joss started to mention getting Tessa home.

Tessa might be pregnant with that asshole's baby?

TWENTY-EIGHT

Tessa

MATEO NEVER MENTIONED IF HE SAW ME PASS A NOTE TO AUTUMN. Though it would probably look bad to Sebastian if Mateo allowed me to pass a note, so maybe he was just keeping his mouth shut?

Every day since my appointment, I waited, hoping someone would show up. It had been a week and still nothing. A week of Sebastian and Valentina acting as though the baby was coming the next day. They had already changed one of the spare bedrooms into a nursery, and to my surprise, Sebastian put the crib together.

It was the start of a new week of my third month in hell when—finally—hope came knocking. Sebastian and Mateo were at the club, as usual. When Valentina answered the phone, my ears perked up.

"But Mr. Delarosa isn't here." There was a pause. "We're instructed to not let anyone in." Another pause. "You have to? Si, okay." Valentina's eyes met mine, and I waited for her to say something, but she didn't. She went to the front door and spoke to the guard who was always posted outside.

How were the neighbors okay with a guy standing outside all day? It was weird, and even though he was on Sebastian's property, the neighbors had to wonder why he had a guard. Maybe he paid the neighbors off? I was slowly learning that money was the moving power for everyone.

Valentina came back. "Ms. Tessa, you and Colton need to go to your room."

"Why?" I questioned, looking at Helen who was in the middle of teaching Colt.

"Because the FBI is here, and it's best you get Colton and go to your room."

The FBI was here? Was it Joss? Please let it be Joss. "I'm not going anywhere. This is my house now."

"Please, cariño. I don't want Mr. Delarosa angry with me," she begged.

If I were to go upstairs and hide, the FBI wouldn't know I was here unless they checked all the rooms. "What about Helen?" I asked.

"You can go," Valentina stated to her.

Helen didn't hesitate before grabbing her purse and going for the door.

"Please, cariño. Please," Valentina begged again.

"I can't," I whispered. I had to see if it was Joss. If it wasn't, then I would tread lightly because whoever it was could also be on Sebastian's payroll and I didn't want to take the chance of telling the wrong person. Joss was the only one I trusted.

She glared at me, and it was the first time she had ever shown one ounce of anger toward me. "I will tell him, and he will punish you."

I walked toward her and lowered my voice so Colton couldn't hear, "I get punished every day I'm in this place. Do you think I'd let this opportunity pass?"

Before Valentina could respond, the doorbell rang. I started to move toward the front door, but she held a hand back, making me stop. I sighed and watched her go to the entryway, hoping Joss was on the other side. When the one side of the door was fully open, I saw a man in a black suit standing there. It wasn't Joss. But then, someone stepped around the guy, and it was her. My heart started to race, a lump formed in my throat, and I wanted to run to her. But then the guy spoke, and my world came crashing down around me—again.

"Sorry to bother you this afternoon. I'm Special Agent Montana, and this is Special Agent Jackson. We need to ask Mr. Delarosa some questions." The man and Joss both flashed their badges.

"He's not here," Valentina replied.

Joss's gaze met mine, and she gave me a tight smile. What did that mean? Did she not remember me? Was she not here for me?

"Then, I'd like to ask you some questions," Agent Montana said to Valentina.

"About what?" she asked.

"Please, if you don't mind, this Vegas heat is brutal."

Valentina hesitated, but then allowed Joss and her partner to enter.

"Thank you," Agent Montana said. "May we go into the kitchen and talk?" He met my gaze, making Valentina turn toward me.

"Si, right this way."

I expected Joss and the other agent to both go into the kitchen, but instead, Joss moved to me.

Valentina spoke, "She knows nothing. She is a guest."

"That's for my partner to decide," Agent Montana affirmed.

Valentina opened her mouth to protest, and I gave her the saddest look I could possibly muster. She had to know this was my chance. Even if I didn't know Joss, this was a moment for me to tell them I was in danger. Valentina closed her eyes briefly and then stepped into the open kitchen. She could still see me from where she stood at the island, but then Joss stepped in front of me.

"Are you okay?" she asked quietly as she looked over at the guard who was by the front door.

"No." I shook my head slightly, trying not to respond too much so that Valentina and the guard couldn't see me. I looked down to see Colton on his iPad, and I took a few steps away so he couldn't hear either.

"We need to make this fast. We're telling the help that we're here asking questions about a guy named Tony Martinez—"

"I met him," I confirmed.

"He's dead."

"What?" My eyes became huge.

"Doesn't matter. When Sebastian asks, tell him I asked you questions about girls being trafficked at Red Diamond."

I nodded. "Okay, but I don't think they are."

"I know, but we'll get into that another day. We need to figure out how to get you out of here."

"You can't take us now?"

She shook her head. "If this were a simple kidnapping case, I wouldn't hesitate, but it's more, Tessa."

"More?"

"You do know who Sebastian is, right?"

I nodded.

"We need him, but we're still doing surveillance on him, and we need time before we can make the bust."

"I saw him kill a guy," I stated.

"You did?"

I bobbed my head again. "That's why I'm here. He's worried I'll tell the police, but some of the officers with Metro are working for him."

"We can use that, but I need you to stay here until we can make the arrest."

"Why?"

"There's a lot of moving pieces, and we just don't have the evidence right now."

"Me seeing a guy being killed by him isn't enough?"

"It would be your word against his, and I'd rather not take the chance of putting you in even more danger."

"Okay, so what do I do? Just pretend everything's good?"

"Yes," she said.

"Everything's not good, Joss. I'm pregnant."

She smiled warmly at me. "We assumed as much since Autumn saw you at the OB. Is it Vinny's?"

I shrugged. "I don't know."

Joss stared at me for a beat. "I was hoping he wasn't doing that to you."

She didn't need to clarify. I knew she understood Sebastian was raping me. "Almost every night."

"I'm sorry. I'll get you out of here as soon as I can."

"When?" I wanted to crumple to the floor and cry. When I gave Autumn my note, I expected the cavalry to come in. Now help was here, but Joss wasn't taking Colton and me away. She was leaving us here to continue our misery.

"I've actually thought about this a lot in the last three months since Vinny told me."

"You've talked to Vinny?"

"Of course."

"How is he?"

"Not so good, but I can't get into that right now. I'm certain they've called Sebastian, and he's on his way. It's only a matter of time."

"Okay, so what have you thought about?"

"We need a way to bring down all his men with him."

"How are you going to do that?"

"When is his next party?"

I shrugged. "I don't think he will ever have one again since I'm locked up here. He doesn't want me talking to anyone. I can't even leave the house. My doctor's appointment was the first time."

"Does Sebastian think the baby is his?"

"Yes. He's already turned a room into a nursery. Colton doesn't even have his own room with toys."

"We need to get all of his men in one room. That will be for the best." Joss thought for a moment. "This may be because I'm a newly-wed, but do you think you can convince him to have a wedding?"

My eyes widened, and I hissed, low, "You want me to marry the guy?"

"No," she corrected. "I want you to *pretend* you're going to marry him. We'll stop it."

"How will you know when it is?"

"We will. Trust me."

Before we could go any further, Sebastian stormed in through the doors. Everything stopped as he stalked toward us, anger radiating off of him. Mateo wasn't far behind him. "You have no right coming into my home when I'm not here. Now, get out."

Joss held up her hands. "Please, Mr. Delarosa, we're just here about Tony Martinez."

Sebastian stopped short, and I moved to him, wrapping my arms around his waist, hoping he would think that I was on his side. "What about him? He's dead." His hand tightened on my waist.

"If you'd like, may we step into another room?" Joss asked.

Sebastian looked down at me, and then back to Joss. "Fine. We can go up to my office."

Sebastian kissed the top of my head, and then we broke apart before he started to walk. Joss turned to follow him, but I stopped her with a quick touch of my hand on her shoulder and whispered, "Tell Vinny I love him."

"You can tell him yourself soon enough." She winked.

As she walked up the curved staircase with her partner and Sebastian, I hoped she was right. I wasn't sure what was going to happen in Sebastian's office because that was where I assumed he took all the people to kill them.

While I waited for them to talk to Sebastian, Valentina questioned me about what I'd said. I stuck to what Joss had told me to say and only spoke of Red Diamond. Thirty minutes later, Joss and her partner returned down the stairs with Sebastian and Mateo following them. I didn't know what was said, of course, but Joss knew the truth about me being here, and now we had a plan.

I just had to figure out how to get Sebastian to want to marry me and plan a wedding. A wedding I wanted to hold tomorrow if it meant I could be rescued sooner. I'd always thought that when I was engaged, I'd do the standard planning that took a year. But that wasn't going to happen. I couldn't survive another year pretending I was okay with everything Sebastian was doing. Someone would end up dead.

And that was probably going to be me.

TWENTY-NINE

Vinny

A WEEK LATER, THERE STILL WASN'T ANY NEWS ABOUT TESSA.

I was starting to hate the line "I'm working on it" with a passion. Joss and Paul should have been back from Italy already, and I needed answers. And because I'd taken the summer off from teaching, hadn't volunteered at the Special Olympics, and had taken a break from S&R, I'd spent most of my time thinking about Tessa and hoping she was okay.

Every day I texted Melony, and every day was the same.

Me: *Heard anything?*

Melony: *Nope, you?*

Me: *No.*

Apparently, Melony tried to talk to Sebastian, but Melony was told —just like I was—that Tessa was at his house on her own. He also went so far as to tell her that Tessa didn't want to see anyone from the club and to just forget about her because Tessa had a new life now and was no longer dancing. He might have thought we'd believe that shit, but we knew it wasn't true. His days were numbered. I just hated that it was taking fucking forever. Also, Melony had said that everything in Tessa's apartment had been taken out and it was getting rented to someone else.

I fucking hated this situation.

I was watching a Dodgers game and was about to pour myself a drink when my cell rang. It was Paul, and I instantly sat up, swiping the call button. "Hey!"

"Gabe is a father!" he boomed.

My body sagged at the news. Not because I wasn't happy for Gabe, but because I wanted an update on Tessa. "That's awesome," I replied.

"Come to the hospital. Meet my nephew."

"Now?"

"Yes, now. Everyone's coming. Well, besides Seth and Cat. They're back in Florida."

I hadn't seen Seth since the night of the wedding. Paul had alluded to shit going down during their mission, and Cat had been involved. It wasn't that I didn't care about them, but how could I care about anything except getting Tessa back?

"Yeah, I'm on my way. Text me the details."

I arrived at the hospital, and when I finally found the room number where Paul told me they were, everyone was there: Paul, Joss, Brad, Nick, Leah, Nina, Mark, and his wife, Tracy. It was an S&R reunion and shit.

"Vinny!" Paul boomed when he saw me walk in through the door.

"If you wake Liam, I will hurt you," Autumn warned from the hospital bed. Gabe, who was standing beside her, gave Paul an evil glare.

"How are all of you in one room?" I asked.

"Not like we don't like tight spaces." Nick winked as he turned his head toward me.

"But we should all step into the hall and let you meet the newest member of the S&R family," Brad stated as he slapped me on the shoulder and walked to the door.

Everyone followed Brad's lead, and one by one, we exchanged hellos as they passed. The only people left in the room were me, Autumn, Gabe, and their little guy. "Congrats, you two."

"You look like shit," Gabe advised.

"Gabe!" Autumn scolded. "Language."

"Liam isn't even a day old. He has no clue what I'm saying," Gabe countered.

I moved closer and ran my finger along the little guy's cheek as Autumn held him. "He's bald like you," I teased, and looked up at Gabe.

"Runs in the family." He smiled.

"Do you want to hold him?" Autumn asked.

I smiled, and it felt as though it was the first time in three long ass months. "Yeah, I would love that." Autumn handed me the baby boy, and I looked down, watching him sleep as I held him.

"You know I saw Tessa at the doctor's, right?" Autumn asked.

Why would she bring this up? Of course I knew, but it was a sensitive subject. She had to know that.

"Yeah, I heard," I replied.

"I know we don't know if she is pregnant, but if she is, I'm hoping it's yours."

"What makes you think she's pregnant?"

"Because you usually don't go to the doctor's for your first appointment until after eight weeks. And she's been gone about that long, right?"

"Yeah, but maybe she was there for something else?"

"Like what? Birth control?" she questioned.

I wasn't sure if that thought was better or worse than the thought of her being pregnant with the asshole's baby. "Can we not talk about this?" I asked instead of answering her.

"Yeah, sorry. I just want you to know I'm here for her when she's out of that place. My ex-husband forced sex from me ..."

I nodded, already knowing that because Gabe and Paul had gone toe to toe with that asshole. He ended up dead, and Gabe and Paul were questioned by the police. Over drinks, they told the guys what had happened, and when they decided to start their self-defense business, it all made sense.

"Maybe I should have gotten you to show her some moves instead of using a gun," I stated.

"We don't know the circumstances," Gabe reminded me. "She might not have even had a chance to do anything. Given what you've said, and how I saw Tessa with you, she isn't there on her own."

"I know." I sighed. I had to keep believing it because that was the only thing that made sense still.

"Joss is working on it," Gabe assured. "Shit will go down, and you'll get your girl back."

"I'm sick of hearing that," I muttered, looking down at the baby in my arms. "Not the getting my girl back part, but Joss keeps telling me she's working on it and I don't believe her because nothing has happened."

"She opened an investigation, Vin. She can't tell you details because of that fact. It goes way deeper than just a friend checking on another friend," Gabe countered.

"But *you* know. Why is it that you know?"

"I know because Paul talks while at the range."

"So you know what's going on?"

He shook his head. "No, but like I said, it's an investigation. It only makes sense she can't tell you."

"Everything will work out," Autumn said, reaching up to cup my fingers that were holding her baby's head.

I looked down at Liam. If Tessa were pregnant, and if it were mine, I'd be over the fucking moon. Kids were never in my plan, but my plan changed when I met Tessa, and I was slowly realizing it. Spending time with Colton, and now this little guy, made me realize that no matter what happened, I wanted it all with Tessa. I didn't need the baby to be mine. I'd raise it as if it were my own. What I needed was Tessa and Colt back in my life, and then everything else would work itself out.

"Yeah, let's hope so," I replied.

"Lookie what we brought," Paul cooed as he and the gang walked back into the room. He was holding cigars.

"You can't smoke that in here," Autumn protested.

"It's chocolate, Auttie. Smoking will kill you, don't you know that?"

She rolled her eyes, and I looked over at Joss. She gave me a tight smile, and I wanted to ask her what was happening with the alleged case, but now that Gabe confirmed there was an investigation, I realized I needed to let my nagging rest.

"Want to hold him?" I asked Joss.

"Yes!" Paul boomed. "Give her baby fever."

Joss rolled her eyes in the direction of her husband. "We just got married."

"So?" He motioned to Gabe and Autumn. "These two ain't even married."

"Speaking of," Autumn spoke up. "Wedding will be in November. Maybe a week or so before Thanksgiving."

When I left the hospital to head home, I felt different.

Joss had told me she'd looked into Sebastian and red flags came up, but I didn't take it to mean there would be an investigation. Now that I knew there was, I was hopeful things would progress faster.

I opened up my texts to send one to Melony and share the news with her but stopped myself. I trusted her—she was Tessa's best friend

—but she also still worked for the asshole. I didn't want her to somehow slip and tell him or someone else that the Feds were looking into him.

That night I still didn't sleep like a baby, but I slept better knowing that one day soon, Tessa would be in my arms again.

THIRTY

Tessa

THE MOMENT THE DOOR SHUT BEHIND JOSS AND HER PARTNER, Sebastian turned to me, eyes glaring. "Office. Now!" he barked.

I didn't hesitate. I knew he was pissed, but since I also knew Joss was working on getting me out, I felt as though I could play up my façade with Sebastian. Somehow I needed him to want to marry me.

When we got up the stairs of his office, he spun me around and wrapped a hand around my throat. He growled, "So help me God, Tessa. If you fucking told the Feds anything, I will squeeze the life out of you right now."

"I didn't say anything," I lied.

"Are you fucking lying to me?"

Yes. "Don't you think if I told them anything about your business and what I saw that night, they would have taken you in?"

"What did you say then?"

"Can you let go of my neck and talk to me normally?"

He stared at me for a few beats, and I thought he wasn't going to let go, but then he did. He walked over to where he had a decanter of alcohol next to the bookshelves and poured himself two fingers of the amber liquor. He turned.

"I'm waiting."

"The woman fed asked me who I was and stuff. I told her I used to work for you at Red Diamond before we got involved. Then she asked me about my time there and what I did and yada-yada. She asked me if I knew Tony. I told her I met him once at a party here, and she asked if he ever went to the club and talked to me or any of the other girls. I told her no repeatedly and that I only met him that one time."

"What else?"

I thought for a moment trying to come up with more. "That's all."

He stared at me again, and I hoped Scarlett's acting was believable. "Are you lying to me?"

"No." I shook my head and walked the few feet to him. His gaze stayed glued to mine as I ran my hand down his chest. I needed to be sweet Tessa *and* seductive Scarlett at the same time. I needed him to think I was coming around and I wanted to be with him. Fuck, somehow I needed him to think I wanted to get married. "Why would I lie to you?"

"Because you want to leave me."

"I *wanted* to leave you," I fibbed. "But now that I'm pregnant, I want to stay."

"You do?"

"Colton needs a father figure in his life. So will this baby. I want a family and not a broken one either." That was the truth. But I didn't want to raise a child with this man. Even if he could provide for me like Valentina had said, my life wasn't crime. My life was watching *PAW Patrol* and baseball games. My life was lobster and steak dinners cooked by the only man I wanted to be with. My life was Vinny.

Sebastian took a sip of his drink and then set it on the cherrywood table between the two brown leather chairs near us. "You have a family now. You don't have to raise either of your kids alone again."

I smiled, trying to make it seem as real as possible. "Okay. I've also been talking to Valentina, and she told me what you did for her. You're a good man, and I know you'll be a good father." Just those twelve words on my tongue felt wrong, foreign. He may be a good man to some, but he wasn't to me. And there was no way I'd ever let him raise either one of my babies.

"I have to admit, Tessa Baby. The Feds coming here isn't good for me."

"Shh." I silenced him with a finger to his lips. "I don't want to know anything. It's better I don't so if they question me again, I have nothing to say."

He cupped my cheek. "You're learning. I like that."

And then I went for it. To get him to think I wanted to marry him, I needed to make the first move on occasion. At least, I hoped it worked. "You know what else you'd like?"

"What's that?" He slowly smiled.

I gently lowered to my knees.

For the next few days, I tried to help Valentina around the house. She was my ticket to freedom even if she didn't know it. She was the one who could get Sebastian to want to marry me if it was *her* idea. So, I was trying to be content. I was anything but happy, but the more I seemed to want to be here, the better my chances were.

"Whatcha makin'?" I asked Valentina, coming into the kitchen while Colt watched his latest *PAW Patrol* obsession.

"Arroz con pollo," she replied as she cut up a whole chicken.

"What's that?"

"Rice with chicken."

"Sounds delicious."

"Si, cariño. It's one of my favorites."

"Why haven't you made it before?" I asked, leaning a hip on the counter.

"It was my oldest son's favorite too, and it makes me sad."

"Oh? Why are you making it then?"

"Today would have been his birthday."

I smiled warmly at her and rubbed her back. "I'm sorry, Valentina. I don't know what I would do if something happened to Colt. What was his name?"

"Santiago."

"That sounds like a strong name."

"Si, he was very strong." She started to dice a red bell pepper after she washed her hands.

I moved to take the knife from her in a silent gesture for me to help. "How old would he have been today?"

"Thirty-five."

"Do you mind if I ask how he died?"

"No." She shook her head and started to dice a yellow onion. "He was shot."

The knife I was holding stopped mid-chop. "How?"

"My sons were in the business too."

"The coke business?"

"Si." Well, that made even more sense as to why she was loyal to Sebastian. "They ran the largest cocaine operation in Colombia, and other cartels wanted a piece of it. There was a war, and almost everyone died."

"I'm so sorry."

"I knew it would happen one day. My country isn't like your country. It's very dangerous."

"I'm sorry," I said again. "How did Sebastian get involved?"

"He was a buyer for here in Las Vegas, and when he heard what happened, he went to my country and saw the devastation, the people, the dead people. He cleaned up my town and helped a lot of people."

"So, he did it to keep his cocaine flowing?"

Valentina stopped chopping, and instead of answering me, she said, "Santiago's favorite dessert was Merengón de Fresas. I make for dessert."

I didn't ask why she was changing the subject. "What is merengue de frittata?"

She chuckled. "Merengón de Fresas. It's meringue, whipped cream, and strawberries—Santiago's favorite."

"Sounds delicious too."

"Si. It melts in your mouth."

"Can't wait. I'm happy to be learning all these recipes. Then I can make them for my kids and husband one day." Yes, I went there. Fingers were crossed.

"Husband?"

I shrugged. "Hopefully one day."

She started to pat the chicken with a paper towel and then seasoned it with salt and pepper. "You mean with Mr. Delarosa?"

I shrugged again. "Maybe? I'm hoping I don't keep having children out of wedlock. I've always wanted to get married. Have the big fancy wedding and honeymoon."

"That would be nice." She smiled.

"Yeah, and maybe before I get too fat to look good in a wedding dress." I laughed, pretending I thought it was funny when really I just wanted the *wedding* to be soon. I wasn't sure how Joss would know, but I had to trust her. Though, if this really happened and she didn't show, I'd have to marry the devil.

"You'll never be fat, cariño. Being with child is a beautiful thing."

"True. I can't wait to eat your strawberry dessert. Calories don't count now."

I wasn't sure if that was true or not. When I was pregnant before, I wasn't stuck in a house, so I was able to burn calories. Now, I probably didn't take three thousand steps each day. But the dessert sounded delicious, and I couldn't wait to try it.

"Put your faith in God's will, Jefe. You'll see that this is the best decision."

I only caught that line coming from Valentina's room as I passed by on my way to put Colton to bed. I didn't know who she was talking to, but Sebastian was the only other person here besides the guard at the front door.

I hurried to my room to put Colt to bed before I was caught eavesdropping.

Three long days later, Sebastian came home, smiling. It was unusual, to say the least. Not because I didn't see him smile, but because he was usually all business. In the time I'd been there, we'd never watched TV together, never had a glass of wine together—which was good considering I was pregnant, and I didn't like wine. In fact, we never did anything together except have sex. Colton and I had dinner with Valentina each night, and honestly, I didn't know when Sebastian ate because I rarely saw him in the kitchen. He'd come home, go to his office, do whatever he did, and then call for me to pleasure him. After he was done with me, he'd fall asleep, or sometimes he'd leave. Of course, I never asked questions. I didn't care.

But now he was smiling.

"You seem happy today," I observed as he poured himself a drink from the bar in the living room.

"It's because I am," he replied.

"Why's that?"

"That's for me to know and you to find out later."

I arched my brows. "Okay?"

He grinned some more. "Trust me, Tessa Baby."

I returned to helping Colton do an animal sound puzzle.

"In fact, let's do this now." Sebastian downed the amber liquor.

"Do what?" I questioned.

"Come." He reached out his hand for me.

I swallowed and took his hand. His office was a bad place to me and nothing good ever truly happened there, but I was trying to show him I wasn't scared of him anymore, so I let him help me off the couch and then lead me up the stairs and to his office while Valentina watched Colt. I was on alert as I watched him walk behind his desk.

"Sit." He gestured for me to take one of the high back chairs in front of his desk. I did. "Do you know I'm Catholic?" he asked.

I shook my head. "No. Do you go to church?"

He smiled. "Not as often as I should."

"Okay?"

"Do you know what's frowned upon in the Catholic church?"

"Murder?" I sassed.

He chuckled. "There's my feisty Tessa. I knew you were still in there."

"Just stating the obvious." For the past few days, I'd been really trying to make the first move, and even though I wanted to throw hateful words at him for just breathing, I hadn't because I needed the plan to work.

"Yes, I guess you're right. But do you know what else?"

I shrugged. "I'm not really religious."

"But you believe in God, yes?"

"Of course." I wasn't sure why he was bringing up God. Did murderers think that just because they were religious, God would save their souls when they died? I didn't think so.

"So do I, even though I don't go to Mass to recite a bunch of Hail Marys."

"Why are you talking to me about God?"

"Because." He stood and walked around the desk toward me. "We're having a baby, and I don't want to have a baby out of wedlock."

My mouth fell open. The plan worked. It fucking worked like a charm. "You want to marry me?"

He dropped to one knee and held up a massive oval cut diamond ring on a gold band. I didn't know how big the main diamond was, but I was sure it was going to cover two fingers. "I've always wanted to be a father, and I'm certain you will grow to love me. We can be a happy family."

Our gazes stayed locked, and I waited a few moments, pretending I was thinking it over. The sad part was I'd manipulated Valentina because she missed her sons. But I needed this. I just hoped Joss followed through.

"Well?" he prompted.

My gaze moved to the diamond and then back up to his blue eyes. I started to smile slowly. "Okay."

His eyes became huge. "You will?"

I nodded and smiled wider. "Yes."

Before I realized it, he engulfed me in a hug. "Our relationship might have started off on the wrong foot, but like you once told me, things happen for a reason. You won't regret this."

I hoped I wouldn't. This plan would either hasten my escape or seal my death, because if I had to marry him, there was only one way out. I couldn't live under his control forever.

"They do," I replied to the first part of his statement. "When do you want to get married? I'll be showing before we know it."

He slipped the ring onto my left hand. "Then we will make it soon."

"Will we have it here?" I questioned.

He thought for a moment. "No. There are too many people I want to invite to have it here."

I nodded. "Okay, then when?"

"I know a place. It can hold five hundred people."

"Five hundred people?" My eyes widened in shock.

"I know a lot of people, Tessa Baby."

"Okay, five hundred people then."

"And that includes your friends and family too."

I gave a tight smile, not because I didn't like the idea of my friends and family sharing my big day, but because if things went according to plan, this wouldn't be my big day. "It's okay," I replied. "They're my *old* friends and family. You and Valentina are my new ones."

"Even Melony?" he asked.

"Yes. I just used her to get my job at Red Diamond." I swallowed down my lie.

"Good. Now, because I'm not a very good Catholic boy, go get naked."

THIRTY-ONE

Vinny

Present Day

I looked around at the guests at Tessa's wedding. No one looked familiar. In the short amount of time I'd known her, the only people I'd met were Melony and Sophia, and I didn't see either one of them.

Melony hadn't told me she'd heard from Tessa. Maybe she didn't want to tell me Tessa was getting married? The last I heard from anyone was when Gabe told me he learned from Paul that Joss had opened an investigation. Sure, Joss had said she was looking into it and shit, but she'd failed. Tessa was getting married to this asshole, and I didn't know what would happen afterward.

As I looked around, I wondered why I was invited. Sebastian clearly knew about me since my little trip to his office at Red Diamond, so how would he *allow* me to be invited? And because the universe hated me, Sebastian walked down the aisle next to me with an older woman on his arm. I watched him lead her to the front row and then, like a beacon in the dead of night, he turned and locked eyes with me. He grinned, and I went rigid. Fuck, I hated him.

I narrowed my eyes as he walked toward me. I expected him to keep going, get ready for his fucking wedding, but instead, he stopped.

"I see you got the invitation."

Anger flowed through me. "Yeah, thanks for the invite."

"I have to admit, I didn't think you'd show."

I crossed my arms over my chest. "Then why did you invite me?"

He shrugged and said hello to someone who was passing by, then turned back to me. "To see how you still felt about her."

"Does she know I'm here?"

He slowly shook his head. "Nope. I want to see how she reacts to you, too."

"Is this a game to you?"

He grinned and stepped closer, getting within a few inches of my face as he whispered, "I admit that at first, it was. But this game has been taken to another level now that Tessa is pregnant with my baby."

"This isn't a game," I growled.

"Maybe. Maybe not. But who won her?" He took a step back and then turned and walked away, not letting me respond.

I wanted to go after him, tackle him to the ground and punch him repeatedly until he was on the brink of death. Instead, I watched Sebastian walk into the hotel and out of sight.

I'd had enough. My heart could no longer take the pain I was putting it through. Plus, he'd just confirmed Tessa was pregnant with *his* baby. I started to walk toward the door that Sebastian had entered but stopped when I heard a whistle. I turned around, looking for the source, and then grinned when I saw it. Instead of going through the door, I turned and walked down a walkway around the building.

"What are you doing here?" I asked.

Paul grinned. "I could ask you the same."

"I got an invitation," I advised.

"Really? I kinda did too."

"What does that mean?"

"Walk with me." He started walking toward the front of the building.

"The wedding's starting soon."

"I know," he called over his shoulder.

"Where are we going?" Paul didn't respond as I followed him. He walked into the front doors of the hotel and then into another door off to the side. At first, I didn't know what the room was, but then I noticed there were rows of luggage. "Are we in the bellman's closet?"

"Yep," he replied.

"Why—"

Joss stepped out from the back of the room. "Why didn't you tell me you were coming?"

I balked. "Tell you I was coming?"

"Well, tell me you had contact with her."

"I didn't have contact with Tessa. The invitation appeared on my doorstep last night." I crossed my arms over my chest. I didn't like that she was interrogating me.

"You should have told me."

"Honestly, I wasn't sure I'd come," I admitted and looked to the ground. I made the decision this morning when I was staring at the names on the invitation of Teresa Stewart marrying Sebastian Delarosa. I needed to see her one last time.

"I'm glad you did come."

My eyes snapped back to her. "What?"

"I couldn't tell you before, but we have a plan." Joss grabbed an earpiece off of the desk behind her.

"What plan?"

"A plan to get Sebastian and his associates together so we can bust them."

"Tessa knows the plan?" I questioned.

"More or less. She doesn't know the details."

"Okay, so what's the plan?"

Joss walked toward me. "Let me get you mic'd up, and then we'll go over what I need you to do."

THIRTY-TWO
Tessa

I'D DREAMED ABOUT THIS DAY AS A LITTLE GIRL.

Over the last week, my life had gone from doing nothing in a house all day to trying to plan a wedding in a week. Yes, a week. Sebastian had gotten it in his mind that I was going to blow up to the size of the house. He didn't say those words exactly, but when I mentioned that I hoped it would be sooner rather than later because I wasn't showing yet, he put the wedding on a fast-track.

That was what I needed. Even so, I worried it wasn't enough time for Joss to find out and come up with a plan. I hadn't heard from her, which was expected, but I also hadn't seen her while I was getting dressed in the bridal suite at the hotel. Joss had told me she'd know when the wedding would be, but I had no idea how.

While I was getting my hair done, I hoped Joss would come in and tell me she was here. She didn't. While a makeup artist did my makeup, I constantly looked in the mirror to see if Joss would walk in. She didn't. And as I slipped on the white dress that looked like something out of a Disney princess movie, I wanted Joss to come in. She didn't.

"Oh, cariño. You look so beautiful." Valentina beamed.

I smiled at her through the reflection of the floor length mirror. "Thank you."

"I can't believe this happened so fast."

"Me either," I admitted.

The day after Sebastian proposed, Valentina and a guard took me to get a dress. It was off the rack, and honestly, I didn't care. Nothing I planned for this wedding would be what I ultimately wanted. The dress was a halter style princess dress. After it was purchased, I was measured, and the dress was sent to be altered. When we got home, a wedding planner came knocking, and flowers were picked. I chose white roses. I thought it was only going to be my bouquet, but Valentina made sure to order a shitload for the reception tables and the ceremony. When she was told how much it would cost to rush the order, she didn't bat an eye.

The planner helped me pick a cake, told me she'd get a DJ, and I chose the invitations with her. The one thing I didn't pick was the location. Sebastian had done that himself because he said someone owed him. I didn't question him. The next day, the invitations arrived, and Sebastian gave Valentina a list of who he wanted to invite. Because money was no object, she overnighted all the invitations since the wedding was fast approaching. No one from my side was invited, but it had to be that way. My parents knew nothing about what was going on, and the only people I'd want to come were Melony and Sophia, and I couldn't have them involved.

"And this guy is so handsome." Valentina bent in front of Colton.

There was a knock on the door, and I held my breath, hoping it was Joss. Mateo entered after Valentina opened the door.

"It's time."

Everything stopped, and I wanted to cry.

Joss didn't come through.

Joss didn't stop this.

Joss wasn't here.

A tear slid down my cheek before I realized it and I wiped it away.

"Don't cry, cariño," Valentina said. "You'll mess up your makeup."

"I know. I'm just so ... happy," I lied.

She hugged me. "This will be the happiest day of your life. Mr. Delarosa is taking you somewhere special for your honeymoon."

"He is?" I looked into her eyes.

"Si."

"But ..." I looked down at Colton who was playing with a fidget spinner.

"You and Colton of course. He's made arrangements."

"He has?"

"Si."

"Okay." I smiled. "Can you give me a minute?"

"I'll stay with her," Mateo spoke up.

"Okay. I'll see you down there." She hugged me again and then turned to leave. Another guard was standing outside the doors and started to escort her toward the elevators.

I expected Mateo to step into the hall and close the door behind him, but he didn't. "I'll just be a minute."

He closed the door with him still inside the room. "We don't have long."

"What?" I whispered. I looked at Colton, who had switched from his spinner to his iPad.

Mateo walked toward me, and I took a few steps back. "When you go down there, everything's going to change."

"Okay?" I questioned, still retreating.

"I did some digging and learned that the FBI agent who came to visit you a few weeks ago is the wife of your boyfriend's friend."

Oh shit! "Does Sebastian know who she is too?"

He stopped walking and shook his head. "No. I'm undercover DEA and sent word to the FBI that I was working the case. Told them about the wedding, and my handler informed me a bust was going down today."

"You're DEA?"

"Yes."

"Wow," I breathed, trying to wrap my head around who he really was. "And Joss came through?"

"Yes."

I perked up. "What do we do?"

"In a few minutes, an agent is going to come in for Colton. They will take him, and you will proceed with the wedding. When Sebastian asks where Colton is, tell him he was having a meltdown and was overwhelmed, so a staff member is watching him. He won't question it because he doesn't understand the difference between a child with autism and a child without it. He doesn't realize you can't just let anyone watch your child because they have to know how to take care of him and communicate with him, so any staff member would be okay in his book."

I nodded. "Yes, but I have to marry Sebastian?"

Mateo shook his head. "No. Everything will happen before you exchange vows. When it does, an agent will be there to protect you and take you to where Colton is in a safe room."

"Okay." I instantly became nervous. My palms were sweaty, my heart was racing, and I was excited. "I'm ready."

"Let me—" There was a knock on the door, and Mateo went to it. He opened it silently, and I heard him ask, "What are you doing here?"

I couldn't hear what was said or who was at the door, but then Mateo stepped back and opened it fully.

My world stopped.

"Miss me?" Vinny asked.

I stared at him for a few beats, not able to move my feet. How was he here? Why was he here? "Yes," I whispered.

"I've missed you too," he admitted as he walked toward me.

"You have?" I faintly heard the door close, but all I could focus on was the man in front of me. The man I thought I'd never see again.

"Like fucking crazy."

A happy tear slid down my cheek. "You have no idea how much I need to hear that."

"What if I tell you I'm here to help get you out?"

"I'd say I better not be dreaming. Because if it's a dream, I hope I never wake up from it."

He grinned, and my heart melted. "It's not a dream."

"How?"

"How about you kiss me, and then I tell you?"

I didn't hesitate any longer. I rushed into his arms and planted my mouth on his. The kiss was demanding.

Like our lives depended on it.

Like it had been years since our lips had last met.

Like our mouths were starving for one another.

His tongue slipped into my mouth and I melted. I liquefied into a puddle of mush because no kiss I'd ever had with Sebastian could or would compare to the way Vinny was kissing me now.

My fingers gripped the back of his head, pulling him closer. I had never wanted anyone as much as I wanted Vinny and I needed him closer to me. So close that no air could come between us. So close that we were breathing the same oxygen to live. We didn't break apart until someone cleared his throat. I'd been too wrapped up in this man to hear the door open.

We pulled apart, and I looked over Vinny's shoulder to see Mateo was back. "We need to go before Sebastian wonders what's going on."

I looked up into Vinny's brown eyes. "I have to go pretend to marry another guy."

He smiled tightly. "I know, but I'm going to be waiting with Colt for you. I'm never letting you out of my sight again."

We gazed at each other, and something told me to tell him, tell him how I felt about him. Because even though there was a plan, anything could happen. What if I was shot? What if Sebastian grabbed me and held me like a hostage and the nightmare didn't end? What if I never got to tell Vinny I loved him? I couldn't let this moment pass.

"Vin—"

"Before you say anything, I want to tell you I've never loved anyone except you, sweets. I don't care that we haven't been together in the last few months, I've loved you every minute of every day since the night your Giants beat my Dodgers and we almost kissed. I knew then that I never wanted to let you go."

Tears started to stream down my face again, and Vinny brushed them away with his thumbs, leaving both of his hands cupping my cheeks. He kissed me softly.

"I've loved you since the first time I watched you carry Colton to your car."

"Yeah?"

I nodded slightly. "And I haven't stopped."

"Good. Let's get this situation over with so I can *show* you how much I love you."

I hesitated for a moment. "I'm pregnant."

He smiled tightly. "I know."

"I don't know whose it is."

"We can figure it out later."

"What if it's his?"

"No matter what, sweets, I will love you and both of your children until the day I die. It doesn't matter if my blood runs through their veins or not. What matters is that I'm not going anywhere."

"Okay." I nodded.

Mateo cleared his throat again. "We really need to go."

I stepped out of Vinny's embrace and turned to Colton, who was still engrossed in his iPad. I compressed his ears so he'd look into my eyes. "Vinny's going to take you to get some juice. Do you want some juice?"

He started to flap his little hands.

"Come on, little man." Vinny scooped him up and then kissed my lips briefly.

Before he stepped away, I kissed Colton on the cheek and then watched the two people who held my heart in their hands walk out of the suite.

"You need to make sure you don't let on that you know what's going to happen," Mateo stated as we rode the elevator down to the main floor.

"I know. Will there be a sign or something?"

"No, but when the agents move in, you need to get behind the priest."

"Really?"

"Have you seen the area where you're getting married?"

"No." I shook my head.

"Sebastian set it up so there's a square stage in the center where you will be so everyone can see you. The chairs are in a circle."

"But why do I need to get behind the priest?"

"He's an agent."

"Really?"

"All the staff have been replaced with either FBI or DEA."

"Wow," I breathed.

"You can do this, Tessa. I've watched you be strong for months. Just hang in there for a few more minutes."

"I will," I assured him. "There's nothing I would like to see more than Sebastian behind bars."

The doors opened after the elevator stopped on the main floor. I felt different, more confident, more aware of what the future held. Sebastian no longer held all the cards. *I* was about to fuck his life up.

Just before Mateo and I were about to step outside, I stopped and looked up at him. "Maybe you should walk me down the aisle?"

He grinned. "I would love to."

I hooked my arm in his, and he gave a nod to someone. Music started to play in the courtyard, and we began walking. I smiled as we walked, and it was the first one in over three and a half months that was real. When my gaze met Sebastian's at the other end of the aisle, it didn't falter. Things were finally going my way. I'd finally outsmarted him.

When Mateo and I got to the end of the aisle, Sebastian took my arm. "You look stunning," he stated.

"Thank you," I replied with another huge grin on my face.

"Where's Colton?"

"He was having a moment and needed to stay in the room."

"Oh, okay."

Sebastian walked me up the stairs, and I briefly wondered as I

looked at the priest how the Feds were able to put an agent undercover as the officiant. Surely Sebastian had to know who he'd hired to
marry us, especially since he was supposed to be Catholic. But maybe
he didn't because we weren't getting married in a church. In fact,
since the wedding was planned on such short notice, we hadn't met
with a priest beforehand.

It didn't matter because the wedding was about to be canceled.

Sebastian and I turned toward each other and held hands. A
moment of panic went through me as I realized he was going to hold
my hands for the ceremony. We never had a rehearsal, never did any
of the traditional things to get prepared for the wedding, and his
friends, I assumed, were in the crowd because neither one of us had
bridesmaids or groomsmen.

"Heavenly father, we're gathered here today ..." I tuned the *priest*
out as he said a prayer. I wondered when everything was going to go
down. The minutes felt like hours as I waited and waited and waited
some more. When Mateo told me the plan, I expected everything to
happen quickly. Maybe they were waiting to get Sebastian's guard
down? I didn't know, but finally, just when I thought nothing was
going to happen, all hell broke loose.

"Freeze, FBI!"

I turned in the direction of the voice to see that it was Joss. The
sound of people moving and weapons being drawn echoed in the air,
and I moved. I moved so fast, breaking my grasp from Sebastian, and
running behind the *priest*, his weapon drawn on Sebastian. Sebastian
had his hands up, and so did the other people who had guns pointed
at them too. Hands grabbed my waist from behind, and I turned and
screamed before realizing it was Paul. I didn't know where he had
come from or how he had gotten up onto the raised stage.

"Come with me," he ordered. Paul stepped off the stage and turned
to help me down. Just before we ran to the door, I turned to see
Sebastian looking at me. I lifted my left hand and wished him goodbye
with my middle finger.

Checkmate, asshole.

THIRTY-THREE
Vinny

KISSING TESSA AGAIN WAS LIKE A WEIGHT BEING LIFTED OFF MY shoulders. Telling Tessa I loved her was a weight off my heart. But having Tessa tell me that she loved me was everything.

Colton and I waited in a hotel room that Joss gave me a key for. I wasn't sure how long it was going to take for everything to go down, but I'd wait forever. For so long I had been angry Joss didn't tell me what was going on. I thought nothing would ever happen. It made sense she couldn't tell me everything because it was an open investigation; I just wished she would have let me know something.

About twenty-five minutes later, there was a knock on the door. I moved to it, looked in the peephole and smiled as I opened the door.

"That was amazing!" Paul boomed from behind Tessa.

I didn't pay him any mind as I grabbed Tessa's hand and pulled her to me, bringing her against my body in a hug. "Are you okay?"

She nodded against my chest. "Better than okay."

Paul closed the door behind him. "Joss said to stay here until she comes."

Tessa and I broke apart. She moved to Colton, who was sitting in the center of the bed with his iPad. "Hey, Slugger. Did you have fun with Vinny?"

While Tessa made sure Colton was fine, I turned to Paul. "How were you even involved today? You're FBI now?"

"No." He shook his head. "Plan was for me to get Colton, remember?"

"But you got Tessa," I countered. "That was part of the mission?"

"Not originally, but since you took care of Colton, Joss figured it would be better if Tessa went with someone she knew."

"Makes sense."

"I wish I could get out of this dress," Tessa muttered as she walked toward the closet near the bathroom. She opened the door. "Yes! They have a robe. I'm going to slip into that, okay?"

I grinned. "Need help?"

"Actually, I do." She winked.

I didn't hesitate to follow her into the bathroom. Once the door was closed, I pulled her into my arms and pressed my lips to hers. I'd gone too many days without her. There was a lot of catching up to do.

When we'd first met, I'd felt as though she was looking into my soul. Maybe it was because I was looking into the eyes of the woman who I'd fall in love with. "I really missed you, more than you can imagine. I was going crazy."

"I've missed you so much. You have no idea," she replied.

"We can talk about all that later. Let's get you out of this dress."

"Please." She turned around, and I unzipped it. She started to step out of the poofy thing.

"I never thought I'd be taking you out of a wedding dress you were going to marry another guy in."

"I was never going to marry him."

"I'm glad it all worked out."

"Me too. Since that night, I kept trying to figure out how to leave."

"I kept trying to figure out how to get you back."

"I'm sorry." She sighed and hung her head.

I spun her to face me and lifted her chin with my finger. "It's not your fault."

"It is."

"How?" I furrowed my brows.

"Because I went to check out his bathroom to compare it to Mark's and ..." She paused and looked off to the side. "It was stupid, a silly idea that made my life a nightmare. I walked in on him killing a guy."

"You saw him kill a guy?" I asked, my eyes wide.

She nodded.

"We really don't need to talk about this until you're ready."

"Okay," Tessa whispered.

I pulled her against me, wrapping my arms around her, and inhaled her cotton candy scent. "Still smell fucking delicious."

She chuckled against my chest. "So do you."

After a few moments more, we broke apart, and I handed her the white terry cloth robe that was sitting on the counter, and she slipped it on. We kissed once more before I opened the door and we went back into the room. Paul was looking at his phone in a chair by the window, and Colt was still watching his cartoon on the bed.

"Joss just texted. They've made all the arrests, and she'll come up here soon," Paul stated as he put his phone back in his pocket.

"What's the plan after she gets here?" Tessa asked as she sat on the end of the bed.

"I don't know," Paul replied.

I walked to Colton. "You hungry, little man?" He started to flap his hands. "You want chicken strips?" He started to hum and rock back and forth in excitement. I turned my head toward Paul. "Can we order room service?"

Paul shrugged. "Sure. FBI's paying."

My gaze moved to Tessa, and I was about to ask her if she was hungry, but I realized she was staring at me. "What?" I asked.

"Nothing." She wiped her cheeks.

"Are you crying?"

"No." She started to cry some more.

I moved to her and brought her in for another hug. "Hey, it's okay. You're safe."

"It's not that."

"What's the matter then?"

She looked up at me. "It's nothing bad."

"Then why are you crying?"

"You."

"Me?" I balked.

"You're so good with Colt. Sebastian didn't even utter a word to him or try to the entire time we were at his house."

I brought her against my chest again. "That's because he's an idiot."

"I can think of worse words than *idiot* to describe him," she muttered.

I chuckled slightly. "Me, too."

"Me three," Paul chimed in.

"Let's get us some room service and wait for Joss. Then we'll go home," I suggested.

Tessa looked up at me again. "Do I even have a home?"

"You don't know about your apartment?" She shook her head. "All your stuff was moved, and it's been rented to someone else."

She was silent for a few moments. "I figured something like that would happen, but I didn't know for sure. Do you know where my belongs and furniture are?"

"No," I admitted.

"What am I going to do? I have nothing."

"You and Colt can stay with me."

"We can't impose."

"Tessa." I sighed. "Do you think I'd let you out of my sight right now?"

"I mean, we can't just live with you."

"You can until you get back on your feet."

"Back on my feet?" She chuckled sarcastically. "I'm homeless, clothes-less, and jobless. Plus, I'm pregnant."

"We'll figure this out."

"You have a lot of friends, Tessa. None of us are going to let you and Colton live on the street or starve," Paul stated.

"See? Don't worry." I kissed her lips. "Let's—"

There was a knock on the door, and Paul got out of the chair and went to it. After checking the peephole, he opened it. "Gorgeous."

He stepped aside, and Joss entered. "How are you?" she asked Tessa.

"I'm good. Probably in shock, but I'm good."

"You're free to go home now. I'll be in touch later tonight or tomorrow to get your statement."

"We'll stop and get some food, and then we'll head to my place," I stated.

"You want me to go like this?" Tessa stepped back and motioned the length of her body.

"Do you want to put your dress back on?" I asked.

"Hell no," she snapped.

I grabbed my suit jacket that was lying next to the TV. "Put this on, and we'll hurry you downstairs. We'll go through a drive-thru for food." Tessa took the jacket from me and went into the bathroom.

"What happened down there?" I asked Joss.

"Actually, everything went smoothly and according to plan. I'm sure it's because if they started shooting, they'd look guilty, but we have a lot of evidence. Mateo has worked for Sebastian for a long time and has gathered a lot. Plus ..." Joss trailed off.

"Plus what?" I questioned.

"Did Tessa tell you why Sebastian kept her?"

"Because she saw him kill a guy?"

Joss nodded. "We have a solid case."

"Good."

Tessa stepped out of the bathroom, and I almost fell over. She was stunning with her hair up and what looked to be only my jacket on her. It went to her knees, and lord, if the sight didn't make me hard.

"Ready?" I asked. She nodded and went to gather up Colton, but I stopped her. "I'll carry him."

"Okay."

After we said our goodbyes to Paul and Joss, Tessa, Colton and I got into my car. Mateo had given Joss Colton's car seat.

"I can't believe Mateo was undercover DEA," Tessa stated as I drove us toward Las Vegas. Colton was in the backseat on his iPad.

"That's the guy who let me in the room you were getting dressed in?"

"Yeah." She nodded. "He was like the main bodyguard."

"Really?"

"Yeah. I'm still in shock about everything."

"Joss mentioned he worked for Sebastian for a long time."

"What I don't understand is how he let Sebastian ..."

"Let him do what?" I questioned. Tessa started to cry, and I squeezed her knee. "Hey, it's okay. It's all over."

"I know." She sniffed. "It's just ... Every night ..."

"You don't need to continue. I think I understand what you mean."

Tessa's tear-stained face turned toward me. "You're not mad?"

"How can I be mad?"

"That I ..."

"Whatever happened in that place was out of your control."

"I know, but—"

"But let's talk about something else."

She paused for a moment. "Okay. What?"

"Well, Autumn had her baby."

Tessa's eyes brightened. "She did?"

"Last week."

"Oh my God, I want to go see them."

"We can go tomorrow maybe."

She gasped. "Oh my God, how are Melony and Sophia?"

"They're hanging in there. They were as confused as I was about the whole ordeal."

"I want to see them too."

"We can do whatever you want." I patted her knee. I didn't know exactly what she went through at Sebastian's, but feeling her skin after all this time made me want to be buried deep inside her again. I hadn't been with anyone since our night together. I couldn't.

"You know, Sebastian had this housekeeper I kinda got close with. I hope she's okay."

"If she wasn't involved in anything criminal, I'm sure Mateo took care of her. From what I gather, he's got a handle on things."

"If she isn't involved in anything, I think she and Sophia would be good friends."

"Oh yeah?"

Tessa smiled. "I can picture them like the *Golden Girls*."

"Sophia needs someone. Hopefully, it will work out."

"Yeah."

We were silent for a few miles. "What do you want to eat?"

She thought for a moment. "Raising Cane's. I've been craving it since that night."

"What the lady wants, the lady gets." I winked.

After going through the drive-thru, we headed toward my house. As we got closer, it dawned on me that I'd never had a woman over to my place before. Except for my housecleaner, of course.

"So, ahh—" I started as I pulled into my garage.

"Wait. Colton doesn't have his nightlight. He can't sleep without it."

A thought popped into my head as we sat in my SUV in the garage. "I have an idea. Let's get inside, eat, and all that needs to be done before bed. I'll take care of it."

"I don't even have clothes or anything."

"You know who would bring you clothes?"

She stared at me for a beat. "Who?"

"Your best friend." I reached into my pocket and pulled out my cell. "Here, call her. Ask her to bring you some clothes. I'll grab Colton."

Tessa smiled and took the phone. "Okay."

While she made the call, I carried Colton and the food into the house. "So, buddy, this is where you're going to live. It's not like your two last places, but we'll have fun. I love your mommy more than anything, and all the bad stuff is behind us. I'm also your teacher, and I'm going to teach you everything. Starting with volleyball."

I sat Colton in a chair at my kitchen island and took out the chicken strip meal that was his. When I got up this morning, I thought I would watch Tessa marry the devil. Instead, she was back with me, and I was feeding her son fried chicken.

Today was amazing.

THIRTY-FOUR

Tessa

I HUNG UP THE PHONE AFTER TALKING TO MELONY FOR TEN MINUTES. She was getting both Colton and me the necessities and then she would be on her way.

When I walked into the house from the garage door, I walked into a kitchen and stopped at the sight. Vinny was sitting across from Colton, both of them eating chicken, and my heart swelled. I'd seen them eat together before, but it still made me happy. The longer I stared, the more I thought about how this could have been my last three and a half months.

Instead, it wasn't.

"Come on. It's getting cold," Vinny stated with a mouthful of food. In the time I was on the phone with Melony, Vinny had changed into a pair of basketball shorts and a tank top that displayed his muscles. I'd missed those arms.

I grinned and moved to him, grabbed his face and planted my lips on his.

"What was that for?" he asked.

"Everything." I moved to my seat to see a T-shirt and a pair of boxers sitting next to my food.

"I figured you'd be more comfortable in that instead of my jacket until Melony gets here."

"See?" I beamed. "You're the best."

"The best is yet to come, sweets." He grinned at me and then took a bite of his chicken.

God, I hoped he was right.

There was a knock on the door. I stood back, anxiously waiting to make sure it was Melony. To my surprise, it was Mel and Sophia. I rushed to them and gave them both the biggest hugs I could manage.

"I missed you both so much." A tear slid down my cheek.

"We're happy you're back," Sophia replied.

"It really hasn't been the same without you," Melony stated.

"You have no idea." I moved back to allow them to come into Vinny's house. It was a two-story tract home. I hadn't been upstairs yet, but what I could tell was it was a standard home with granite countertops and a two-car garage. To be honest, I expected it to be more lavish, given that he drove a nice car. It was nice, but at the same time, typical. Like a teacher would own.

Melony handed the bag from Target to me. "You two sit while I change and get Colton ready for bed."

Vinny showed me upstairs where Colton could sleep. After his bath, I put Colt to bed. When I entered the room, it was like Christmas. Red and green lights danced on the ceiling and walls, and I almost cried again. It might not be the blue waves from Colton's night light, but the movement of the lights would calm him. It was perfect. Vinny was perfect.

When I returned back downstairs, dressed in pajamas, my three friends were in Vinny's living room laughing. I had to pause for a minute and remind myself that I wasn't dreaming. I was home. I was with my people.

I was back where I belonged.

I stood at the bottom of the stairs, taking them all in. Vinny's gaze moved to mine, and he motioned for me to come to him. I didn't hesitate. I sat down beside him on his leather couch, and he pulled me against him, wrapping his arms around me.

"Vinny was just telling us what happened this evening," Melony stated.

"And you thought it was funny?"

"No," Sophia replied. "We laughed because Sebastian thought he'd won."

"He invited me," Vinny stated.

My eyes became huge. "He did? I thought you were there because of Joss?"

"Nope. Sebastian put the invitation on my doorstep because he wanted me to watch you marry him. Paul saw me there and took me to Joss, and then I found out the plan and was able to help."

"I hope Sebastian doesn't know where you live," I confessed. "But Mateo did a lot of stuff for him, so he probably delivered it, and given that Mateo was undercover ..."

"Well, hopefully, you'll never have to see that fucker again," Melony responded.

"What about you?" I asked. "Are you still dancing?"

"Yeah, but I'm starting at another club Thursday."

"Which one?"

"Silverthorne."

"I don't know what I'm going to do," I confessed. "I'm obviously not going back to Red Diamond, but I have nothing else."

"We don't need to think about that right now," Vinny stated. He'd said that to me before, but I was still worried. "We just need to focus on getting you and Colton back in the groove of things. Plus, Colt needs to go back to school."

"Sebastian had a teacher for him. We tried to keep up with his previous goals."

"Really?" Vinny balked. "Also, don't forget I'm still his kindergarten teacher."

"You are?"

"Of course. The school year started a few weeks ago, and since you said he's had a teacher, he'll be on track to meet his goals. It's you I'm worried about."

"I'm fine," I lied.

Sophia leaned forward and placed her hand on my knee. "You're not. Whatever happened blew out the light in your eyes, but we'll get it back just like everything else. You have us, and we're here to take care of you."

I smiled warmly at her. "Thank you."

"And," Melony cut in, "when you're ready to tell us what happened, we're here for you then too."

I stared at the two women for a few moments as I thought about everything. "I'll tell you now. While I hated every minute of it, I don't think everything has sunk in. Maybe I need to get it off my chest?"

"Okay." Sophia leaned back against the couch she and Melony were on. "Take your time."

I proceeded to tell them everything from the night of the party when I went to look for the bathroom until the moment Vinny walked into the hotel suite this evening. I didn't go into details about the sex with Sebastian because it wasn't needed and they knew better than to think I would sleep with him willingly. The entire time I recounted the ordeal, Vinny held me as tight as he could. I couldn't imagine what he must have been thinking to know I'd been with another man, but there was nothing we could do about it since it was never my choice.

That night after Melony and Sophia went home, I took a shower in

Vinny's master bath. I needed to wash off everything from the last three and a half months. When I crawled into Vinny's bed, and he wrapped his strong arms around me, I instantly fell asleep and had the best night's sleep in over three months.

A week passed, and I realized Vinny was right: Colton was more resilient with the bouncing around than I was. He was starting to smile more as though he knew we were in a good place again. I no longer felt as though I was walking on eggshells, worried that a man would order me to his room, and when Vinny came home each night, I was excited to see him walk through the doors.

I still had no job, but my days weren't spent sitting around doing nothing. While Colton and Vinny were at school, I researched online colleges for hotel management. I even put in applications at all the hotels on the Strip to work the front desks. I was hopeful that one of those would pan out.

I sold the diamond engagement ring from Sebastian through a jewelry broker. The money I received for the massive diamond was enough to keep Colton and me afloat for a few months, but Vinny still insisted we live with him. I didn't argue because I was certain if I didn't have his arms around me each night, I would wake up back at Sebastian's.

Joss took my statement, and I recounted everything for her. Because Sebastian was a drug lord, there was fear I might be in danger. However, Joss had somehow worked it that my statement was sealed. If they needed it for Sebastian's trial, then I would be put into protective custody until it was over. Joss didn't go into detail, but she was hopeful that Mateo's evidence and testimony would be enough.

Also, I found out Mateo never killed Brent. Mateo used my pregnancy as a distraction and took Brent home, telling him to never show his face at Red Diamond again because if Sebastian ever saw him again, he wouldn't hesitate to kill him *and* Mateo. Melony said his friends still came in, but she never saw Brent.

Also, through victim services, I had to have an STD test, given my ordeal. Thankfully, it came back clean. I still have to meet with a therapist for a few weeks or more, depending on how everything goes. I've only had one appointment, but it was good. I was able to recount everything and get it off my chest. While all my friends and Vinny were there for me, I still couldn't tell them the details. But the therapist had no emotional connection with me and I was able to let it all out. When I left the appointment, it was as though a tiny bit of everything was lifted.

After putting Colton to bed, Vinny and I started a ritual of climbing into *our* bed. He made sure to tell me he'd never shared it with another woman before. That made me feel special. Most nights we watched either the Giants or the Dodgers, or we flipped between the two games, but the season was coming to an end in just another month.

Tonight, as Vinny and I laid in bed, I knew it was time. He'd been supportive the entire time, hadn't even mentioned sex, but I wanted it, and I wanted it with him. I wanted Vinny to erase Sebastian's touch.

Figuring I had to make the first move, I went into the walk-in closet and stripped myself of my pajamas. I grabbed my Giants jersey, slipped it on and walked back into the bedroom where Vinny was watching *his* Dodgers.

His brown gaze slid from the TV to where I stood with my arm on the wall and my hand on my hip. "What are you doing?"

"I just want to make sure you know where I stand."

"What do you mean?"

"I lied to you when I said we'd always have the Dodgers."

He grinned. "I know. You've been making me watch the Giants on and off for a week now."

"But you have to admit, I look better in orange and black, right?"

Vinny hesitated for a moment. "Well, to be fair, I haven't seen you in Dodger blue."

"And you never will." I chuckled.

"Come on? Don't you want to see if blue would look better on you?"

"Don't you want to see if *nothing* would look better on me?" I countered.

His eyes widened, and he whispered, "Yes."

I moved toward him and lifted my arms above my head. "Then let's see if you're right."

Vinny faltered for a moment, and then reached down and lifted the jersey off of me. "I'm right."

He pulled the covers back, and I crawled onto the bed and straddled his hips after sliding his basketball shorts off, leaving him naked like I was. "You look better in nothing too."

"Are you sure about this?"

I nodded. "I need this. I need *you*."

"You have me, sweets."

"I know," I agreed. "But I need all of you. I need to remember your touch and not his."

He stared at me for a beat. "I'll do whatever you need me to do."

"Then make love to me. Make it so that you're the last man to touch me everywhere."

Without further hesitation, Vinny lifted me and flipped us so I was on my back looking up at him. His mouth descended on mine, his tongue urgent as it parted my lips. "I'm going to taste you everywhere."

I moaned in response. His mouth returned to my lips, tasting, devouring, claiming. He continued down to the valley between my breasts, stopping to suck each one into his mouth again. His lips felt right, perfect against my skin as he sucked each nipple into his mouth, making each one pucker. With each swipe of his tongue, I tried to focus on Vinny and not the past. Of course it was different, and honestly, not hard to focus on the man currently loving on my body.

Vinny's hand reached between my legs, and I gasped as he touched my clit with his finger. I arched my back off the bed. While it had been months since I felt his fingers between my legs, my body reacted as though it knew it was him. My arousal flowed and coating his hand, and while he rubbed the nub of nerves, he continued his trail with his tongue. He licked his way to my stomach, dipping into my belly button and going further south until his lips met my center.

At the first swipe of his tongue against my pussy, he noted, "Sweet like fucking candy."

I didn't respond as I enjoyed the feel of him working and tasting me. He flicked my clit, nipped it with his teeth and brought me closer and closer to coming with each second. He spread me open wider, and while he used his fingers to work my core, he continued to use his mouth too.

"I've fucking missed this," he stated against my heat.

"Me, too," I panted.

My body started to tighten as I was on the verge of shattering. Vinny pumped his fingers faster, hooking them just right to make my back arch off the bed again as his tongue worked my bud. I clenched his head with my thighs as my orgasm raced through me, and I moaned with pleasure.

Vinny rose off his belly, licked his lips and crawled back up my body. Our eyes were locked as he bent his head down, capturing my mouth with his. My tongue darted out to taste myself on his lips and tongue. I moaned again, running my hands over the light hair on his chest and down his rippling washboard abs to grab his cock. I pumped him a few times with my hand, and he pulled out of my grasp and eased himself between my thighs. He pressed the tip of his shaft against my entrance while looking into my eyes.

"You okay?" Inch by inch he slid inside.

I nodded. "Yes. This is what I need."

He kissed my lips again. "Me, too, sweets."

He increased his speed, working me deep, and I knew at that

moment it was Vinny, not Duane, who was making love to me. I wasn't sure if I'd actually ever meet Duane Wood in bed because he was on a break—hopefully for good—and Scarlett was no longer in existence. I never wanted to be Scarlett again. She died the moment I stepped out of that wedding dress.

Our bodies had a light coating of sweat as our hips rocked in sync. I moaned, and he groaned, and the pleasure grew so intense that I knew another orgasm was coming.

"I'm close," I panted.

"Me, too," he groaned.

Vinny rested his weight on his left forearm, continuing to pump into me as he reached between my legs and rubbed my clit. He claimed my mouth again, and while he massaged my nub harder and faster, grinding his hips into me as fast as he could, I moaned his name as I came beneath him. He groaned, and came a few moments after.

"I love you," he said into my ear as we stayed connected.

I smiled. "I love you too. Always have and always will."

He leaned up and stared into my eyes. "Forever?"

I nodded. "Forever."

THIRTY-FIVE

Vinny

Four Months Later ...

A LOT HAD HAPPENED IN THE LAST FOUR MONTHS.

Gabe and Autumn got married three weeks ago, Tessa was about to pop, and Seth and Cat moved to Las Vegas and were planning a wedding. Colton started making even greater strides in his progress. He began to verbalize here and there, which was huge. It meant he was hopefully going to be able to one day verbally communicate with us. We also threw him a birthday party and everyone came, including some kids from school. Neither the Giants nor the Dodgers won the World Series, but it didn't keep Tessa and me from having our continued rivalry. Even in the off-season.

Tessa and Colton still lived with me, and honestly, I was okay with that. I didn't want them to leave. My nights without Tessa in my arms and bed were the worst nights of my life. I never wanted to feel that emptiness again.

And that was why I was going to ask her to marry me tonight. I even had Colton's permission.

"Hey, buddy, before we head home to Mommy, we need to make a quick stop." I looked at Colt through the rearview mirror to where he sat in his car seat in the back seat of my SUV.

He didn't respond, but I knew he heard me, or if he didn't, I'd deal with it when I got to the jewelry store. I needed to hurry because Tessa might worry if we weren't home at our usual time after school. Based on Gabe's advice, I had designed and ordered the ring online, and I just needed to run in and pick it up.

When I pulled into the parking lot, my heart rate kicked up a beat. I never thought I'd be buying an engagement ring, but I also never thought I'd ever have the desire to be with one woman for the rest of my life. But, here I was, grabbing my girlfriend's son from the back seat and walking into a jewelry store.

After giving the sales clerk my name, I told them I had a ring to pick up. I looked around at the people looking into the glass cases. Most of the men looked as though they were going to get choked by the collars of their shirt because they were nervously tugging at the hems or cracking their necks when the women they were with would point to a ring she liked. I didn't know what kind of ring Tessa liked, but if she didn't like the one I'd designed, I'd buy her whichever one she wanted.

"Do you know why we're here?" I asked, looking at Colton still in my arms. He shook his head, and I bent down, setting him on his little legs. Crouching in front of him, I gazed into his blue eyes that matched his mother's. "I'm going to ask your mommy to marry me. How does that sound? Can I be your dad?"

His little hands started to flap excitingly, and he nodded his head. "Dad—dy."

My heart swelled at his progress, and I was beaming because we were on the same page.

I just hoped his mother was too.

Tessa and I hadn't known each other for even a year yet, but I knew I wanted her to be with me and only me for the rest of my life. If you were to bet me a year ago that I would be living with a woman and her son and ready to pop the question, I would have gladly taken that bet because nothing like that was even on my radar. I never saw it coming, and I never realized being in love would bring me more joy than traveling to new places and living a life of luxury. I still wanted those things, but I wanted Tessa more. I wanted to be a father, and it didn't matter that we didn't know if the baby she was carrying was mine or *his*. What mattered was I was going to raise it as my own. Of course, there was a part of me that wanted to know, and eventually, we would, but we'd made the decision to wait until the baby was born to find out.

"Are you almost ready?" I asked, coming into the bathroom where Tessa was getting ready for Seth and Cat's wedding. I brushed her hair off her shoulder and kissed her bare skin that smelled of cotton candy.

"Almost. Are Sophia and Valentina here?"

"Yep."

Valentina was cleared by the FBI. When Tessa found out, she and Tessa had a heart to heart. I wasn't sure what was said, but I knew Valentina assured Tessa she was only loyal to Sebastian because she thought she'd have to live with him forever. She feared he'd send her back to Colombia. Then Tessa introduced Valentina and Sophia. Those two ladies hit it off instantly, and since Sophia had lived in her apartment for several years and her lease was month to month, she and Valentina got a place together. Once a week they came over for dinner, and on Saturday nights they watched Colton so Tessa and I could have a date night. It really worked out for all of us.

All of us except Sebastian, who was still awaiting his trial.

I went back downstairs to the kitchen where both ladies were preparing dinner for themselves and Colton.

"Do you have the ring?" Sophia asked.

"Of course," I replied, and patted my suit jacket.

"I'm glad my cariño is marrying the one she loves," Valentina stated.

I chuckled. "She has to say yes first."

"She will." Sophia winked.

Tessa walked into the kitchen. "She who?"

All of our eyes became huge. "You," I replied.

"Me?" Tessa questioned, her hands to her chest.

"You're going to make us late, and Seth will kill me if we are. After last night, I'm sure he's pissed at all of us."

The night before, for Seth's bachelor party, the guys and I, including Seth's best man, Gibbs, took a limo around town and got him wasted. I only had a few rum and Cokes because I didn't want to forget coming home to Tessa. I'd never take a day for granted again. We never knew if it would be our last night together because that was life. You just didn't know. One minute you meet a girl you can't get out of your head, and the next she's being held hostage because she witnessed a murder. Or in some people's cases, you drive to work and get into a fatal car accident. We never knew what our future held, and I wasn't taking a second for granted. Of course, I was never letting Tessa go to a party without me or at least Joss since she was an FBI agent. The girls went out the night before too, but at the end of it, Tessa and I fell asleep in each other's arms.

"Well, let's go. I'm ready," Tessa stated. She moved to Colton. "You be a good boy, and in the morning we can have waffles before school."

He nodded and made an exaggerated "O" which we knew meant "Okay." My heart beamed each time I heard him talk. He was amazing.

And yes, Seth and Cat got married on a school night because Seth wasn't wasting any more time being without the one he loved and because venues booked up fast and all the weekend dates were booked solid for at least a year. That was okay because after what I had planned, I wanted it to be an early night.

Tessa and I held hands as we watched the happy couple say their vows in the primrose garden courtyard at The Wynn. For once I wasn't in the wedding party. Both Paul and Gabe had asked me to be a groomsman, and while I didn't mind, I loved sitting next to Tessa in the audience more.

The entire time we waited for Cat to walk in, Mark gave me a look. I hadn't told him I was officially leaving S&R, but it had been over seven months since I'd had a date. Galen more or less became my replacement after Red Diamond closed due to the owner being locked up and then losing its liquor license as a result. Mark had to know I was quitting the game.

Seth and Cat said their goodbyes after dinner. Since the wedding was booked super-fast, there was no reception—just the ceremony and dinner.

"Walk with me?" I asked, looking down at Tessa after the happy couple made their escape.

"Where are we going?"

"You'll see." I smiled and grabbed her hand. Both Gabe and Paul gave me a nod because they knew what I was about to do.

We walked out of the restaurant, which faced the Lake of Dreams at the hotel, and I led Tessa down the walkway and to the next restaurant.

"We're eating again?" she asked.

"No, I figured we could get a cup of coffee or something."

"Coffee?"

I smiled down at her. "Well, decaf for you."

"Here?"

"Yep." I stepped up to the hostess stand. "Reservation for Reed."

The hostess looked at her list and then grinned. "Right this way."

"We need reservations for coffee?" Tessa asked as we followed the hostess through the restaurant.

"I didn't want to take a chance there wouldn't be a table."

"You know we can just go to Starbucks, right?"

"Yes," I replied, and left it at that.

The hostess took us to a private cabana overlooking a small man-made lake with almost forty silver spheres that appeared to be floating. "All this for coffee?" Tessa asked after I helped her into her seat and then went around to my side.

"You know I like nice things." I smirked.

She chuckled. "Yeah, but I didn't take you for a guy who wanted to have coffee in a cabana with a chandelier."

"We were next door." I shrugged.

"True."

"Want dessert?" I handed Tessa a menu to distract her from the fact that I'd pre-planned *coffee*.

"We just had cake."

"But we didn't have ice cream, and you can't have cake without ice cream."

"So you want to get ice cream and coffee?"

"Sure, why not?"

She laughed. "Okay."

While Tessa looked at the menu, my palms started to sweat. I wasn't sure why I was nervous. This was Tessa, the only woman I'd ever loved, and we more or less lived together. I was certain she was going to say yes, but in the back of my mind, I thought about how this wasn't her first marriage proposal. What if it was too much for her too soon?

As I started to have a mini panic attack, I saw a waiter approaching with a tray of two champagne flutes. One had champagne, and the other was sparkling apple cider. He set them on the table.

"I thought we were going to have coffee?" Tessa asked.

I nodded to the guy, and he turned and left.

"Vin—"

I got out of my seat, smoothed my tie down, and knelt on one knee beside her. Her hands flew to her mouth. The menu fluttered underneath the table, and my heart started to pound in my chest. I pulled the princess-cut diamond solitaire ring from my pocket and held it out in front of me.

"Sweets, I promise I will love you until there are no more stars burning in the sky. I want to spend forever with you. Will you marry me?"

She didn't hesitate as she stood, her chair falling backward as she threw her arms around my neck. "Yes!"

My lips found hers as I held her in my lap squatting like a catcher. My thighs burned, but nothing in the entire world would burn more than the love I had for this woman.

EPILOGUE

Tessa

Forty-Five Days Later ...

THEY SAY EVERYTHING HAPPENS FOR A REASON, AND THAT WHATEVER doesn't kill you makes you stronger. After everything I went through, I realized it was all true. Granted, I wished my story was different. Autumn, Joss, and Cat all had scary stories to tell too, but thankfully, we all had strong men in our lives who were there when we needed them. And now, I was engaged to mine.

But *right* now, I was barefoot and pregnant in the kitchen —literally.

"Sweets, let me do that," Vinny offered as he came into the kitchen where I was making Colton a grilled cheese.

"I can still cook."

"You need to be off your feet."

"It takes—" I doubled over as pain radiated through my stomach.

"Tess ..."

"I'm okay," I groaned.

He bent down so he was eye level with me. "You don't look okay."

"Just Braxton Hicks."

"No." He shook his head. "From everything I've read, those don't hurt."

The pain went away, and I straightened. "See? I'm fine."

He eyed me and then left the room. I finished Colton's sandwich and brought it to where he sat in front of the TV. Yes, I was one of those moms. I didn't care. Colton had been through a lot, and if he wanted to eat a grilled cheese while watching *PAW Patrol*, he could.

Vinny walked back into the room and sat next to me on the couch. "I was thinking for our wedding colors—"

"*You* were thinking of our wedding colors?" I asked.

"Well, I was thinking that since you won't let us get married at Dodger Stadium, that we could have blue and—"

"No!" I held up my hand. "No blu—" Another wave of a cramp raced through me.

"That's it." Vinny stood. "We're going to the hospital."

"I'm fine. I've done this before, remember?"

He didn't answer as he ran up the stairs. While he was gone, another cramp washed over me. Just as I was about to grab my phone to look up Braxton Hicks, he ran back downstairs.

"Sophia and Valentina are meeting us at the hospital."

"Vin—"

"Sweets, don't fight me on this. If it's Braxton Hicks, we'll just come home. No harm in going."

"Fine," I huffed.

By the time I waddled to the car, Vinny had already put our bag and Colton into it.

Ten Hours Later ...

. . .

So, Vinny was right. It wasn't Braxton Hicks. Luckily, my labor was only nine hours versus the eighteen hour labor I'd had with Colton.

"You can't have this many people in this room at once," the nurse scolded as everyone piled into the room. And I mean everyone including my parents and Vinny's parents—whom I'd yet to officially meet because they were waiting for the baby to be born before they came from Arizona.

"Just for a second," Vinny replied.

She nodded briefly. "You have until I get back." Then she left.

"Everyone," Vinny started as he moved to my side where I held our daughter, "meet Riley Lucille Reed."

"Aw, that's a pretty name," Sophia stated. "Who picked it out?"

Vinny and I looked at each other and then I answered. "We compromised and named her after the Giants *and* the Dodgers." More specifically, the mascots: Rally Bear and Lou Seal.

"You two and your rivalry." Melony laughed.

Vinny and I shrugged at each other. Like he had once told me, it made our relationship interesting.

The time had come. The nurse had sent Riley's umbilical cord to the lab with a DNA sample from both Vinny and me to test to see if she was his or Sebastian's. They put a rush on it because they refused to put Vinny's name on the birth certificate since we weren't sure who the father was.

Whatever the test stated, Vinny would always be her dad.

"While we wait to be discharged," Vinny said, moving to a bag and digging in it, "I have something for you."

"Oh yeah?"

"Well, more for us." He pulled out a manila envelope. "I had these drawn up. If you don't want to, that's okay."

"What is it?" I asked and stuck out my hand for the envelope.

He handed it to me. "Just open it."

I pulled out the stack of papers and read the three words that stuck out to me. "You want to adopt Colton?"

Vinny nodded. "Of course I do."

Tears instantly stung my eyes and then rolled down my cheeks. "Thank you."

"Don't cry." He brushed the tears off my face.

"I'm happy. I never expected this."

"Me either, but we're a family now, and we might as well make it official, right?"

I nodded just as the nurse came into the room. "Am I interrupting?"

"It's okay," I replied.

"I have the paternity results. I had them printed so you could read them for yourself." She handed Vinny the folded up paper.

I smiled and wiped at the tears still flowing down my cheeks. "Okay."

"You ready for this?" he asked, looking down at me.

"No matter what, you'll always be her father." I could no longer keep my tears at bay. They streamed heavily now.

Vinny started to tear up as he lifted the flap of the trifold document. I knew exactly the moment he found out the results because his face lit up and he started to cry harder.

"99.9998%."

That was now my new favorite number.

Life had thrown me one too many curve balls, but no matter what the future held for me and Vinny, we'd always have the Dodgers *and* the Giants.

THE END.

Bradley's story is next in *Gin & Jewels*!
To stay up-to-date on release information, join Kimberly's newsletter.

AUTHOR NOTE

Dear Reader,

I hope you've enjoyed *Rum & Coke*. Please take a moment to spread the word so everyone can discover Vinny and Tessa and the men and women of Saddles & Racks.

Please also sign up for my newsletter so you can stay up to date on all the Knight news. You can find the link on my website.

You can also follow me on Facebook.

Thank you again, and I hope these two have captured a place in your heart. You can really help me out by leaving a review where you bought the book as well as on Goodreads and Bookbub.

Your love and support mean everything to me, and I cherish you all!

xoxo,

Kimberly Knight

ACKNOWLEDGMENTS

I always start with my husband because he's the one who has supported me through this journey. So, Mr. Knight, thank you for making my lunch and dinner when I was stressing over the deadline for this book and also for brainstorming with me. I love you, you know?

To my editor, Jennifer Roberts-Hall: Thank you for always making me sound good and for helping me master the dreaded blurb. You're amazing and I'm happy I can call you my friend! Now, let's get together so we can have more than one picture of us that's not just from 2013.

To Lara Hull, The Red Pen Princess: Thank you for proofreading this baby and making it perfect!

To my alphas: Stephanie Brown, Kristin Jones, Kerri Mirabella, Stacy Nickleson, and Carrie Waltenbaugh. Thank you for taking this journey with me and for telling me if an idea works or not. I truly appreciate all of you and what you bring to my tribe.

To my betas: Dianne Sweeney Metzmeier, Heather Hopkins Miller, Leanne Tuley, Lisa Petty and Stephanie Lorentz Cross. Thank you for being my eyes and making sure this story and timeline made sense. You ladies are amazing, and I'm lucky to have you willing to help me out. Thank you so much.

To my PA, Sara Cunningham: Thank you so much for all the time you spend with anything and everything I need to keep this train rolling. You're incredible and I'm so lucky to have found you.

To Verlene Landon: Even though I dedicated this book to you, I wanted to also thank you for your continued love and support of this series. To have another author praise your work is so surreal and no amount of thanks will ever be enough.

To Christie Harris: Thank you for helping make Tessa the person she is. You truly helped me out a bunch and so thankful to have you as a fan and reader.

To Blanca Esquivel: Thank you for helping me with my Spanish! Next time I'm in the Lone Star state, we should meet up. Or maybe Chicago again?

To my Steamy Knights: Thank you for your continued love and support and always being willing to help promote me. You all rock!

To all the bloggers and authors who participated in my cover reveal, release day blitz, review tour, and release day party, thank you! I can't tell you how much I appreciate it each and every one of you that are willing to help me spread the word about my books. Without you, I wouldn't be living my dream.

And finally, to my readers: Thank you for believing in me and taking a chance on my books again and again. Without you guys, I wouldn't still be writing and bringing you all the stories that captivate my brain on a daily basis.

BOOKS BY KIMBERLY KNIGHT

Club 24 Series – Romantic Suspense

Perfect Together – The Club 24 Series Box Set

Halo Series – Contemporary Romance

Saddles & Racks Series – Romantic Suspense

By Invitation Only – Erotic Romance Standalone

Use Me – Romantic Suspense Standalone

Burn Falls – Paranormal Romance Standalone

And more ...

ABOUT KIMBERLY KNIGHT

Kimberly Knight is a USA Today Bestselling Author who lives in the mountains near a lake with her loving husband and spoiled cat, Precious. In her spare time, she enjoys watching her favorite reality TV shows, watching the San Francisco Giants win World Series and the San Jose Sharks kick butt. She's also a two time desmoid tumor/cancer fighter, which has made her stronger and an inspiration to her fans. Now that she lives near a lake, she's working on her tan and doing more outdoor stuff like watching hot guys waterski. However, the bulk of her time is dedicated to writing and reading romance and erotic fiction.

KIMBERLY KNIGHT

www.authorkimberlyknight.com